ALIENIST

Other Books

ALIENIST

Laurence M. Janifer

WILDSIDE PRESS

ALIENIST

An original publication of Wildside Press.

First Wildside Press edition: November 2001

This one is for
(as I am)
my dearest Exactly—
and for the entire
Basement
with love

PART ONE

FOLLA

ONE

There are some very strange people in the universe. I don't mean human beings—human beings are strange, God knows, but we're *used* to human beings. We've had less than two hundred years to get used to the others—the aliens, as people used to call them before we met some—and now and then it does take just a little doing. There are the Berigot, for instance—nice enough folk, true, but you do have to allow for that passionate interest in information-collecting, and the lack of interest in anything else. There are the Vibich, too, whom we've never figured out at all, and who seem to have no interest in us whatever—which simplifies matters without clarifying them any. The Kelans aren't exactly strange; they're more like the Wise Old Uncles (and Aunts) of the Universe—but the Tocks, who may know almost as much (in their own weird way), are anybody's strong contenders for the Strange Award, and name your year. There are, as we'll see further along, the Gielli, who take a little more getting used to than you think they're going to.

Well, even the small piece of the universe we've managed to get to see, so far, as 2300 A. D. has come and gone, is the Hell of a big place, and you can expect Strange to crop up anywhere. No real problem, and some of my best friends, if I may preen a little, are among the strangest.

Or at least, they used to be—before the *real* aliens popped up.

You may not have heard much about them yet—Folla and Dube and all the others. The Comity was the Hell of a long distance from where they did pop up, and the Comity had no official authority over the matter; but the actual (not official) authority of a government is as stretchable as an old girdle, if every bit as smelly, and Colonization, External Affairs and the entire damn Dichtung turn out to have a reach that makes the ancient Long Hand of the Law look like your favorite carnival's Armless Wonder. The lid has been put on, and soldered damn well shut, and there is a general feeling that maybe, just maybe, if nobody mentions anything, the whole situation will give us one small embarrassed smile, and fade into the wood-work.

If you've got this report in your hands—or feet, or mouth, or beam—you know better Or you will, by the time I'm through here. Because Folla and Dube and all their friends and associates are not, I assure you, likely to fade into any kind of woodwork at all, and we had better know something about them. One way or another, we're going to have to live with them.

If possible.

Let's start from the beginning, shall we?

I was going from Here to There through space-four, which I do a lot of. The specs don't matter, because I never did arrive at There, and it took me several hours of sweat and fret to locate Here all over again, from a position that turned out to be eleven thousand light-years from anyplace any human being had ever seen before—astronomical surveys excepted. What I was, God damn it, was lost.

This is not supposed to happen, but of course it does; uncertainty is built into space-four, and everybody knows it, and everybody figures it will bite some other body. I popped back into normal space on schedule, looked around for the field and towers, and found out that, this time, it had by God bitten *me*: I was traveling at the Hell of a clip, my instruments told me, through what my viewboards told me was empty space.

Well, as empty as space gets—littered as it mostly is with hydrogen atoms, radiation, and occasional junk. And I was not at all sure I could trust the boards; I punched up my locator and got, instead, a lovely 3D graph that didn't seem at first glance—or at eleventh—to make any sense. The graph was labeled (lower right front, as usual): INFORMATION CONSUMPTION (PRELIMINARY), and it was scaled in minutes, parsecs and kilojoules.

I shut my eyes and uttered something or other—prayer, curse or simple steam—and when I opened them the graph hadn't changed, but the label had. PRELIMINARY had been replaced by EXIGENT. While I watched, EXIGENT faded away, and was replaced by FIFTH READ.

9

Four seconds ticked by. Then the label vanished, taking the damn graph with it, and a blinking sign appeared.

FORMAL ERROR, it said: PLEASE RECHECK DATA FEED.

It took the words right out of my mouth; the data feed, and the data, were what I was going to check, and recheck, till Hell wouldn't have it. I needed some solid answers, and I needed them in a hurry.

Step one: define "hurry."

All right: I was still breathing, and the air did not seem noticeably odd in any way. Water and food supplies were computer mediated, of course, and if I did a full readout to find out what I had, I'd get figures I couldn't trust, given what the boards had been doing. But I did have two water bottles, and iron rations, stowed under the never-used co-pilot's couch (well, never used in flight; there are always a few rosebuds who find a tour of your ship an exciting way to spend an evening). Thirty-six hours was my best figure for what the supplies to hand meant.

Unless, of course, the damn ship took it into its head to explode. That, I reflected, might happen at any second.

It might not happen, too, and there was nothing whatever I could do about it, pro or con. I fished a portable tester out of the pilot's locker and it told me the air was air, normal for composition and pressure, at the temperature I'd set it for—78F/25.3C, if it matters. There are people who claim that a cold ship increases alertness, and I make it a point not to travel with these people if I can help it.

Conditionally, then, I had thirty-six hours to figure out where I was, and how I was going to get to some specific someplace else. It didn't really seem like enough time.

I had that portable tester, by the way—running on its own power source, unconnected to the ship—and the water, and the rations—and a few other things here and there around the cabin—for reasons related to my trade. My business cards read: *Gerald Knave: Survivor*, and a Survivor is, among other things, the kind of person who wears suspenders and a belt—with jogging pants. A certain amount of caution is built into the job: when what you do professionally is wander out to a brand-new planet, alone, and try to stay alive on it for a Standard year, you do get into the habit of putting safeties on your safeties. I had not been expecting to get myself lost—who ever does?—but, just in case I did—or was forced to hole up for a while in a ship whose machinery couldn't be worked, say—or sixty other odd and unlikely emergency situations—I'd have something to fall back on. Not much, but just maybe enough.

All right: immediate survival as assured as I could make it, I had two questions.

1. Where the Hell was I?
2. What instruments could I trust to tell me the answer to 1?

TWO

After a brief pause, and a little more steam let off, I punched for the locator again. This time I got it, but what the Hell did that mean? All was illusion, or might be; step two had to be an attempt to see what, in the thoroughly complicated innards of the ship, actually worked, and what had gone out for a long lunch.

The pilot's locker (and the co-pilot's locker) had a fair assortment of instruments with their own power supplies, but there's a limit to what you can build into a portable tool, and there are limits to what even a cautious Survivor type is likely to want to carry around. I could check my air, I could do some basic diagnostics on my engines, and I could debug a few programs built into the boards. Most of those did not immediately look useful—I carry a fair number of interactives to while away trip time, and I could debug most of those, some letter-writing equipment, and my several files of music tapes.

And even they, I realized after the first few seconds, had some use for me, right there and then. I could check what the boards told me those programs were doing against what (according to the portables) they actually *were* doing—and get some idea of where my machinery was playing games.

First things first, though: I was still, apparently, going at the Hell of a clip toward God knew where. Was this illusion?

I dragged out a large, unwieldy box with snake attachments, thumbed its primary switch, showed it the relevant boards, and set it down at the rear of the cabin. The thing weighed about sixty pounds, and, I hoped, was going to be worth every last ounce.

The snakes fished around, found connections, sockets and shielded holes, flipped shields open where indicated, settled into the sockets and connections, and hummed for what felt like ten or twelve years, and was actually (its little topside clock told me) thirty-eight seconds. Then its dials and displays began to read out.

My engines, according to the tester, were putting out

eight-tenths of max power, and exhaust was encountering minimal resistance.

This defines as going at the Hell of a clip through empty space. I punched in a stop command, waited, punched in a stop-fuel-feed command, waited, punched in a stop-fusion-run command, and waited some more. Any one of the three should act to stop my engines, and perhaps, by some wild mischance, one of them would.

The tester told me, a few seconds later, that one of them had. I was now, at least, not *increasing* the clip I was going at. Slowing down was going to be something else again, and putting the ship into braking mode might, it occurred to me, do something fatal to the works. I might be left with a ship I couldn't control at all—or, if an explosion decided to happen, with no ship whatever.

Well, what else was new? I punched in braking orders. By that time, I was holding my breath, and when I noticed the fact I told myself firmly that breathing was a necessary and even a desirable function, and climbed slowly back to something within hailing distance of normal.

The tester couldn't quite tell me that the brakes were on, but it could tell me that engine function had resumed, and that the direction of exhaust had changed. What I needed was a way of finding out what my speed was relative to the rest of the universe, so to speak, and I wished, a little bemusedly, for Sherlock Holmes' tools. On a train from somewhere to somewhere—en route to Baskerville Hall, if memory served, where he was going to investigate a Houn' Dog—Holmes had calculated the speed of the train he was on because the telegraph poles it passed were a quarter-mile apart, and "the calculation," he told his publicist, a fellow named Whatsis, "is a simple one."

So it would be, if I could find some telegraph poles out there, at known distances. My locator would show me the local star field, and just possibly identify one or two of the handier objects—but how could I trust the information it gave me? There is no way to run a check on a locator, short of a full field shop; locators are what you expect to run checks *with*.

Well, there might be a way.

The board clock had gone on automatically when I'd dropped out of space-four, but I didn't have to trust it; the big engine tester had a clock, and my alarm is a portable, because I can rig it to wake me and not disturb anyone else who happens to be sleeping aboard. Neither could tell me the precise millisecond I'd come back to normal space—the board clock would do that—but if both agreed not only with each other (which they did) but with the board clock, too, about what time it was being, I could then take the board figure for return to normal space as a first approximation. What eight-tenths max would give me for initial speed I knew without much thought, and the millisecond at which I'd got response to my brake command, the tester clock and my portable alarm *would* tell me—had told me, in fact, and identically, and I'd filed the readings, noticing both out of an eye-corner, without having to think about it. I would then have initial speed, and a start from which to measure duration of my braking burn.

So I could find out just when I'd be at a dead stop, and could at that point (I hoped) turn off the braking I'd just turned on.

The calculation was a simple one—for a good hand calculator, suitably instructed. I watched my alarm, handier than the tester clock at the rear of the cabin, like a hawk, or a bandsaw, or something or other, and punched in all the stop commands at time zero.

The tester told me there was no engine function.

Cheers and applause. I was now somewhere, and I would be at the same somewhere for a while. Step two, at last, coming up.

I fed in two interactives—the first two I happened to grab, Conversational Saurian and a little thing called Old Earth Burleycue—some Kurt Weill tapes (after reaching for Laura Quink's *Songs from the 20th*, and deciding I wasn't at all in the mood for charming antique folk guitar), and my letter-writer, one at a time. The debug programs told me that the things were doing what my boards showed me they were doing—but the boards insisted they were, each and all, doing their things perfectly. This was not quite the case.

That was worrisome. There were some fascinating small

oddities. The letter-writer worked just as specified, except that it did everything in duplicate. The Saurian tape—I was doing a refresher course, in hopes of getting back to Rasmussen some time soon—seemed to be all right.

The Kurt Weill bits I tried—*Surabaya Johnny* and the *Army Song*—played at something like twice normal speed, boosting everything into a manic sprint and turning the rough baritones of the *Army Song* into chirping little sopranos. And Old Earth Burleycue did its usual cheery and stimulating job with the stage show, selecting two lovely and accomplished strippers from its varied cast, but kept going into freeze during my visits to the backstage dressing rooms.

I punched for some beef, rolls, horseradish and the makings for coffee, added in iced mango as a dessert, and was faintly surprised that it all arrived at speed. I made myself a small scratch dinner and thought things over while I chewed.

Uncertainty is built into space-four, as everybody knows. Figuring out what had done the damage was a job for a mathematician and a space-four theorist, and could wait any amount of time. Figuring out what damage had been done was something else again.

Circuitry and wave guidance had been hurt, somehow; that much was clear. But what had changed, as far as I could trace, was in response circuitry: speed response for the Weill, singularity for my letters program, rate of response for the Burleycue. I wasn't getting material out of left field; I was getting the material my boards said I was getting, delivered a little oddly.

That, I could live with. It gave me some hope that my locator would provide answers I could trust, though possibly not at its usual speed.

At any rate, it gave me enough hope to punch up the locator again, point it at the surround, and instruct it to tell me where the Hell I was.

It took four full minutes to respond—not unheard-of, but very unusual. The response time for my rig averages about eighteen seconds; in difficult cases, perhaps thirty-one.

And the response (I translate freely from the program) was, when it finally did arrive:

15

"Damned if I know."

I did not scream and curse. Somehow, I'd been expecting as much; whatever had bit me was not, I had been assuming, going to be satisfied with dumping me, say, in orbit around Kingsley, or Alphacent, or within shouting distance of Mars Dome.

No, it was going to do what it *had* done—the complete job. If I was going to be lost, it had decided, I was going to be *entirely* lost.

The first query for any locator is Where am I? The second is Star Ident. If you need the second, you are in trouble, but how serious the trouble is you can't know until the thing checks in with a set of idents. Or, of course, doesn't—if there is nothing whatever that can be identified for H-R placement and spectral signature, you are in more trouble than you ever wanted to imagine.

Given my locator, and the stats I had lovingly fed into it over many weeks of maintenance, a total lack of star ident would mean that I was sitting somewhere not only outside the galaxy, but (at best) at the further edge of one of the local group. You never do know, but I hoped for better news than that, and I began to get it.

I was, as I've said, eleven thousand light-years (and change) from the furthest-out spot humanity had yet managed—a planet called Debrett, which I'd never visited. It didn't take me two minutes to find that out; once the locator had begun feeding me star idents, it took three hours.

Few of the idents were tagged Absolutely Certain. At the distances involved, some fuzz had crept into the readings—and though a completely detailed spectrum is as individual as a fingerprint, I wasn't getting complete details. The job was a long process of if-then: if that star over there was 1491 in my handbook, and that other one was 2200A, and the third little dot was Haven, then I was *right here*. If, on the other hand, 1491 and Haven were right, but 2200A was really 590B, I was, instead, *over there*. And if Haven and 2200A were right, but 1491 was really Cuchinar, then I was *someplace else*.

What I had to do was to cross-check a large pile of such triples against each other, tossing out contradictory results as they turned up, and hoping that, in the end, I'd be left with one and only one possible location. Even with a lot of help from the boards, this is not a fast and simple kind of job, and I punched for, and carefully brewed, and slowly emptied, two complete pots of Indigo Hill coffee—why not go with the best?—before I had a location I was satisfied with.

All right. I was at rest, and I knew where I was resting.

Next step: find my way back.

This was going to have to be done through space-four, whether I liked it or not: hopping eleven thousand light-years through normal space would take me something over eleven thousand years, no matter how hard I boosted for how long, and I didn't feel I had that much time to spend.

Through space-four, it might take me twenty minutes (unlikely) or five days (just as unlikely). But a course plotted to anywhere, from where I had painfully found out I was, didn't exist; instructing my ship was going to be a very interesting job. Space-four routes are usually figured by teams of theorists, sitting at ease in large, airy rooms, over a period of weeks. All your usual traveler has to know is where to feed in his trip card; his ship reads the bumps on it, and does the work.

I am not exactly your usual traveler, but I am not a space-four theorist either, and while my cabin is a little larger and airier than most, I didn't have weeks to spend on the job. There had to be a quick-and-dirty emergency answer somewhere, and I dug out a Pilot's Manual and an unreasonably thick book of space-four routings (limited edition, for official use only), and got myself some lox and cream cheese on thick rye bread, along with a jug of iced tea—any more coffee, and I'd be awake for five days, and jittering for seven.

An hour later, I had three possible routings, none of which looked especially helpful. I sighed deeply, finished the last of the tea, and decided to try for two more before arranging them in any sort of order. I flipped through the book of routings again, came to the section I wanted (headed, if you care, "Transductions in d, dx and e"), and began punching in numbers.

I had been doing this for about four minutes, varied by an occasional stare at my boards and a muttered *hmm* or two, when I was interrupted by a voice.

It was a fairly loud, medium-tenor voice, with no discernible accent (which means it had mine), and it said, and I swear it to you:

"Lonely? Ready for company? Punch 117-62-97, and rejoin your friends and neighbors at their preferred locations. This is a service of Path, Ltd."

THREE

All right. The strain of my situation had been too much for me, and I was having hallucinations.

Well, what would you have thought? I took several deep breaths. Then I said, to the air around me: "What the Hell?"

"Human," the same voice said. "Planet resident. Occupying three per cent of locations suitable for growth, within one galaxy only. Resident of three spatial dimensions and one temporal dimension. Visitor to one additional spatial dimension. Limited sensory equipment. Cognition unknown. This is a first cut."

Obviously, my ship was acting up again. Something had got into the speaker system, and I was fascinated by what the Hell it might be. It didn't sound like any interactive I had aboard, or had ever had aboard; it didn't even sound a lot like any interactive I had ever so much as heard of.

Though it is hard to tell, it didn't sound like random selections from any interactive I was at all likely to own, either. *Sensory* and *cognition* are not words I expect to find lying around among my amusements. Concepts, yes; vocabulary, no.

I punched for a sound check, and as I did that the voice said:

"Response inappropriate."

"All right," I muttered. "What would be appropriate, you damn fool? Appropriate for a voice coming out of the everywhere, into the here."

"Identification and reply, of course," the voice told me promptly.

I was staring at my sound check board. It had informed me, accurately, that I had just muttered something. (I got a db reading and a plot of overtones.)

It was now also informing me, with certainty, that no other sound had existed in the cabin over the previous eighty seconds.

Maybe my sound check had fallen ill. Maybe I was hallucinating.

And just maybe, I told myself, something brand-new was happening in my ship. Or in my head. Or both.

So I said: "Who am I replying to, and what kind of identification?" I have no idea whether I really expected an answer.

But I got one, though not an immediately helpful one. "Who. Does there exist specific individuation?"

"There exist individuals," I said. "They have identities. I made a request regarding that identity."

"Individuals," the voice said. "Sound-coded individuation. Call me Mishmael. Mosh. Kabibble." A slight pause. "Sound-coded as Folla. Sufficient. Call me Folla."

I felt as if I'd fallen into somebody's notion of Surrealism. I felt, in fact, thoroughly cuckoo, and the notion set off an association, somewhere in my collection of scrappy Classical Learning. "Oh cuckoo," I said, "shall I call thee bird, or but a wand'ring voice?"

The wand'ring voice said: "Response inappropriate," again, which I suppose it was. I said:

"Translation: who the Hell is Folla, and what are you doing on my ship?"

The voice said: "Reply in series. One: Folla is now an inhabitant of these spaces. Two: I am occupying no space in your ship."

All right. "Where is your voice coming from?"

I got the answer I should have been expecting. "Out of the everywhere—" it said.

"Into the here. Yes. I said that myself, two minutes ago. Any particular kind of everywhere? And your voice is not affecting my instrumentation."

"Reply in series," the voice—Folla, I supposed—said. "One: a non-specific and other everywhere. Two: I will correct, within six seconds of time flow."

Well, I was getting answers, but the answers did not, for some reason, seem to be helpful. I tried again. "Where is your ship?"

"These spaces are my ship," Folla said. "Do you wish to change your location, and rejoin your friends and neighbors?" My sound check now told me that the voice was coming from inside my cabin, centered on a point five inches over my head.

There was nothing visible five inches over my head.

Beware, the old saying goes, of geeks bearing grifts. Whether Folla was or was not a geek I was not prepared to say; but the offer did sound a lot like a grift. A con. What would happen if I said Yes, get me home?

"I am preparing to do that myself," I said.

"It can be done without disturbance," Folla said. "Fret not, and it will be arranged. No payment will be requested at this time."

"A service of Path, Ltd.," I said, to fill in time while I thought. Hard.

A slight pause. "What is the planet of your residence?"

"Ravenal," I lied. "You probably won't know the coordinates. But let's discuss this for a—"

I stopped right there, because my boards were showing me that I had changed location. I thought I knew where I'd come to.

"Folla?" I said.

No reply.

"Folla, damn it?"

No reply.

I punched up my locator again, and queried it.

It told me I was in close orbit around Ravenal.

I didn't believe it for a second. But I punched for Approach Control on-planet anyhow, made some adjustments, and got myself into an approach path.

FOUR

Ravenal is the hard-science center of the galaxy, as far as human beings are concerned—which is putting it mildly. I've spent time there on a small variety of occasions, and I have some friends there. It is not my planet of residence, but it was, very definitely, the place I wanted to go. If you need dependable answers, Ravenal is the first place to go and look for them, and some of the people I know there are the first ones to ask.

What had happened to me out there in the unknown had no explanation I could come up with, and no ancestors I could think of; I had never heard of such a thing happening to anybody, anywhere. People do hear voices, of course, but not quite like that.

There is the old joke, for instance. Psychologist to patient: "Do you ever hear voices, and you don't know whose voices they are, or where they're coming from?"

Patient. "Yes."

Psychologist: "Aha. And when does this happen?"

Patient: "When I answer the telephone."

And there are, of course, people who really do hear voices from the unknown. Some of these people have become heroes of one religion or another, and some of them have become patients in facilities for the helpless, and a very few of them have become respected poets.

These were not, on the whole, groups I was comfortable about belonging to. And the experience I'd had hadn't quite been theirs: my voice had told me that something absolutely impossible was going to happen, and it had then, and very quickly, happened. Even the voices that had come to religious heroes hadn't been quite that efficient.

I had traveled about sixteen thousand light years in either zero time, or a time interval small enough to measure in eyeblinks. I couldn't tell which, because I was not sure either that I'd noticed what my boards had told me at the precise millisecond they'd begun to tell me—I'd been just a little distracted—or that the boards had responded instantaneously to my change in location.

It didn't, as far as I could see, make much difference; either was impossible, Space-four doesn't work like that; trip time is a fairly large number of minutes, at a minimum, and is usually measured in days. There are studies that seem to have established that the minimum theoretical trip time through space-four is just over eighteen minutes—no trip whatever, from anywhere to anywhere, can ever be shorter than that.

Mine had been—by something over eighteen minutes.

The voice I'd heard, obviously, knew some different theories.

And they'd worked out, in the real world. I got my signals from Tower for Ravenal's City Two, punched in the course, braking and so on, and was on the ground in ninety minutes; even the landing people on Ravenal are efficient, and there is very little fuzz or delay to the process.

The fuzz and delay happened after I'd left and sealed my ship, of course, and is known everywhere as Customs. I bore up under the various idiocies and indignities gamely, and, a couple of hours later, by now late at night by my body clock, found that a hotel I remembered visiting during my last visit—with the typical Ravenal lack of any literary imagination at all, it was called City Two Rooms and Services—was happy to board me. I settled in, and then, even before I began any serious unpacking, I reached for the phone.

The rasp that answered gave me the feeling that some things never change. "Who?" Master Higsbee said, in a voice like an unoiled camshaft with attitude.

"Gerald Knave, Master," I said.

"Ah," he said. "Gerald. I am glad to hear your voice. It has been too long—nearly eight months Standard. Where are you, and why do you call? It is not, surely, to cheer an old blind man."

"Well," I said, trying not to sound either sympathetic or irritated, "any cheering I can do, you're welcome to. But something strange has happened. Very strange. I'm right here on Ravenal, and I've got a story I don't think you've heard before."

"Indeed," he said. "You have come to ask me questions, Gerald? It should not be necessary; you have the wit to provide your own answers."

I sighed. "Not this time, I don't," I said. "You may not have any answers either."

He said it again: "Indeed." And then: "It is nearly time for my dinner, Gerald. I will come to your hotel, if I may."

"City Two Rooms and Services," I said, not bothering about the fairly obvious deduction that I was in a hotel. "We'll find a restaurant."

"Room Service will be sufficient for an old and helpless man," he said. "If you are serious about your story, Gerald, we shall want no distractions."

An old and helpless man. Oh, God. But though being around the Master meant you had to put up with a lot—you also had to put up with being called Gerald, for instance—it was worth it; he was, after all, the Master.

"I'll look for you," I said.

"Do that. Look for a blind and lamed old man, Gerald."

"Lamed?"

"It is unimportant," he said. "A small accident, and I am assured temporary. Finished."

Click. The Master wasted no phone time whatever.

He has been blind for thirty years and more, but I had never seen him with a cane before. He didn't lean on it unduly and he didn't flourish it; he used it, with as little waste motion as possible. He stalked into the hotel lobby, a big barrel-shaped man with a large, Roman head and a crown of fine white hair, moving a little slowly but not with a noticeable limp—and when he got to the middle of it he stopped and cocked his big head. The place was full of bustle and movement, for City Two—which, while a full city, is not as crowded as City One, where the bureaucracy lives—but when I said: "Over here," he heard me without effort. He stalked toward me. People in his path got out of his path.

I think the Master has memorized the entire ground plan of any place on Ravenal he's at all likely to be; he's never used a cane for location that I know of. He came within two inches or so of a pillar, on the way to me, but no closer. When he got to me, he said: "I thought you might come down to meet me, Gerald."

"Of course I would," I said. "And not because you have difficulties—"

"Blind," he said. "Not because I am blind. Periphrasis does not become you, Gerald."

"At any rate," I said uncomfortably, "simple politeness. What happened to your leg?"

"The room," he said. "I dislike to chat in large open spaces."

"Sorry," I said, and headed for the elevators. He followed me without trouble. A couple of large men walking across the lobby and arguing with each other nearly bumped into him, but they did see him at the last second, and turned aside just enough. A little more than just enough. He affected not to notice, and let them live.

In the room, we got settled into chairs, and he said: "If I remember this establishment, the steak au poivre is edible. We will accept their usual accompaniments. That, and any decent red wine."

I seconded the motion, called for Room Service, added coffee and a warmer to the menu—well, it would do for a midnight supper, for me, and the coffee would be welcome (though much earlier I'd been filling up on it), after the last few hours of Customs.

I put down the phone, and the Master said: "Tell me."

"The leg first," I said. "What happened?"

He shrugged, just a little. "I was examining some files, at the request of a friend," he said. "Instances of minor theft in specialty shops—unusual lingerie."

I nodded, trying not to look surprised; God knows what he can notice. "Unusual lingerie?"

"What seem to be called Playtime Wispies," he said flatly. "I had not myself previously encountered the objects. The records of theft were among several boxes of reader spools."

I was trying hard not to picture the Master encountering a delicate handful of Playtime Wispies. Some of them are edible. Some play music. Some are rigged to vanish into thin air after set periods of wear—say two hours. Some—well, there are a lot of variations. "And the boxes of spools—"

"Just so," he said. "A particularly heavy box fell on my foot. There is injured musculature, a small broken bone, a swollen ankle. All, I am assured, quite temporary."

"Good," I said. "And the thefts—"

"A very minor matter," he said. "But my friend was curious as to patterns in the timing as well as in the objects stolen. A private matter, not for police inquiry. It will be settled easily enough, there is no real complexity involved."

"Well," I said, "I hope the foot's better soon."

"Indeed," he said, and then: "Tell me."

So I did. In careful detail, and word for word, second for second. It wasn't at all the sort of thing I had trouble remembering. He asked no questions until the end, which was pleasing; it meant I was doing a thorough job of reporting events.

When I had brought him to the point at which I was orbiting Ravenal, I stopped. He said nothing at all for over a full minute—which was not usual.

Then he said: "You have left nothing out, and have added nothing?"

"Of course not."

"Then we have an extraordinary situation," he said. "You were quite right, Gerald: this is a story I have not heard before, and one for which I do not have any immediately final answers. There are, of course, a number of suggestive points."

I said: "I've seen a few of them. But I'd like to hear your—" and there was a polite little rap at my door.

Room Service, of course. I got up and let the Totum in, told it where to set up the table and arrange the plates and food and so on, and punched my accept code into its shield. It buzzed faintly, said: "Ank you, Sir, and a pleas evening."

Well, that it talked at all was evidence of the high ranking of my hotel; expecting perfection, in a machine that saw the kind of heavy use a hotel Totum had to see, would have been silly. "Thank *you*," I said, and it went away, and I shut and locked the door and we got down to eating.

"Suggestive points," I said after a while.

"Let us assume that what you experienced was objectively real," he said. "In that case—though I hesitate greatly over the conclusion, and of course this Folla may have been lying, or mistaken, or mad—you were hearing the voice—produced I do not know how—of someone who was not, so to speak, from this universe."

"Not from this galaxy, you mean," I said. "A total stranger. I did get that. A very strange stranger, too."

"Not from this universe," the Master said flatly. "So he claims. Not from this—little sheaf of spaces. Three dimensions of space, and one of time—as Folla said. With visitations, of course, to a fourth dimension of space—which would describe, loosely to be sure, our travels in or through or with space-four."

I nodded—very tentatively. "He described—space-time—as if it were something special. Odd. Not the kind of thing he's used to."

"God alone knows what he might be used to," the Master said. He cut the last bit of steak au poivre and began to chew. "'Sensory equipment limited'," he said. "I wonder what unlimited sensory data would be."

"Maybe his is limited too," I said. I chased some peas around my plate, caught them and ate a forkful. "But in different ways."

"Anything is possible," the Master said. "He said 'these spaces' are his ship—that is, these spaces are where he now resides, and through which, or by which, he now travels. These three—or four—spatial dimensions."

"As opposed to what?"

"Other dimensions?" he said. "I say that very hesitantly, Gerald—and, indeed, without any clear idea of what such a phrase might in fact mean to us." He shook his head. "I sound as if I were talking about a very bad piece of science-fiction. A dimension is a heuristic convenience; it is not, if we except the ones we normally live in, an object, a thing one can point to and so define."

"Space-four can't be pointed to," I said.

"And space-four is a dimension by definition only," he said at once. "We cannot in fact point to time, Gerald. We can define, practically, so to speak, three dimensions of space, and those only." He drank off some wine. "What do we mean by 'dimension'—and what can it possibly mean to say that this creature, this voice, this Folla lives in some other one or ones?"

I poured out the last of the wine for him, and emptied my own glass. "Damned if I know," I said.

There was quite a lot to be dug out of the comparatively few words I'd had with Folla, whoever or whatever he was. (He, she or it, I suppose—but "it" doesn't seem to cover the case, somehow, and since Folla is not really a nice sort of being, I'd rather include him in my own gender than insult my companions of another g.) It was somewhere after midnight by City Two clocks, and positively into early morning by mine, when the Master sighed: "This shall have to be continued. I must leave."

I agreed that it was getting late. He got up, grabbed his cane from beside his chair—he'd had it leaning against the portable table—and headed for the door. He wastes very little time on polite goodbyes.

But at the door—I trailed him by a few feet, politely—he turned. "Gerald," he said, "I would like you to talk to a psychiatrist. An expert in Psychological Statics."

I took a second to digest that. "Well," I said, not wanting to burst out with objections, of which I had several hundred on immediate call, "why would you want me to do that? If we're to accept the experience as objectively real—"

"That is why," he said. "Euglane has an interest in such matters. He may prove quite valuable, if we are to inquire into what has happened at all. We could of course simply drop the whole matter."

"And spend the rest of my life wondering what the Hell had happened," I said. "Thanks. But why a psychiatrist? I may have a few bats in my personal belfry, but—"

"Your bats are your affair," the Master said, "as mine are my affair; that is what it means to be human, and adult. But I believe you will find his insights helpful, as regards this particular problem."

I was doubtful—but he was, after all, the Master. "If you say so," I told him.

"I do," he said. "I will call him in the morning, and he will then call you. By the way, Gerald—he's a Giell."

I blinked. "A what?"

He gave me his chuckle—a dry sound, part muted trumpet and part creak. "Not a gel," he aid. "A Giell. You may not have heard of the race. There has been very little contact as yet between humans and Gielli, though they have found a place here. In City One they are become, even, fashionable."

"A new race?"

"New to humans," he said. "Or to most of them."

He chuckled again. I said: "I can hardly wait."

FIVE

Euglane explained a little about the Gielli to me, after we'd had a chance to talk about my problem, and when we met the next evening. He'd had, he told me, appointments right through the day, "and it would be unkind in me to break them, if I can avoid doing that," he said. "There's a certain dependence, you know." His voice was middle-register for a male human, pleasant and even and just a little gruff.

I nodded at that, and I didn't press it. I agreed to meet him at his home at what Ravenal calls eighteen-thirty and I call six-thirty P. M. I was there about eight minutes early, but when I thumbed the entry switch the little bell-announce had barely stopped chiming inside when he opened the door. He was smiling, or he looked as if he were smiling. With a face like his, it was hard to tell, and mostly in the eyes.

Two eyes, a rather small head, and a beak. The head was tan, the beak dark and glossy, either brown or black. His eyes were large, looked almost human—the irises were narrow upright ovals—and bright blue.

Imagine a koala with the head of an eagle. Wearing, by the way, a short-sleeved white shirt, a pair of shorts, and slippers, and standing about five feet eleven inches tall. That isn't it—Euglane wasn't as puffy as a koala, and his head was larger and longer than an eagle's—but it will give you a fast idea. I said: "Mr. Euglane?" and he said:

"Euglane, please. You're Knave?"

Despite its hard, glossy appearance, the beak was mobile enough to shape vowels. "I am," I said. He stepped aside, and I went in, to a small, light entry hall panelled in expensive dark wood. He shut the door—which was also wood; apparently this particular Giell was doing all right for himself financially—and then led the way to a big, airy living room. There were couches, tables, overstuffed chairs; he indicated a small couch and I sat down, and he dropped into a big chair nearby.

"I don't know what Master Higsbee has told you about me," he said.

"Not a lot," I said. "To be frank, I'd never heard of the Gielli till he mentioned you last night. He said you might be helpful."

"Well," he said, "I will be if I can. That's my nature, being helpful. It's what I do, you know."

"I suppose so," I said. "A psychiatrist, after all."

At that point he remembered his manners, or something, and offered me drinks. I said fruit juice, to be friendly, and he went away and came back with a couple of tall glasses on a tray. I took one, he sat down again and said:

"Do you mind if I relax?"

"Not at all," I said.

He nodded, put his own glass on the tray, which sat on a nearby small table, and sighed. A second went by.

Then his arms and legs started to extend.

When each limb was about four feet long, he sighed again. "Thanks," he said. "It's a strain, but it is best to seem as non-threatening as possible. Long arms mean a long reach, long legs an overpowering height. Not always the best or most reassuring picture for a human."

Accordion limbs? They seemed to be boneless, with strong muscles for motion. Expandable cartilage? Standing upright looked to be a problem without anything as hard as bones to take the weight over four feet of leg, and I thought, when fully relaxed, he probably got around on all fours, in a sort of sea-lion crawl. "I can see where it might be a strain," I said. "Holding yourself in like that."

"Well," he said, thrashing his arms and legs a little, just loosening up after a long day, "it's worth it, if it keeps my patients calm. But of course you're not a patient."

"To tell you the truth," I said, "I wasn't quite sure. The Master was—a little vague."

"He was very vague with me." Euglane said. "He told me he wanted me to form my own impressions—a good idea generally, but I'm pretty much a blank at the moment; anything you tell me is going to be news."

I nodded. "What do you know about dimensions?" I said.

"Dimensions?"

I explained, as briefly as possible—which was not very. I finished: "What I ran into recently—not anywhere near here, though I am not at all sure 'near' has any meaning in this context—is, then, and among other things, a claim to live in terms of 'other dimensions'. I am damned if I know what that means."

He shut his eyes. His arms began to twine around each other, not tightly. I waited for a long minute.

"I assume," he said without opening his eyes, "you heard this claim as something literal. Not some sort of figurative, poetic statement."

"The speaker didn't strike me as the poetic type," I said.

He hummed for a second. Not an unpleasant sound—a little distant. Then his eyes opened. "A dimension is a mathematical convenience," he said. "N-dimensional space is a common enough theoretical concept. But to speak of living in some—other set of dimensions—well, we can define a dimension in terms of right angles."

"Go ahead." The easiest way to consult an expert is to let him explain to you, even if you know most of what he's going to tell you.

"Take a line—one-dimensional, assume it's a mathematical line, without width. Erect another line at right angles to it and you have a two-dimensional structure. Erect still another at right angles to *both* of those, and you have an object in three dimensions."

I nodded. "Clear so far," I said. "And a fourth line, at right angles to all the other three, defines a fourth spatial dimension—space-four, in fact."

"That's the theory," he said, "and since we do travel in terms of space-four, we can accept the theory as having some sort of practical existence."

"Line, square, cube, tesseract," I said. "So far I'm with you."

"Now, if we continue to erect lines, each at right angles to all of the previous lines, we will be creating objects of more and more dimensions."

"We can deal with the objects mathematically," I said. "We can't picture them. Not that picturing them is a final test of anything."

"It is some sort of test in this case, though," he said. "This being—Folla?"

"Folla."

"Folla was able to interact—massively, he moved your ship—in terms of our four spatial dimensions. While he was doing that, he must have been—in a way—picturable. If you see what I mean."

"He must have existed in this space."

"At least in part," Euglane said. His arms twined again. "The question is: does he exist in terms of *more* than our dimensions—three spatial dimensions, we can travel by means of space-four, but we can't *do* anything in it, so to speak, or with it, we just pass through—or merely a different three?"

He had said something I hadn't expected, for the first time. And I had only one reply, though I seemed to have been saying it a lot lately. "I am damned if I know."

"It must be one or the other," he said, and as he said it I held up a hand. Something had occurred to me, something interesting. Just perhaps . . .

"He said he was now existing in these spaces, and implied he'd been existing in different ones, or a different combination," I said. "But does this involve a different set of dimensions?"

Euglane raised an arm over his head, and turned it. A shrug?. "What else can it mean, after all? It sounds like science-fiction, as I understand such stuff—it sounds, even, like very bad science-fiction—but there it is."

"Maybe," I said, "just maybe, there it isn't."

He left his chair. I'd been right; he didn't stand upright. He eased himself to the carpet, which was expensive-looking but thin and comparatively stiff, and got around in a sort of combination crawl and all-fours. He went over to another table, where there was a small pile of papers. He levered himself up to a chair next to the table, picked a paper off the top of the pile, and said: "I've been thinking about this general subject for some time."

What a psychological-statics expert had been doing thinking about other dimensions I couldn't really imagine, and, as politely as possible, I said so.

"A few of my patients report contact with alien intelligences from other dimensions," he said.

I blinked. "But—"

"But they're mad," he said. "Crazy. Mentally many degrees out of true. Yes. And I do not for a second believe that any report I've heard has any foundation in objective fact."

"Well, then—"

"But my habit is to look everywhere," he said. "Let me give you an example."

I took a swallow of fruit juice. "Go ahead."

"A few years ago," he said, "a patient of mine reported that she was being spied on by aliens. From some 'other dimension', I don't doubt. They patrolled her building, she said. They had a set of signals that told them which room of her little apartment she was in—she lived at the top floor of a small building—so they could train their spy-rays on her at any time."

"And you found the aliens?" I said.

He laughed. He had a musical sort of laugh, with an undertone of the gruffness that was in his voice. "I did not," he said. "I never expected to. But I looked. I hired some people to look."

"And?"

"There were no aliens," he said. "Of course there weren't, and never had been. But—on the roof of a building near hers, with a good view of three of her windows—there was a human. A peeping tom."

I nodded. "Everybody needs a hobby."

"I suppose so," he said. "A little talk with him stopped the practice, at least as far as my patient was concerned—and perhaps altogether, I can't be sure."

"And that relieved your patient?" I said.

"Not by itself, though it certainly helped," he said. "Humans do tend to feel that they're being watched—when they're being watched. Sometimes, as well, when they're not—but the feeling diminished greatly for my patient when the practice stopped. Some further work with her helped relieve her of her delusion about the aliens."

I took a second with it. "So when people report contact with aliens from other dimensions—" I began.

With his patients, he was probably quieter. But he was one of those people who seldom let you finish a sentence. "I look into the contacts they've had with beings from *these* dimensions," he said. "Friends, business associates, relatives—and so on. And," he went on, lifting the paper again, "I look, generally, into the idea of other dimensions as well." He went to the floor again, and came over to me, holding the paper in one hand. He gave me the paper, and went back to the chair near me. "The fact is, Knave, very little about the universe is certain. It's a good idea to check everything you can—however odd it seems to do so."

It's an attitude I'm very fond of, and one I never expect to meet in anybody else—except Master Higsbee, of course. I nodded at him. "The damnedest things do turn up," I said.

"Exactly," he said.

SIX

"Before we go on," I said, "and I do want to go on with this, if you've got the time—tell me a little bit about—well, about you. About the Gielli. And about what a non-human being is doing practicing as a psychiatrist for humans. It seems just a little strange, and I'd like to know, so to speak, who I'm talking with."

He smiled at me. The beak did move, a little, but the effect was mostly eyes and cheeks. "It's a consequence of Troutman's Theorem," he said, "which you don't know, and don't want to hear about. Psychological Statics. But I can put it, more or less, into standard speech."

"By all means," I said.

"Most psychiatric work with patients is built on the very ancient idea—among humans—of transference. That is, the patient treats his doctor, his psychiatrist—they used to be called psychoanalysts, you know, long before rigid methods of analysis were even possible, before Psychological Statics really existed—"

"Before the Clean Slate War."

"So I understand," he said. "The term's a little threatening, for many patients, and we don't use it now. 'Analyst' has rather menacing overtones, and 'anal', which some patients respond to without being fully conscious of the fact, is of course even worse. 'Psychiatrist' is comparatively neutral."

"You were saying something about transference."

"So I was," he said. "In a transference, the patient treats his doctor the way he'd treat—his mother, his father, his brother or sister—someone close to him during an early period of his life, when attitudes were being formed."

I nodded. "I see," I said. Always let an expert be an expert.

"Some psychiatrists use the transference, for all sorts of purposes," he said. "Good ones. We have little use for it among ourselves—the Gielli are—strongly empathic, you might say. We're interested in attitudes rather than objects; it might be put that way."

"Not an unusual kind of interest for a psychiatrist," I said.

36

"You might say that the Gielli were born to be psychiatrists, though less often for, or among, ourselves," he said. "But to go on: in transference, among humans," he said, "there are difficulties—it's hard to establish the distance you need for treatment. You're always juggling the doctor-patient relationship and the transference relationship, whatever that transference relationship is."

"Human doctors seem to manage it," I said.

"They do," he said, and nodded. "But it's always a difficulty—and if the doctor is—non-human, deep transference is less likely to occur. Other means develop, and are in fact as useful."

"So a non-human doctor—"

"Is much less likely to have to deal with the difficulties of deep transference," he said. "Distance is easier to establish, and work becomes much simpler. Of course, there is the question of initial trust—very important—but humans seem to find us likeable people. We are trustworthy, and it's our good luck that we also seem to be trustworthy."

"And your patients don't—well, confuse you with these alien beings they're in contact with?"

He laughed. "We're not aliens," he said. "We're Gielli. We're a known quantity, now." He paused, and smiled once more. "We're not extensive travelers, you know—we've had space-four travel for a few hundred of your Standard years, but we've never been much for exploring. We ran into a human ship—whose pilot *was* exploring, scouting a new area a few light-years from the inhabited planet humans call Rimshot—forty-four Standard years ago, and began talks. Some of us decided to settle here on Ravenal fifteen years ago; our physical requirements are similar to yours, though at home we do have a lighter gravity. The weight here is a bother, but not a great bother."

"I'd never heard of you people," I said.

"Well," he said, "we're really rather quiet sorts."

And then he gestured at the paper.

"Do take a look," he said. "You may notice something interesting."

"Before I do that," I said again, "let me go back to all this about dimensions. We might not be looking at a question of different dimensions at all."

"You're assuming that this being was telling lies?" Euglane said. "It's possible—of course it is. But as a primary assumption—"

My turn to interrupt. "I'm assuming he said exactly what he meant, and nothing else," I said. "He didn't say he was coming from other dimensions."

"But surely—"

"There is a lot of empty space," I said. "Even in crowded places, there's a lot of empty space."

"Between the atoms, to so speak," he said.

"Everything we know," I said, "is nine-tenths nothing. There are forces traveling that nothing, from one particle to another. But there doesn't seem to be anything else. Ten per cent of the space has particles in it—speaking loosely. Quarks, subquarks, and all the things built of quarks—protons and electrons and so on, right up to us. The other ninety per cent—nothing."

He nodded, very slowly. "I do see the point," he said.

"It's not a new idea," I said. "It's been out of fashion the last few centuries—space-four, which *does* call for a fourth spatial dimension, started people looking in another direction, so to speak. But even back before the Clean Slate War, some people had theories involving something, God knows what, existing in the empty space between what we can detect. In the ninety per cent."

He stared at me. "How very ingenious," he said. "Not at all the sort of thing a Giell would think of. An actual, physical universe, co-existing with this one, and undetectable by it."

"At least," I said, "there may have been such theories. Everything got so damn scrambled when the War happened—"

"So I understand," he said. "A shame, to let such destructive emotions loose. But I do understand that humans are like that."

"Some of us, and some of the time," I said, and he nodded again. "Not 'other dimensions' at all, but just what this Folla said—other spaces."

"Fascinating," he said. "Though of course there's no way to establish—"

"No way in the world," I said. "At least, until Folla pops up again."

"You think he will?" He looked eager, as closely as I could read his face. Not worried, not puzzled. Something new to experience, something new to look at.

"He met me," I said. "Somehow or other, he picked up enough of the language to make himself both understood and confusing. He flipped me thousands of light-years in no time I could measure. He must have expended some sort of work on all that. Maybe he wants to follow it up—for whatever reason. Maybe he just wants to see what happened, or what my 'friends and neighbors' are like, from somewhere nearby. I think he'll pop up—sooner or later."

After which, of course, nothing whatever happened for six weeks.

PART TWO

HARRIS FRANCE

SEVEN

I mean, of course, that nothing happened involving Folla, or other dimensions, or other spaces. In fact, the Hell of a lot happened, and I was right in the middle of most of it.

Not the shooting, though. I was out of range for that, and I would have heard about it eventually, I suppose, but in fact I got the news about as fast as anybody did, except the victim. Until then, I was working with Master Higsbee on the idea of other spaces. The math for such a concept had been worked out before the Clean Slate War, "as a theoretical exercise, Gerald," he said. "You must remember that the ancients had no idea anything existed that was completely unmeasurable."

"If you can't measure it, it isn't science," I quoted.

"Exactly," he said. "A silly attitude, but quite typical of the time. The saying spread so widely and rapidly that we have, to-day, no idea who originated it. People seemed to like it."

"Well," I said, "they had some excuse. Even psychology works better when you can put the numbers in—that's what Psychological Statics is all about."

"Ah," he said. "You enjoyed your talk with Euglane?"

I nodded. "An interesting fellow. It was while we were talking that this other-spaces notion bit me."

"You were bitten well," the Master said. "It is an idea too long laid aside, Gerald. Such other spaces would be wholly in-tangible—not even detectable as forces, particles or waves or whatever the ancients called such things—I don't recall."

"Wavicles," I said.

He shrugged. "To be sure. Deciding that a compromise is an object. Typical."

"Well—"

"An object that cannot be detected in any way cannot be measured," the Master said. "Therefore, it was not science; therefore it could not exist."

"We can't measure space-four,." I said. "But the ancients didn't know there *was* a space-four. They have some excuse."

"They knew that Cantorian infinities existed," he said.

"Cantor, Dedekind, many others lived and died before space flight. Such infinities are not mensurable in any usual sense; they can be measured in terms of each other, but not in terms of any objects themselves not infinite."

"Well," I said, "they were the ancients, after all."

"They were a strange collection of people," he said. "But let us leave them, and apply ourselves to something more interesting—to this idea of other spaces."

We discussed it up, down, and sideways, and kept running up against the central puzzle: how in Hell could we contact anything that existed in the ninety per cent of the universe that was, for us, nothing at all except a passageway for forces? We came up with some notions, many of them complicated and all of them too silly to bother you with—but if you don't hunt for all the notions, silly or not, you are not going to find the good ones.

And a few weeks went by. And I did other things—renewed an acquaintance here and there, went to a meeting of a club I'm a member of—spun time out, in other words, in the company of my friends and neighbors. And then, early one evening, Euglane called me.

I was, in fact, dressing for dinner, and looking forward to it, since a rosebud named Gjenda Cass, an expert in some arcane aspects of physical chemistry (which was not, for me, her major attraction, but I have no prejudice against physical chemists), had agreed to share it with me, and had suggested a restaurant I'd never tried.

"It's rather a new idea, Knave," she'd said, "and I think you'll like it."

I am all for new ideas, or at any rate some of them, and I was looking forward to suggesting to Gjenda some rather old ideas of my own, later on in the evening. I was putting some plain black studs into a lovely and expensive off-white shirt when the phone blipped at me.

I went and got it, keyed in Remote and said: "Hello?" as I put in another stud.

"I need you," a voice said. Not, unfortunately, Gjenda's.

"Euglane?" I hadn't heard from him, nor had I called him; Master Higsbee and I had been off on another track, and I assumed that, if Euglane had any news about other dimensions, alien beings or the like, he'd be in touch. Until something happened, I wasn't on any deadline.

"I dislike to ask it, Knave," he said, "but I need to see you as soon as possible."

His voice was still pleasant, just a bit gruff, but there was a lot of strain in it. "What's happened?" I said.

He made an odd sound. In a human being I'd have called it a moan, and maybe it was one. "Death and destruction," he said. "I am at home. You remember the address?"

Euglane hadn't struck me as the kind of person who was given to random hysteria. I checked my watch. All right. "Give me forty minutes," I said, and hung up without waiting for a reply.

Damn. There was just time to find Gjenda at home, I hoped, and I got back on the phone. Gjenda answered, and she did not take it well, and I was in too much of a hurry to smooth things over.

Well . . . perhaps some other time, physical chemistry.

Thirty-six minutes later—dressed in a casual jumper, with my dinner clothes still lying around my hotel room—I rang the little bell-announce, and Euglane opened the door just as quickly as before. I wondered briefly if he hid himself right behind the damn door when he was expecting visitors—twice I'd been early, and twice there'd been no delay at all. But probably not; call him speedy and hospitable.

His arms were fully extended—relaxed—but his legs weren't; when tightened up he had rather short, almost stumpy legs, capable of carrying him nicely upright. He didn't look much different, if you passed the eyes, which were wide and staring, and didn't notice the fact that he was breathing just a bit raggedly.

I said: "What's happened?" and stepped inside. He shut and locked the door behind me, and leaned against it, facing me in the entry hall.

"His name is Harris France," he said, "and I'm horribly afraid that he's killed someone."

I nodded, and went on into the big living room I'd seen before He followed me, and when I sat down on the same couch he sat down in the same big chair. He twined his arms over his head. I nodded again.

"Let's take it a step at a time," I said. "It will make more sense that way. Who is this Harris France, who do you think he's killed, why do you think so, and why aren't you sure?"

That seemed an exhaustive enough list to start with; it left out only the question: Why me? which could wait a few minutes. Euglane stared at me, his arms twining and untwining. Nervousness? Panic? Worry?

"Of course you're right," he said. He let his arms fall. Far down by the carpet, his hands clenched and unclenched. "I'll try to—I have a patient, whose name is Harris France. He presented with symptoms of—well, never mind, never mind. We've been working for six months. Almost exactly six months. Progress has been slow; he has some—intractable beliefs. Apparently intractable. They interfere with his perception of the normal world, and—Knave, this isn't getting us anywhere."

"In order to get anywhere," I said, "it is necessary to start from somewhere. I've got to find out where the somewhere is."

"Right," he said. "Right. He came here this afternoon. Not his usual appointment, but he called and said he had an emergency. I was able to clear an hour. He told me that his companion was lying dead in their home."

"He killed his companion?" I said.

The arms went up, twining again. "He doesn't know," Euglane said. "He told me he felt sleepy—it's an escape for him, it's been happening for a month or more now. He went to his bed and lay down, and remembers nothing. He thinks he slept about three hours. That would not be unusual. When he woke and went into his living room, he found her body. He told me she had been killed by a beamer, fired from a distance of between four and eight feet, tightest focus and maximum power. The beam had gone through her heart. He knows little more. He called me, he says, within minutes—when he was able to function at all. The shock was massive."

"He noticed a good deal, for a man in a state of shock," I said. "Weapon, range, focus, power. He must have spent some time examining the body."

"He would recognize such things rapidly," Euglane said. "He's a Detective-Colonel with the Homicide detachment of the police."

EIGHT

It took a little while, but some facts emerged. Let me give you a few of them in summary, just for openers:

Harris France: age 53, career police officer, current rank Detective-Colonel, head of Homicide Four (which was the—reasonably extensive—Lavoisier section of Ravenal Scholarte, plus twenty square blocks of expensive houses, and a small park) for City Two. Twenty-two years with the police, steadily climbing the ladder. Bright, a little slow physically, medium height and a tad overweight. Living with Cornelia Rasczak for the past nine years; before that he'd been a bachelor, with a few short-term liaisons here and there but nothing serious. He'd had some kind of unhappy love-affair in his early twenties, and the details, Euglane told me, were private—"if at all possible," he added.

"I won't pry if I don't have to," I said. As it happens, I never did have to. "This Cornelia—"

"Rasczak," he said. "Yes. She's the one whose body he just found."

I nodded. By then we had coffee in front of us. Euglane had pulled his arms in, and kept extending them and pulling them back. It was a little disconcerting, but at least both arms changed at the same time. I wondered if he could extend only one, and put the question aside for a more peaceful moment.

"He wouldn't have heard the beamer," I said. "Even awake, with a shut door between them, he might not have heard it. But he would have heard somebody come in. When he went to sleep, nobody else was in the house?"

"Just Cornelia," he said. "Knave, I'm not used to violence. It's not—a part of our natures, really. Gielli are not hunters, not eaters of animal life."

"It isn't easy," I said. "But surely some of your patients—"

"Troubles in ideation," he said. "Emotional difficulties. There is violence in the mix, of course there is. For humans, violence is a given, like rigidity or love. But it's—a factor. Not an object in itself. It's an idea, a drive."

"Not a thing lying right out there in actual, physical, bloody existence," I said.

"Exactly," he said. His arms shrank and lengthened, rapidly. "I tried to persuade Harris to stay. I told him I would get help, we would discuss this fully, we would conclude—something. I was—not very effective." His arms twined. His eyes shut and opened. "Knave, I was ill. Physically ill." He made that sound again, the moan. "Violence," he said.

I nodded. "I'm a little easier with it," I said. "You don't have to carry this by yourself. You can hand it off. And just by the way—why *haven't* you handed it off?"

"But I called you."

"I don't mean me," I said. "I don't know what I'm doing here, in fact. The police will know—probably know already—"

"He called them from this house," Euglane said. "He explained that the shock had been very great, and he had had to come here and talk for a bit before being able to make the call. He had wanted to try to find out what had happened, he said. But we could not find that out, Knave."

"The police will," I said. "He was an important man there. They'll be extra-careful. They'll figure it out. You don't need me."

"You don't understand," he said. "The police—this will be a subject for the news readers. Of course it will. And the police will be anxious to make clear that Harris committed this horror. They will do everything possible to convict him."

I opened my mouth, thought for half a second, and then nodded. "They're afraid of being accused of covering up for one of their own," I said. "If everything looks clear and simple—"

"They'll fight to keep it simple," he said. "Yes. It's *because* he's an important police figure that we can't leave it to them to investigate thoroughly enough. They'll see what they want to see—as humans do a good deal—and that will be the end of it."

"So you want me to investigate."

"I want you to find out what really did happen, Knave," he said. "Someone has to."

I did not rush eagerly into agreement. I knew a few police officials in City Two, and they were no fonder of me than most police officials are, anywhere. I am not a detective by trade, and taking apart a murder was not my favorite occupation.

"There's no doubt it *was* murder?" I said at one point.

"No doubt at all," Euglane said. "The only beamer found in the house belonged to Harris, and had not been fired in several weeks. He had had it on a practice range then. It was fully charged. The beamer that—that blotted out Cornelia's life was not to be found in the living room, according to Harris. His own beamer was in the bedroom, in his holster, hanging over a chair."

"He's sure he didn't use that one, clean it, recharge it, erase the counter, and put it back before he—woke up?"

Euglane shook his head. His arms quivered a little, retracted, then extended again. "He's sure of nothing," he said. "But I'm sure. Harris might conceivably perform some single, directed act without full consciousness. A series of complex acts—cleaning, recharging, revising the shot counter, returning the beamer—would be impossible. Absolutely."

I nodded. "All right, then," I said. "No suicide, no accident, or where's the weapon? Either Harris got rid of it—could he have done that?"

"If he got rid of it in some simple, direct way, yes," Euglane said. "Knave, you see why I need you. You're thinking. Analyzing events."

"I'm saying the obvious things," I told him. "There must be detectives on Ravenal, professional people who could—"

"With no ties to the police?" he said. "With no need to see the police view, no matter what the facts? I doubt it."

"It really isn't my sort of—"

"There would be payment, of course," he said. I gestured at him.

"Payment isn't the thing," I said. "But I might not help as much as a professional could."

"Please try," he said. "Harris will need you. And I—I am undone by this. I will need you, Knave."

Gjenda saying she needed me would have been a lot more pleasant. But what the Hell could I do? Plead a previous engagement?

And maybe the Master would help out. I might be better than a detective. Better than the local police, no question.

47

The Master would be, I told myself, a lot better than that; he always was.

I sighed. "Tell me about it," I said. "All about it. Everything."

NINE

I'm not going to tell you about it, not all of it. It would take more time than either of us has to spare, whoever you are and whatever spare time you have lying around. As far as I could get the picture without going over to Harris France's house and poking around in it for a few hours, Euglane gave it to me, in detail.

I was going to have to go over there, and I knew it, but I wasn't really fond of the idea. The police would be an occupying army, of course, and though I could probably run a good enough bluff to give me some standing, it would be the Hell of a complicated job to manage. It was just possible I could get some real standing, if I called a few people here and there, and once I had that I could check through the police files for anything they'd managed to turn up at the scene. Not satisfactory—I don't like trusting anybody's judgment but my own, having had some experience of what the average range of judgment is likely to be, anywhere in the universe—but it was going to have to do.

Meanwhile, I had to take Euglane's report on trust. I didn't like doing that, either, and filed it in my head under Provisional, but I got everything I could. What I'll give you is a short tour of the high spots.

Many of which were barely spots at all. The couple had had no disagreements to speak of recently, and there were, Euglane assured me, no long-standing items smoldering away anywhere. "There are difficulties, of course," he said. "Harris sometimes identifies Cornelia—identified Cornelia—with his mother, as many husbands do; and as his mother was not a pleasant woman there was friction. But not serious friction, nothing that seemed to point to real trouble. His major difficulties were outside that relationship. Much more general."

They had involved, for God's sake, alien beings. He'd had the idea that alien beings (beings who were both invisible and had, he said, no permanent shape, though they had identities and, in his head at least, voices) were watching him—not to harm him, exactly, nor to help him; they were (Euglane said) grading him daily on his performance in every area of his life. "As if his life were one long school-term, with constant exams and constant supervision," Euglane said. "What the grading meant—what could result if, at some point, he received a C or an F or an A in some area for a given week or month—he has never been wholly sure; but it is important, he feels, that he do well, that his grades be good ones. He fears greatly some unidentified calamity if they should drop."

"He must be in great shape just now," I said.

"He's very worried," Euglane said. "Very disturbed—not that they will think he has done this thing—they will of course know, they're always watching—but that he has done it, and they will disapprove. He is almost as much afraid of their disapproval—of poor grades—as he is forlorn at the loss of Cornelia."

"It's a shame we can't ask them," I said. "If the damn beings existed, they could fill us in on exactly what the Hell *did* happen."

He nodded, and we moved on to other matters.

Harris France, when in one of his naps, slept like the dead. If you'd set off a reasonably large bomb within a few inches of his head (while somehow managing not to shred the head), he might have awakened. He might not, too. During the night, Euglane told me, he slept normally, and wasn't terribly hard to awaken. But the naps were different.

"They're escapes for him," he said. "He needs them, and he has been having them often enough, the last month—perhaps five weeks—so that, to your human ancients, he'd look like a case of narcolepsy. They are not normal sleep—though he dreams in normal sleep, in these naps he is simply, as he expresses it, 'turned off'; if there are dreams he has no memory of them, and I suspect that perhaps there are none. It might well appear, to someone without sufficient knowledge, that he is a narcolept."

"But he isn't?"

"Physically he's normal," Euglane said. "Or within normal limits for his age and condition—which is a little above human average. But the sleeping—well, we've been working on it. Before this, I thought another few weeks might see the end of it, the replacement of this sleeping by a different, less harmful and demanding, escape. The need for some such escape would be likely to last longer—by a factor of ten or twenty."

"Sleep doesn't seem all that demanding," I said.

"It robs anyone of time," he said. "Sleep is a good, in anything like normal amounts. It is a great good."

"Knits up the ravel'd sleave of care," I said. "Or something."

He nodded. "Very expressive," he said.

"I'm quoting an ancient," I told him. "Shakespeare."

"Ah," he said. "Yes. I have read some of the plays and the poems. Not all. A terrible waste, you know."

"A what?"

"Think of it," he said. "What a psychiatrist the man would have made, if only he'd had the chance. But he had to settle for plays and poems."

Well, it was a viewpoint I hadn't run into before. I nodded and let it pass. "But getting more sleep than usual—"

"The body tries hard to adjust," he said, "but adjustment's difficult. Activity is needed, and not really available; there's a lot of muscular motion during sleep, but of a very limited nature."

That brought up something. "Maybe not all that limited," I said. "Did France sleepwalk?"

"Not to his knowledge," Euglane said, "and since he did not sleep alone—his naps occurred either when he was at work, in which case he would retire to a resting-area, a room that was always occupied by some officer or other lying down for a bit—or at home, where Cornelia would be present—he would have known; someone would have told him."

"Always?"

"As far as I know," he said, "and I think I would know; we've been working in some detail on this."

I thought of a small list of ways for a man to sleepwalk without anyone's knowing about it, including the man himself. But they were all a little tricksy, and I'd look into them later. "It's about nine o'clock now," I said. We'd been at it for hours by then. "What time did he wake up to find Cornelia Rasczak?"

"He told me he checked his watch within seconds—professional habit, I suppose," Euglane said. "It was then—as you say it—four-thirty-seven A. D. Sixteen-thirty-seven, we say here."

"P. M.," I said, and he nodded. "What did he do? I mean for the next few minutes. Everything."

He had, Euglane said, stared for an undetermined time, perhaps a minute. Beyond checking his watch he hadn't moved. When he did he'd gone to her, seen for certain that she was in fact dead—he hadn't had any doubt of it, the charred wound over her heart, perhaps an inch and a half in diameter, was a fairly good convincer—and, though he'd dropped to his knees and touched her, mostly around the head and face and hair, he hadn't moved her body at all.

The wound had made him check his beamer, and he'd gone back to the bedroom and done that, taken it out of its holster and read the counter, checked the charge and put it back.

Then he'd called Euglane and come over. He'd taken a cab, being a little afraid of doing his own driving.

"Nothing else?" I said.

"Nothing, until he started to leave. I wish he had cried, then or when he arrived here. He did not."

"He was dressed when he woke up?"

"Yes. That was usual for his naps. He didn't even remove shoes, just lay down."

"All right," I said. I sighed. "Tell me: why the Hell does he think he might have done this? Somebody got in—he wouldn't have heard that—killed her and got out."

"When he called me, he was only distraught over the death. The violence. The loss," Euglane said. "When he went to the door to leave, he saw that it was not only locked, but chained from the inside. He took a minute or so then, to check the windows. He's fully air-conditioned, and the windows were shut and locked; some are sealed shut, and none were open or readily openable. None had been broken."

"Wonderful," I said. "We have a classic locked room."

"If Harris did not himself commit the crime."

"Just possibly, even if he did," I said. "If he sleepwalked—he'd have to get rid of the beamer simply. Unchaining the door, say, and chaining it up again, anything like that— would that have been too complex a job for him?"

Euglane thought for a minute, his arms twining. "I'm not sure," he said.

"So either the beamer is somewhere in the house—or he managed to get it out while sleepwalking—or somebody else got in and out like a ghost. Or, of course," I added, "like an alien being."

Euglane nodded. "Just so," he said.

TEN

I've read a fair number of Classic detective stories—I have had a scrappy sort of Classical education—and I've run into a lot of locked rooms. They were very popular, back before the Clean Slate War—for readers, of course, who had never heard of space-four.

They were not so popular out in the real world, then or now.

Nor, I told myself on the way back home, were they going to be popular with me. Locked rooms come in two sizes: tricksy, and accidental. This didn't look like an accident, unless Harris France had done the deed and automatically locked up after himself, once he'd disposed of the damn beamer, which sounded unlikely. And if somebody were being tricksy, I had no real love for the job of unraveling the tricks, which was likely to take time, thought and effort, all of which I would be much happier spending on almost anything else.

Well, the basic rule about poking into any murder of *any* kind is, you start with the victim. Comparatively few people are killed by total strangers, and the victim's list of friends, relatives and acquaintances will usually contain the name of her killer. All you have to do, of course, is cobble up that list, and then eliminate everybody on it except the killer. Simplest thing in the world. I had found out a little about Cornelia Rasczak from Euglane, and I was going to find out some more when morning arrived.

When I got back to my hotel room, it was nearly eleven at night—twenty-three hundred, if you like it that way. After putting away my unused dinner outfit, I began to realize that I was hungrier than usual; neither Euglane nor I had thought of finding anything to eat or drink over the hours, except a few cups of coffee apiece. Room Service runs all night, but I wasn't going to have to depend on it, having stocked the place during my first days. I made myself a small pile of beef-and-cheese sandwiches, and a pot of Sumatra Mandheling coffee, and tried to think while I took it all in.

After about forty minutes, it came to me that this was a useless enterprise. I had six thousand new facts in my head, few of them at all sorted or arranged, and as I began to feel less hungry I also began to feel more weary. Well, the morning would do, I thought; without some standing in the case I couldn't go prying either into the France house or into the police files, and there was no way of getting any standing that night.

The damn locked room would wait, then, like Cornelia Rasczak, while a) my brain caught up with the facts it had been fed, and b) it got to be a reasonable hour to start calling people. I took myself off to bed, and went into sleep as if the whole of Ravenal, or at least the City Two Fourth Police Detachment for Homicide, had hit me over the head.

When I woke up, I blamed the beef and cheese. I do remember a dream now and again, but when I do it's always too silly to repeat. But there's a reason for telling this one.

I had dreamed I was sitting in a large lobby somewhere. Possibly a hotel lobby, possibly the lobby of some office building or even apartment tower, but whatever the Hell it was, it was built on the grand scale. It stretched for miles in every direction, and the ceiling seemed to be about forty feet high.

There were people passing by, though not many, but I recall only a fellow in middle age, with a dark-grey jumper and a pair of pince-nez. I had seen pince-nez once in real life, at a costume ball, and three or four times in museums. He wore them just as if he put them on every damn morning.

I didn't talk to him—he was just one of the busy people going by. I was sitting on a white-painted bench in the middle of this expanse of lobby, and I was waiting for a bank president to come and tell me what my savings account was at the moment. For some reason, it was important to me to know this.

I felt impatient, but not violently impatient. I sat, and looked around the lobby, and only fumed very mildly, and silently.

Then I heard someone come up behind me, and when I turned my head I saw a girl about twelve years old, with a small and hairy dog on her head. She said: "I'm from the bank," and I said:

"Bankers don't wear dogs. What have you done with the real banker?"

The dog looked at me, and said: "I'm the real banker."

I was not surprised. I nodded at the dog and said: "Show me some identification."

"My name is Folla," he said, "and your account has a hole in it."

"It can't have," I said.

"A man with a beamer burned a hole in your account, and the money leaked out," the dog said. The little girl wearing him giggled. I said to her:

"It isn't funny, beamers can be dangerous."

Then I said to the dog: "That account was inside a locked safe. No beamer could have burned through."

"The safe was opened," the dog said. "He pulled off the front with a wire."

"Oh," I said. "That's different. Who has my money?"

"I do," he said, "and I'm keeping it."

"But it's mine," I said.

"Not here," the dog said. "Everything here belongs to me."

"Oh," I said.

That's the dream. The emotional tone—which, as you may have noticed yourself, has nothing to do with the events of a dream; in dreams you can watch grisly murders and laugh, and see a box of marshmallows and run screaming—the emotional tone was very calm. In the dream, I was accepting everything that happened as more or less normal.

When I woke up I thought I could explain it all, even a dog named Folla—after all, Harris France had had some delusions about aliens, and I'd recently met one. Why Folla should have turned up as a dog on the head of a twelve-year-old girl I couldn't say, but dreams are like that.

And I went on with my life, which turns out to have been a mistake.

It didn't look like a mistake then. I got up and slowly persuaded myself that I was awake, and while I was having a small and lovingly self-prepared breakfast I began to punch up numbers on the phone.

I know a few people on Ravenal who have influence even on Ravenal—a Ravenal address will give you influence almost anywhere else, no matter who you are, because there's a general feeling that Ravenal people Know Things. In fact, a lot of them do, and new-style Nobels are almost as common on the planet as the greenflower that carpets most of its parks. The first one I called was at a conference on Haven II, but the second turned out to be in. It was ten-thirty by then, and she'd just got home from work, which had started for her, I discovered, at two in the morning.

Her name is Guinevere Jenn, and she's a neurosurgeon. Her day starts early as a rule, but not all that early; there'd been an accident with a taxi and a pedestrian just after midnight, and though the pedestrian wasn't her affair—two broken legs, a cracked rib or two and a variety of things to patch—the taxi-driver was: bone splinters into the right side of the brain. He'd bashed himself very solidly with a metal crate he'd been carrying next to him in the front seat, when he'd swerved to avoid the walker, and piled into a stone building front at (traffic estimates from Watcher films—City Two has its light-posts fully stocked with cameras) something near eighty miles an hour.

"Simply silly," Guin told me over the phone, sounding tired, and every bit of her sixty-odd Standard years old. "A crate that size should have been in stowage, in the trunk." Guin has little patience for normal human idiocy, which is one of the things I've always liked about her.

"Well, maybe the trunk was full up," I said. "People carry things next to them all the time."

"Large metal crates?" Guin said. "I spent seven hours picking splinters. He'll survive—I *think* he'll survive—but there are going to be residuals. Sizable residuals."

"Well," I said, "he'll know better next time."

"Next time," she said, "won't happen. If he can walk, a year from now, I'll be massively surprised. If he can drive a taxi—if he can drive a tricycle— I'll be damn well astonished."

"Well," I said, "he's still breathing."

"So he is," she said. "And if he keeps on breathing—this is not an exact science I've got here, Knave—it'll be more than the fool deserves. Eighty miles an hour—more, because the swerve slowed him—on a public street. Ridiculous. What prompts the call? I'm a bit fagged out here."

"I know," I said, "and I'm sorry, but I need a little help."

"For God's sake," she said. "You haven't gone and damaged somebody again, have you?"

"Nothing like that," I said. "But you did a job once on Michael Morse, didn't you? Got some kind of plaque—I saw your name in a news feed, and read about it."

She chuckled. Indulgently. "How nice of you," she said. "Yes—an aneurysm. Nasty, but not particularly—special, you know. But if you work on a public figure, people do seem to notice."

"I'd appreciate it," I said, "if you'd call him for me. I've got myself into something, and the M. G. of the City Two police could be a big help."

"Knave," she said, with another little chuckle, "what have you done that calls for interference from the police Master General?"

"Not a thing," I said, "not a single damn thing," and explained.

"So you want a pass to the events," she said after I'd done that. "Permission to look round, question people, examine files and evidence—"

"Just so," I said. "If I'm going to do this job at all, I'm going to need it. And my friends among the police are non-existent."

"I'll make a call or two," she said. "You'll want it now, of course. You usually do."

"In this case," I said, "I damn well need it now. Things get cold fast, and if I'm going to go looking—"

"Right," she said. "I was about to shower and collapse. I should love to shower and collapse. I'll make the calls first, and someone will get back to you."

"Thanks," I said. "Thanks very much. Have a lovely shower."

ELEVEN

Then I started punching buttons on the room screens. Cornelia Rasczak (I knew a little of this from Euglane, and got more, as I punched and read, from news files, directories and a few professional yearbooks) had been 42 years old, a tiny brown-haired woman with a fierce expression and, people said, a very mild manner. She'd been a neuropsychologist—which is not much like a neurosurgeon; the emphasis is on the psychologist half, and her field would be a little closer to Euglane's than to Guin Jenn's—attached to a Rehab unit in (Ravenal's flair for names again) Third Injuries Complex, one of the larger hospitals in the city.

She'd been born on Pupil III, blazed her way through schooling there, and managed to get a place at the Scholarte for her graduate work, which meant that she'd been in the top one per cent of her field, for her age and weight. She went on amassing degrees for a while, taking a year off after the Ph. D. to get into practice with a small Rehab facility in City Three, and finally found herself a spot with Third Injuries Complex, in City Two, as an associate. Her family was back on Pupil III, and it had never been one of those close-knit families; on Ravenal she found friends and co-workers, and when she'd been with Third Injuries Complex about four months she met Harris France.

It had been a romantic story, in a way, and it turned up in several features on the couple: a Homicide Detective-Captain had become a patient of Cornelia Rasczak's. He'd had one of the wasting diseases of the nervous system that used to be quickly fatal, a hundred years back, and are now very slowly fatal—which is an improvement, as it gives the patient ten or twelve years in which to find something else to die of—and he needed a lot of physical retraining after the first set of major attacks, and some understanding of what he could expect his nerves and muscles to do, which was where Cornelia had come in.

He hadn't been a good patient—a good patient, as somebody has noticed, is not the patient who causes no trouble, but the patient who gets well. He'd caused no trouble, he'd followed orders and advice, he'd even improved very slightly—but he felt more and more tired of the fight, and he was ready to pack it in. He was thinking of suicide, and came to France for help.

France temporized with him—and called his doctor. Between them, he and Cornelia managed to restore enough of the man's spirit so he went on working, and gradually began to improve mentally and emotionally as well as physically. He lived fairly happily, and with a good deal of normal function, for eight years, and fell out of a boat during a storm, and drowned.

Long before that, Harris France and Cornelia Rasczak had become an Item, and they had remained an Item. France had had, as I've said, a few liaisons here and there, though nothing serious since his early twenties; for Cornelia there had been work, and little else; he was her first and, as things turned out, her only love.

I looked around for any evidence at all of an affair, and found nothing. Euglane had assured me there hadn't been one, but he had to be going on what Harris France knew, and if there had been one, Cornelia wouldn't have been supplying him with bulletins.

But there was nothing. I amassed a pile of small facts, and found nothing in them to chew on. So I reached for the phone to start calling people, and it blipped at me.

A secretarial voice told me I could pick up an official document giving me official permission to look anywhere and question anybody, and only (she emphasized it just a hair) as regarded the murder of Cornelia Rasczak, at police HQ for City Two. I thanked the voice, hung up and made that my first stop. Just about an hour later, document in hand, I was standing at the door of Harris France's two-story house, arguing with an officer.

I'd showed him the document, all neatly printed out on fax paper, and he'd read it. Two or three times, and slowly. "Nobody gets in here," he said, in a lagging, almost smooth baritone. "It's closed to the public."

"I'm not the public," I said wearily. "This paper comes from Michael Morse. Directly. You do know who Michael Morse is?"

"He has to follow the rules, just like everybody else," the officer said. He'd been lounging in front of the brightly painted door when I arrived, looking bored.

"Damn it," I said, "this paper is the rules. It says I can—" and a good alto voice from a second-story window said:

"Paolo, what the Hell's going on down there?"

"Gink wants to get in, Mirella," the officer called back.

"Nobody gets in," Mirella said.

Paolo said: "He's got papers. From the M. G. Says he can look around."

Mirella sighed. A very theatrical sigh, worthy of the voice. "So let him look around," she said.

"But—"

"The M. G. says, so you do," Mirella said. "Let him by."

Paolo raised his hands to heaven, or to Mirella one flight up, and then, reluctantly, opened the door. I took a last look around—the house sat in the middle of a greenflower expanse, surrounded at several hundred feet by a circling double row of walking-trees: that inner row would move along with the sun every day, providing maximum shade for the front of the big lawn; these were the tame variety, and I felt a certain fondness for them. Their cousins, on Rigel IV, had had a nasty habit of stampeding, and I'd managed, after some struggle, to break the habit. They're not trees, of course, but—when not actually stampeding—they're good company, if you like the leafy silent type.

The greenflower came right up to the door, or within inches; at the door itself there was some packed dirt. It looked scuffed or trampled, probably, I thought, by the endless parade of police who'd certainly been visiting since the afternoon before.

Paolo was waiting with exaggerated patience at the open door. I gave him a nod and a smile and went on through.

I shut the door behind me, leaving Paolo to enjoy the sunshine—it was a lovely day in late Spring for City Two—and set about things. I gave the room I was in one look—it was a large living-room, furnished in a plain, almost bare style—and turned right back to the door.

There must be ways to gimmick glassex windows, but I have never heard of one: glassex is unbreakable, and sealed into place by heat and an electric field, and though I was going to look over the locks and sealing with great care I wanted to concentrate on the damn door first. It had been locked when France saw it after the murder—which was easy: many doors lock automatically when closing unless you tell them not to, and most locks can be gimmicked, anyhow, without enormous effort—and it had been chained from the inside, which was not easy at all.

The room was painted almost as brightly as a circus, for all its simplicity. Harris France and Cornelia Rasczak had apparently liked bright colors, because the walls were a staring sky-blue almost the color of Euglane's eyes, the door itself—thin wood, showy just because it was real wood, but thin enough to be kicked in without your having to be a notable athlete about it—a fine, slightly dark yellow, and the chain—which was of fairly heavy metal—bright red.

It was the simplest kind of chain lock, a set of small heavy links hanging from a metal plate bolted to the wall, about four feet from the floor. A knob at the end dropped into a slot in a smaller metal plate bolted to the door. I took out a handkerchief—the odds were enormous that the thing had already been fingerprinted, possibly two or three times, but if so the job had been done very neatly, there was no powder residue, and in any case why take chances?—picked up the chain, and dropped it into the slot. It looped down gracefully a bit, the red standing out against the dark-yellow door. It looked solid, heavy enough not to break under pressure from outside. The bolts holding the metal plates looked solid, too, and showed no sign of tampering

And the chain hadn't been broken. I lifted the knob out of its slot and went over the whole chain visually. I dug out a small magnifier from a side pocket of my jumper, and went over the damn thing link by link. Then I went over it again.

Freshly painted, but not all that freshly—slight signs of wear. No signs of breakage, solder or strain.

I made a note to check the police files for records of heat residue on the chain, on the inside of the door, on the metal plates, and on the wall near the chain. If somebody had touched those within an hour—perhaps within two hours—of examination, there'd be heat residue the police measurements would have turned up.

Not that the touch would tell me anything: if the door had been used, the chain would have to have been touched by *some-body*; the knob was in its slot when France saw it, right after waking up.

Unless, of course, there'd been a visitor present who could walk right through the locked and chained-up door without leaving traces. An alien, in fact—one of Harris France's invisible alien examiners.

Or Folla, for that matter—who might have got in and out through the damn fourth dimension.

God knows that sounded improbable—but then, Folla himself had sounded improbable, and here I was on Ravenal.

I sighed, and vowed to concentrate on heat residue. It made things so much simpler. Then it occurred to me that the subject was really, truly, totally meaningless: Harris France had had to get *out* of the damn house to go see Euglane, and he'd have had to handle the chain then.

Damn.

The door itself got an examination as thorough as I'd given the chain. It had occurred to me that the whole wood door could have been taken off its hinges, or removed in some way, and replaced after the murder. That notion left me with the same problem the chain posed: the hinges were on the inside of the door. But it seemed easier somehow to gimmick large iron hinges (painted the same yellow as the door) than to gimmick a smaller and much more visible chain of the same material.

Removing the door would have been noisy, and visible. But that was not an objection: Harris France, asleep, wouldn't have heard the noise (and if Cornelia had heard it, she might not have lived long enough to do anything about it), and nobody would have seen the removal—the walking-trees would have interfered, and any (remotely possible) spectator would have been standing in an open road hundreds of yards away.

But getting the hinges back, on the inside of the door, would have been a neat trick. They were painted, and the paint showed no cracks or flakes.

Damn.

All right, pass the door. Provisionally. Maybe one of the window locks would offer a clue. Maybe there was another entrance to the place; a back door, a kitchen door, a cellar door— did the place *have* a cellar?

Had Harris France checked the upstairs windows?

Was there a chimney?

There is seldom any shortage of questions. I sighed again, and turned away from the door, and started out to look through the house.

I was almost instantly interrupted.

TWELVE

A voice I recognized—a good alto—said: "All right: what the Hell have you been doing?"

"My job," I said, and nodded at a police officer who had to be Mirella, standing near the foot of the flight leading to the upstairs.

"All right, so Paolo says you've got a paper," she said. She came down to ground level. "Let's see it, buster."

I walked across the big room, took the fax paper out of a pocket and handed it over. Mirella read it—once, and speedily—and handed it back.

"You got to be something very special," she said. "This thing is an open pass to poke your nose in everywhere—which I have never seen before. You don't mind my asking, buster, who the Hell are you?"

She was a short, roundish and muscular woman in her early thirties, with a great mass of tightly curled black hair, and a dark face that was trying hard not to look cheerful, dark shining eyes, pug nose and all. I had the feeling she had to work at not looking cheerful every day she was on duty, and I liked her at once.

"Says so on the paper," I told her. "Gerald Knave."

She nodded, unappeased. "And who the Hell is Gerald Knave?"

"I've been hired to look into things," I said. "The note from the M. G. makes it official for you."

"Hired," she said, and sighed again, almost as theatrically as she'd sighed at her partner. "Oh, God, don't tell me you're private. I thought I knew most of the people work private around here."

"Just a friend," I said.

"A friend of the Master General's," she said. "Riding a hobby, friend?"

"Not exactly," I said. "And I do have work to do."

"You spend half an hour standing at the front door," she said. "Doing what, I don't know, but I heard no steps away from the area. Now what?"

"Now the rest of the place," I said. "You people have had since yesterday afternoon to print and measure, get heat spots and bag anything you found around. Give me a while to do my own version."

"Got no choice, buster," she said. "I don't got to like it, only got to do it. But would you mind telling me what the Hell you're looking *for?*"

I shrugged. Why not? "The woman's dead. Somebody made her dead. Was it Harris France? Maybe something in the house will tell me."

"Right," she said. "And you think maybe it wasn't. I get the door now. There are two others—kitchen door and a little side thing on the right, opens into a kind of garden. Locked, both of them, but no chain." She saw me look interested, and grinned. She had a fine grin. "Bolted, both of them. Nice heavy iron bolts, inside, and tight."

"Well," I said, "he had to get in somehow."

"He was already in," she said. She'd moved across to a chair, and sat down on it. I took another chair, across a little table littered with magazine spools. "Harris France. Why look for somebody else?"

"Because maybe he didn't do it," I said. "He was sleeping."

She nodded, tiredly. "Sure," she said. "He says he was sleeping. What do you want him to say, he was sitting there and watched the whole thing? Look: there was no struggle. Nothing knocked over. All very peaceful, one dead person."

"So whoever came in was somebody she could trust, more or less," I said. "He—or she—didn't come in waving a beamer and foaming at the mouth."

"He was already in," Mirella said. "I told you."

"You found the beamer?" I said.

"We found his," she told me.

"Clean, no recent shots, fully charged."

"So he cleaned it, he fiddled the shot counter, he recharged. This is difficult?"

"According to his doctor," I said, "it's impossible."

"Right, I heard that," she said. "He shot her, went over to this doctor, called it in from there."

"Or he found her dead, went over to the doctor—"

"You buy his story," she said, "you are going to be the one person in City Two who does. I mean, come on, now. Nice locked house, one beamer, one body, one guy walking around."

I nodded. "Who says the house was locked up?"

"He does," Mirella said.

I gestured at her. "And why would he say that? If he killed her—why not say the door was wide open? Why not put on gloves and open two or three windows, too, just to keep things confusing? No prints, and the heat residue could be anybody's— an unknown killer, opened a window and fled. Or walked out the wide-open door, take your pick."

"Do I know why a killer does things?" she said.

"He's not a civilian," I said. "He had to know how it would look. He's been in Homicide a long time."

"This job can make you crazy," she said. "He snapped. End of story."

"There are always a lot of stories," I said. "One of them is the right one. Maybe I can find out which one."

She grinned again. "Good luck," she said. "You go right ahead and poke around, buster. We did that already. Paolo and me are just here on post now. On your way out, you stop for a fast search; for all I know that paper said you can take stuff away, even, but at least we want to know what." She looked at me. Hard. "You won't upset this one," she said. "No chance. That doesn't happen. But you want to look—feel free, buster. Feel free."

So I felt free, and I poked around. Mirella let me work—she ambled over to wherever I was, now and then, just for the company—on post in an empty house can be the dullest of duties—and we exchanged a few words when whatever I was doing at the moment left me any conversational room. I learned a little bit about Mirella, and the Hell of a lot about the house.

The bedroom where Harris France had taken his nap was actually a sort of small den, on the ground floor, a room in the front, to the left of the living room as you came in. The front door led straight into the living room, but a wall only about eight inches to your left had a door in it leading to the sunny little den. which had a small single bed in it. On the ground floor there was also a kitchen, which was extensive, and a bathroom, and a small library. The kitchen had a door—with a nice solid bolt, the kind you slide into its socket and then turn—and there was a door at the far end of the library, also well bolted.

Upstairs, two larger bedrooms—one used as a guest room—a sort of office for Cornelia, and another for France himself, as well as another bathroom.

And I could give you details of the place—I could spend hours doing it, because I took the house about as far apart as I could—and they would be useless. The two bolted doors were impossibilities—maybe somebody cut that front-door chain and restored it undetectably, though I didn't believe it—but cutting large, solid bolts was something else again. The damn windows were glassex, sealed into place, and the window locks were absolutely solid. There was no chimney.

"See?" Mirella said when I'd tested out the locks on the last window (Cornelia's upstairs office, back right). "He was already here. What else could make any sense?"

I'd had a little more pleasure finding out things about Mirella. Her name was Mirella Puffer, she'd been with the police force for seven years, she'd been promoted right on schedule and was looking to speed that up a little, and she was single. "Just your average frustrated old maid," this round, muscular little woman had told me with a big grin.

I sighed. "It might be he was here," I said. "I mean: of course he was here—and sleeping. While somebody else got in, beamed Cornelia, and got out."

She looked at me. She put her fists on her hips. We were standing in Cornelia's office upstairs. It was about four o'clock in the afternoon—I'd spent the whole damn day doing the France house. "Knave," she said, "you believe him when he says that?"

"Well, yes."

"Why?"

It was a good question. I did believe it, and I believed that Harris France had slept right through the killing, whether or not he'd done it—if he had, he'd done it while sleepwalking.

But why did I believe it?

Because Euglane had said so, I discovered. Harris France had told his doctor he'd been sleeping, and his doctor had, even in Euglane's agonized state, sharp enough eyes to know whether the man had been telling the truth.

He'd been treating France for months. Any patient can lie to his psychiatrist, and I suppose most do, at one time or another; but a good psychiatrist is unlikely to be fooled, once he gets to know his patient. Euglane had had the time to do that—and I thought he was probably a good psychiatrist.

I tried explaining some of that to Mirella Puffer. "You think he would know? Man spins him a story, and you think he would know is it true or not?"

"If the man is his patient," I said.

"Maybe he's good," Mirella said. "I mean, he helps sick people. He's a Giell. They're supposed to be pretty good, you know?"

"So I understand."

"But that's sick people. Look, some of us human types are pretty good liars, right? I mean, France is not a kid, he has been around the block. You think a Giell can tell for sure, a human being is lying to him?"

"If the human being's been his patient for a while."

"If the human being's been his patient for forty years, still I don't believe it," she said. "Husbands lie to wives, every day of the week, and the wives do not catch on very quick. People lie to bosses, same thing. I mean, they know each other years and years, and still they can lie good. This Euglane is different?"

"A good doctor, looking at his patient—"

"Can still be fooled," she said. "Believe it. Not even human, how much can he know?"

"The Gielli are supposed to be pretty good," I said.

"Maybe for sick people, yes," she said. "Maybe. For some sick people. But that good? Knave, *I* am not that good, and I am good. Believe it."

Well, she had a point. Maybe not enough of a point—and I was going to ask Euglane about possibilities. Still—damn it, if he'd done the job, why had he told the story he'd told? The bolts and locks and the chain on the front door spotlighted him, and he had to know it. I mentioned that to Mirella, too—again. And she gave me the same answer.

"Who can tell what a crazy person will do?" she said. "The job made him crazy. Maybe Cornelia made him crazy too. Did he know what he was saying? Maybe not. He said it. And he did this, Knave. Take my word."

It was going to be, I realized, a very general opinion.

THIRTEEN

By four-thirty—sixteen-thirty, as they say—I was through with the house, or as through as I could be. Mirella was going off duty at five (seventeen), and I had a sudden impulse, and asked her what she was doing for dinner.

"Eating it," she said. "You mean we should get together to-night?"

"For dinner," I said.

"Sure for dinner, what do you think I am?" she said. "You know— maybe not such a bad idea. Why the Hell not?"

"Fine," I said. "I skipped lunch, and when you're off duty—"

"I skipped it myself," she said, "but I do that. Diet. When I remember, you know? Sure, an early dinner. You got a place in mind? Because I do."

City Two's restaurants had never printed their names on my mind in letters of fire; I was open to any suggestion, and said so.

"It's sort of a new idea," she said. "Maybe you don't take to it."

Gjenda had suggested a new idea, I remembered. Given Ravenal's general feeling for tradition—they're very big on it, making it do instead of imagination, once you get out of the sciences—it was probably the same new idea.

"Let's find out," I said.

I borrowed France's office, which had a phone, and shut the door, leaving Mirella out on post in the rest of the house. I called Euglane, and got him, he told me, just as he'd finished with his last patient for the day.

"What have you found?" he said. "Is there something that clarifies all this, Knave? I spoke to Harris this morning—he's adjusting fairly well, but of course it's very difficult."

"I'm going to have to see him," I said. "But I've been going over the house, and it looks impossible. I mean, impossible that anybody got in."

"Then you're telling me that Harris, while sleeping—sleep-walking—did this thing?"

"No, I'm telling you he didn't," I said. "If he had, he would-n't have had the damn door chained."

"I've been thinking about that," he said. "It's not impossi-ble for him to have done it while sleepwalking. But it is very im-probable; it's a demanding set of actions, physically, finding the socket and then fitting the knob into it. It doesn't actually re-quire sight, but without it, I think it would require prac-tice—which didn't happen."

"You're sure it didn't happen?" I said. "Suppose Harris has been lying to you. Isn't that possible?"

"Knave," he said slowly, "I am very good at what I do. Even for a Giell, I am very good. No Giell could lie to me with success after months of contact. A human being?" He almost chuckled. "No, Knave. No."

"So he didn't do it sleepwalking," I said.

"And you begin to believe he really did not do this awful thing?"

"I do," I said.

They're two dangerous words, in any context at all.

The new idea—and I will say I was curious by this time, having been primed for it, in a way, by Gjenda long before—turned out to be an adaptation of a very old one. And on your av-erage planet, I don't think it would work very well.

On Ravenal, it works as well, I suppose, as it can. Very in-teresting notion, in fact. In a way.

We took the police transportation—a small black car, la-beled POLICE in large light-red letters—back to the precinct station, a large sandstone building with two dark-blue globes outside—tradition again, though whether a tradition of real po-lice stations on preSpace Earth I can't say. Stations that look like it turn up in ancient 2D movies a lot, and maybe there were actually some real ones, not just ancient movie sets; a recon-structive archaeologist I asked about it once says there seem to have been.

Mirella drove—she told me later in the evening that Paolo was a nice enough fellow, but not to be trusted with anything larger or more complex than a nail clipper. "And even with that," she said sadly, "I think he could probably hurt himself a little." She pulled into the station garage, a dim and open place, and we all piled out. I went around to the front of the building and waited, having had my fill of police stations on a previous visit to Ravenal, and knowing that I was going to have to visit them some more, this trip. It wasn't something I looked forward to.

It took her twenty-five minutes to turn up again, which is not bad time for signing out and doing a full change. She'd been in uniform out at the France house, but now she was dressed in a simple, nicely cut dark-blue jumper, and she'd done something or other to her hair. It looked looser and less official, somehow. She swung up to me briskly.

"Want to stop anywhere before this place?" she said. "Or are you set for it?"

"I'm set," I said. "What is this new idea, anyhow?"

"The place is called Murray's Basement," she said. "Kind of neat, right? You'll see."

We took her car. I sometimes drive on-planet, hiring a car as needed, but in City Two I depended on cabs every time. The place has complex traffic laws—six varieties of light, for instance, from red, through orange, purple, yellow and blue, to green, and each color means something different—plus signs and postings, of course; it all seems to work well enough for the natives, but it would take three months of study for me to figure it all out, and I always seem to have something else to do.

But a cab wasn't for Mirella. "Who knows?" she said. "I might want to get the Hell away in a hurry, no offense. And right around Murray's, I would have to phone for a cab. Why bother? End of the evening, I will drop you off where you say."

And she drove. "My car, I am used to how it acts up," she said casually. It didn't seem to act up much, and she got us to a small park hidden away in the center of town, parked at a spot where the street widened out about two cars' worth—there were already a few cars parked there—and led the way to what looked like an iron trap-door smack in the center of the park, surrounded by greenflower cover and maple trees.

"We go in here," she said. "You game?"

"Why not?" I said, and she opened the trap-door, pulling on a big ring set into it. It opened out easily, and was clearly not iron at all but a lightweight stage set. I followed her down some stairs, which were better lit than I'd expected. The door swung slowly and quietly shut again over our heads.

Down at the bottom of the stairway was a large, cheerful room with the Hell of a high ceiling, half-filled with large, cheerful people. The average weight was perhaps two hundred and sixty pounds, and I may be undercalling it. The patrons of Murray's Basement clearly liked to eat—a very good sign.

It took me a minute or so to get the place assorted into my head. Mirella watched me, grinning, while I figured it out; it was not much like your usual restaurant.

There is a thing called fondle. The Swiss invented it, I think—some day when we've all got time I'll explain what the Swiss were—and the basic notion was, you collect some cheese, you melt it carefully in some kind of pot over low heat, and then you put things on long metal sticks, you dip the things in the melted cheese, and you eat the things. The things are cubes of meat, cubes of bread or potato, bits of broccoli or carrots, anything you happen to have around that might work with whatever cheese it is you've melted.

I don't know why this was called fondle, and of course the word may have been scrambled over time. But there are restaurants on a variety of planets that specialize in it: you check in, grab a skewer, amble over to the big platters of whatever-it-is that's available for dipping, and load the skewer. Then you find the cheese pot. You keep on doing this until you are full.

Murray's Basement had taken this simple, basic notion and expanded it right out of sight. There were tables, some with people sitting and eating; there were longer tables loaded with big platters of food and neat piles of skewers; and there were vats. There were no cheese pots—there were very large, steaming vats more or less all over the place, immense low oblongs perhaps six feet long and two feet wide.

Some of them were filled with melted cheeses, bubbling gently in the bright light. Some seemed to be filled with sizzling fat of some kind. Some held boiling water. One or two held what I later found out—at dessert time—was melted chocolate. Each was connected to piping that, obviously, kept the liquid level nice and high.

Totums rolled everywhere, carrying trays of drinks to the diners, replenishing this or that platter of food, and so on. The place was roomy, and needed to be; and even with the high ceiling, and what was clearly a good air system, it was just a bit steamy.

Now, on your average planet, immense vats full of bubbling cheese or fat or water are not what you want in a public restaurant room. People will get drunk and fall in. (If you are going to stick skewers loaded with food into the vats, there is a definite limit on the guard rails you can be provided with.) People will get spattered by the sizzle of something. There are even a few pathogens that live nicely in heat, and work out badly if introduced into human beings.

But this was Ravenal. The pathogens were no worry, I was sure—things on Ravenal tend to be as safe as some very ingenious people can make them—and for sizzle, splatter or the occasional drunk, there were fields. Very sophisticated fields. They'd pass the skewers, they passed air and light—and they'd pass nothing else. If it wasn't attached to a skewer, it couldn't get in or out, and if it were the mass of a human being it was entirely locked out. The skewers were coded for the field somehow—don't ask *me*, for God's sake—and the process worked perfectly.

Mirella waited for me to catch up to the place, and then led the way to a small table not too near the vats. We sat down, and she said: "We wait for a Totum to come for drink orders. That registers us. Then we go pick up stuff."

"Fine," I said, and the Totum was there inside four minutes, though the place was slowly crowding up. Even when the basic idea looks fantastic, Ravenal tends to be efficient.

FOURTEEN

A while after that, we were cleaning up a first portion—I'd had some beef cubes in a sort of cheddar cheese, and chunks of broccoli in a thick white sauce that was more highly spiced than I'd expected, as well as some potato cubes quick-fried in oil, and Mirella had taken the beef, and gone for two basket items. There were metal-mesh baskets you could attach to the skewers. She'd filled one with peas in the white sauce I was trying, and one with slivers of potato for french-frying. We were drinking, at her suggestion, a house wine cooler that came along in a large pitcher, and was surprisingly drinkable, with a good deal of fruit and some spice added to the basic red.

"So tell me," she said, and picked up a potato sliver, "why is it you asked me out to eat?"

"No particular reason," I said, truthfully. "It seemed like a good idea."

"You usually make dates with police?"

I thought back. "Never before in my life," I said.

"And I am so marvelously attractive you just could not resist," she said, and ate the french-fry.

"Well," I said, "you're interesting." I had the feeling Mirella didn't take well to compliments; some don't.

"I'm fascinating," she said. "It wouldn't be you want a friend you can talk into believing Harris France? Because I am not that friend."

"I never thought you were," I said. "This is purely social."

Whereupon, of course, it stopped being.

In the bustle, I wasn't sure I had heard someone come up behind me; it might have been a diner passing through on his way a vat. But Mirella looked up past me, and I turned around.

Master Higsbee, leaning on his cane, said: "Gerald, I thought I recognized your voice."

Mirella said: "Gerald?" and stifled a small laugh. "People call you that?"

"Gerald, damn it," I said. "People call me Knave. Most people." Then: "Master, it's good to see you, but what the Hell are

76

you doing here?"

He chuckled. "It is a new experience," he said, "and an interesting one. This city has several acceptable restaurants, but few if any remarkable ones. I was told that this was an exception, and I am here with a friend. As are you, I think."

"I hope so," I said. "Master Higsbee, this is Mirella Puffer. With the police—Lance-Corporal—but she's off duty just now. Mirella, this is Master Higsbee. He's a Consultant."

"Hey," Mirella said. "What kind consulting? Hi."

"Very various," the Master said. "And you?"

"I work with the police," she said. "You know that, right? I mean, he told you."

I watched the Master's eyebrows go up. "Gerald," he said. "You actually have a friend with the police? I had thought you were spoofing."

"I hope I do," I said again. "But we've just met. Purely social."

He nodded. "Of course," he said, and then: "May we join you?"

Well, I had never met any of the Master's lady friends, though I was sure they had to exist, somewhere or other. "Shall I ask her over?" I said.

"I will perform it, and my thanks, Gerald," he said, and raised an arm, leaning on the cane. "But it is not a female friend with whom I dine."

I was about to say something, and then I caught sight of the Master's friend standing up—he hadn't relaxed, of course, in a crowded restaurant full of people moving around—and only nodded.

Purely social, I told myself, and watched Euglane come on over.

Euglane was happy to meet Mirella, and for a little while the talk was about Murray's Basement. Mirella began to thaw toward the Master after a minute or so—he's intimidating when he wants to be, but now and then he doesn't want to be—and was enthusiastic about the place. The Master called it "unusual, but in its way a fascinating study." Only Euglane (who had a plate of water-cooked vegetables in a very mild sauce, no potatoes or tubers, and of course nothing animal whatever) seemed to dislike the restaurant.

"I do understand that, for humans, ingestion of food and drink is not only a social occasion of sorts, but almost a celebration, a party," he said. "I see the point—a lot of people sharing the fact that their lives are connected to other lives, both plant and animal. But for me—for Gielli generally—eating's no more a social occasion than breathing, if no less. This sort of—mass convocation of eaters—is just a bit disturbing. Like a mass of people gathering somewhere to breathe in and out."

"It's called exercise," Mirella said helpfully, and Euglane laughed.

"I suppose it is at that," he said. "Humans are very odd, in any case. Their dreams, for instance."

Mirella leaned forward. "Don't Gielli dream?" she said. "I thought everything dreamed. Birds, fish, Berigot, people, anybody."

Euglane frowned. "I don't know whether Berigot dream or not," he said. "I've never thought to ask. And if birds or fish dream, we don't know it. Some animals appear to dream—or at least show muscular movement during sleep that can be interpreted as response to dream experience, though, once again, we simply don't know; we can't ask them."

"And Gielli?" the Master put in.

"Oh, Gielli dream," Euglane said. "We—go into a world. Not the real world—at any rate, not our waking world. We know a good deal about that world, though little of it makes connected sense."

Mirella ate her last french-fry, rapidly. She looked fascinated. "You mean you all have the same dream?" she said. "Everybody dreams the same, every night?"

Euglane shook his head. His hands fiddled with each other over his vegetable plate—a suppressed desire to twine his arms? "Not at all," he said. "We have different dreams—different experiences in that odd world. And they don't—match up, so to speak. The world, the background, is consistent as far as we've ever been able to tell. But our individual experiences in it change from dream to dream, and from person to person—and there are small inconsistencies, vaguenesses." He shook his head again. "That for each human dreamer, a different basic world, a different background exists—drawn from his individual experiences, hopes, fears, and different, even, for each dream—is the thing I've had the most trouble getting used to, in my work."

The Master was nodding, slowly. Thinking. "But how is this accomplished?" he said after a second or so. "Is there a telepathic link of some sort? I had not known Gielli possessed that gift."

"We're not telepathic, no," Euglane said. "We've always assumed that some basic substrate of intelligent operation, some general commonalty, provided the background, which the dreamer uses to express his own desires or fears in each dream. It may be so only for Gielli—or there may be another explanation entirely. There's theoretical work being done, but we're not going to come to any conclusion in a hurry. It's—difficult to theorize in this area."

The Master chuckled, and if I didn't read his mind I read his chuckle, and said it for him: "If you can't measure it—"

"It isn't science," he finished. "Exactly. In a dream there is little mensurable material. But dreams are real things—we experience them—and a science worthy the name will find a way to investigate them thoroughly. Some work, of course, has already been done."

"That a dream is emotionally connected to the dreamer's waking experience, yes," Euglane said, "and we have begun to have some ideas about the kinds of connections made. A patient of mine has been very helpful over the past months—he sleeps a good deal, and reports dreams of almost Giell-like basic consistency."

I said, without thinking: "Harris France?"

"I should not discuss any patient casually," Euglane said. "I can't answer such a question, Knave."

Of course he couldn't, and while I was apologizing Mirella said: "You're Harris France's doctor?" and shot me a look that was suddenly and absolutely poisonous.

He smiled at her, when he got her attention again. "I am," he said, "and you'll have to put it down to coincidence, Lance-Corporal. I certainly never arranged to meet Knave here—I was surprised to see him; it's not, as I understand it, his usual haunt—and as certainly, not in the company of a police officer."

"Hell of a coincidence," Mirella said, suspiciously, and Euglane smiled again. Mirella hesitated, and then smiled back. "Jesus, I suppose it is," she said. "But you have to admit, it looks funny."

"Lance-Corporal," Euglane said, "anything in the universe looks funny—if you look at it carefully enough."

FIFTEEN

Harris France's name having been introduced, we couldn't stay off the topic. But we tried not to discuss the murder itself, or whether France had been guilty of it—Euglane was sensitive enough to Mirella's feelings to steer things away a little, and I wasn't about to plunge in. We weren't successful, but the try was made.

Instead, we followed the Master's lead. "About this whole situation," he said, "the unanswered question—and for the most part the unasked question—is, simply: motive. There appears to be none for the murder."

"Motive," Mirella said flatly, "is for stories. People kill people. Sometimes nobody knows why."

Euglane shuddered. "They do indeed," he said. "But there is always a motive—a reason. It may not be obvious—and it may not be the reason the—the killer imagines it to be. But it is not simply an action at random."

"Of course not," the Master said. "If we assume that Harris France is the killer, then his motive must somehow be discoverable. If we assume otherwise—and I am not doing so, save for theory's sake," he added, turning to Mirella with a small, and surprisingly gentle, smile, "then a motive must lie somewhere in the life of Cornelia Racszak. That, too, must be discoverable."

"Or the whole thing is simply nuts," Mirella said. "If he did it—and I say if," she said with a big smile for the Master, "for the sake of a theory, okay?—then maybe he is just plain nuts. If somebody else did it, so why not if it is just theory, then maybe the somebody was also just a nut. Nuts happen. Believe it."

Euglane nodded soberly. "As the expert on—ah—nuts," he said, "so far as there's any expertise involved—this is the one thing that cannot be."

"Nuts don't kill people?" Mirella said. "Maybe you don't get out enough, Euglane. Maybe *Giell* nuts don't kill people."

"Gielli do not, in fact, kill," Euglane said mildly.

"Lovely place your planet must be," Mirella said. "What is it, Rosscapow?"

Euglane laughed. "Ruskpoir," he said. "It seems to be pronounced many ways among humans."

"Whatever," Mirella said. "No killings. Boy."

"Oh, we have our troubles," Euglane said. "But in this case—among humans—a nut did not do this thing. That much is certain."

Mirella nodded, equably enough. "You can prove this?" she said.

"I can," Euglane said. "If Harris France committed this act, then I can testify that he is not a nut, and was not at the time of the act."

"Well—"

"And if he did not," Euglane went on calmly, "then the care involved in—ah—boxing Harris France argues sanity and balance on the part of the boxer."

Mirella blinked. "Boxing?"

I said: "Framing. Slang sometimes gets away from him."

"Framing is slang?" Mirella said. "I thought all this time it was just usual." She shook her head. "Live and learn," she went on. "But a nut can plan careful. Maybe he is a very clever nut."

"The windows were sealed," Euglane said. "The doors were bolted or chained shut. The weapon was either not found, or carefully cleaned, its counter changed, and fully recharged after the act. No trace of the framer remains." He spread his hands. "A—a nut may be careful," he said, "but he will leave traces. He will leave—a signature of some sort. It may not be sufficient to indicate his identity clearly—but it will indicate the presence of *someone*."

Mirella looked very doubtful. "This always happens?"

"It is a consequence of energy focus," Euglane said. "For a—a highly disturbed person, much energy must be spent in maintaining a workable relationship with reality. The energy thus spent is robbed from other sorts of care. For humans, it is expressible in terms of focus tensor relationships: Rome's Theorem. There exist only so many dimensions—theoretical dimensions, Knave, heuristic conveniences only—in which human action can be planned or take place. Some must be dedicated to the relationship with reality, and the more disturbed the person, the more dimensional structure is taken up by that effort."

"Well, if it's mathematics—"

"It is mathematics," Euglane said. "In fact, it is Psychological Statics."

"Okay," Mirella said. "So it wasn't any other nut. So it was our nut, and the Hell with him. It was our boy, what I said."

"But Harris France is not highly disturbed," Euglane said.

Mirella gave him a very short laugh. "He was seeing you," she said. "So this makes him normal?"

Euglane sighed. "Many people are troubled," he said. "They are not highly disturbed."

Mirella shrugged. "I take your word for it," she said. "So he had a reason. So we will find the reason."

Another sigh. "Unfortunately," Euglane said, "as someone conversant with the details of his life, Lance-Corporal, I must tell you that you won't; it isn't there."

SIXTEEN

I credit Euglane with it: Mirella stayed calm, and even friendly. By the time the discussion broke up, she and Euglane were laughing like old friends. The Master joined in, spinning a couple of small stories Mirella found hysterically funny.

I didn't: they involved ancient history—mine. And by the time Mirella drove me home, she had almost stopped making little jokes about one incident or another. We shook hands at the hotel door, like the friends we were becoming, and she said: "Hey, don't take this wrong, my mind is not changed—but good luck, Knave."

"Thanks," I said. "Neither is mine. I'll call you."

By then we had exchanged phone numbers. I went upstairs, realized there was nothing to do till morning, and went to sleep. Morning arrived at its usual speed, and as unpleasantly as it usually does, and I spent most of it at a police station, gathering facts. None of them conflicted with the ones I'd gathered previously, and none of the new ones looked at all helpful. After a quick sandwich lunch at something advertising itself, inaccurately, as a deli, near the precinct, I pulled out my pocket piece and began making calls.

The pass I had, courtesy Guin Jenn (and Michael Morse), allowed me to go and see Harris France, but I didn't want to crash in to his jail quarters unannounced, and I wanted any cooperation, both from him and from the jail personnel, I could manage. So I cleared everything by phone, found out that France was at home and willing to greet visitors, flagged down a passing cab and headed for the jailhouse.

When Ravenal isn't being traditional, it's being state-of-the-art, and then some. The jail was buffed and ridged solid, and very heavy, metal, with a big front hologram door, and windows that were transparent fields—the whole thing, obviously, under a single umbrella field so the metal walls wouldn't go red-hot by noon every sunny day. The umbrella field passed people, though it cut down heavily on atmosphere-mediated heat and UV, and I went on through without noticing anything—I knew the field had to be there, and found out in some later conversation or other that it was, but Ravenal tends to be unobtrusive about its small wonders—and pushed the plate that opened the hologram door.

Inside, there was a single large room with a high ceiling, and a heavy-looking metal desk square in the middle of it. Doors at the back and sides led somewhere, but none of them was marked. A lumpy fat man in a police uniform sat behind the desk, looking at me with no expression whatever on his dark face.

"I'm here to see Harris France," I said, walking up to the desk as gently and calmly as possible.

His voice was small and high. "And you are?"

"Gerald Knave," I said. He asked me to prove it, and I fished out a variety of cards and, just to nail things down, the letter from Michael Morse I'd been carrying around. He looked the collection over, not quickly but not with undue hesitation, nodded and said: "Second door on your left. Wait for the buzz, then slap the plate. Third floor, fourth cell down the corridor."

"Has he had a lot of visitors?" I said.

"Wait for the buzz, then slap the plate," he said. So I did.

The cell looked comfortable, as cells go. Everything in plain sight, of course, and the door was no hologram but old-fashioned glassex. Harris France had a cot, a small table and chair (both bolted down to the floor), a washstand and small toilet, and a metal bar angled in one corner to use as a clothes rack. There was a plain dark-grey jumper hanging from it, and he was wearing another one that looked identical.

He was sitting in the chair, facing the door—a big, broad-shouldered man, an inch or two over my six feet even, with large brown eyes that looked surprisingly expressive for a police official—they seem to run to the small, hard marble kind—and a mop of iron-grey curly hair. He looked through the glassex door and said: "Who are you? Knave?"

"Knave," I said. "How do I get in to talk to you?"

He grinned. "You don't," he said. "Speaker system's pretty good, and somewhere down the corridor you'll find a chair. Drag it back here and sit down."

I said: "What about privacy?"

"There isn't any," he said, and grinned again. "My lawyer can get in, or my doctor. Otherwise, friend, this is the way it is. Pretty good system, as a matter of fact."

"What about your brother?" I said. "Or—"

"Or my wife," he said. "All right—or somebody's wife. A prisoner has to give up something. Minor arrests, there are other cells, cells that do let people walk in. This isn't a minor arrest. They did what they could for me—for comfort. Some." He grinned at me. He seemed to be taking things very well; or, of course, he was putting on a show for his invisible alien examiners.

I went and found a chair and sat down facing the glassex cell door. Any other prisoners, in the cells on either side, were out of sight, and didn't chip in. Maybe the floor was empty except for France; I hadn't noticed anybody in the cells I'd passed. Maybe prisoners up here were just polite.

"You know why I'm here," I said.

He shrugged. "Not exactly," he said. He got up from his chair—he had to slide out from under the overhanging table—and stretched. "I know Euglane sent you, and I know you have a letter from Mike Morse. Impressed Hell out of Robert—he's the duty guard here."

"Euglane didn't actually send me," I said. "He asked me to look into things. I'm looking. It's the Hell of a strange situation."

He nodded. "I'm told I didn't do it," he said. "I don't remember doing it—I'm a blank for the whole thing—and I—" His face changed. He became sober. The big blocky face looked hard, and only the eyes stayed soft. "I can not, just can not, imagine a reason for doing it."

"So Euglane was saying."

"I don't mean me," he said. "I mean anybody. People have enemies—what the Hell, I've been in uniform a long time, and I've seen every kind of killing there is. Everybody has enemies." He paused. "Cornelia didn't," he said.

I nodded. "Somebody did it."

"I know that," he said. "Believe me, I know that. But I—can not imagine it. A reason to—to kill—Cornelia—" He stopped and took a couple of breaths. "Sorry," he said, to me or to his examiners. "But there isn't one. There simply isn't."

"Somebody," I said, "somewhere, thinks there is."

"Oh, Jesus, I know how I sound," he said. He slid into his chair again. "I've heard people who sound like that—she was an angel, everybody loved her, she didn't have an enemy in the world, nobody could do this thing—" He shrugged. "People say that all the time. About Cornelia it was true. She helped people."

"Neuropsychologist," I said.

"Right," he said. "A clinical neuropsychologist—not research, she dealt with therapists and patients. Do you know what that is? A lot of people don't."

"Vaguely," I said. "I've read up a little."

"A neuropsychologist," he said, "works with the physical results of damage to the brain or central nervous system. Damage you're born with, or damage that happens to you. Sometimes it's people who can't use their arms or legs—or eyes, say. Sometimes it's something else—you know that disease where people suddenly start to curse or say weird things? They have muscle jerks, they repeat things sometimes?"

"Tourette's Syndrome," I said. "I've heard of it."

"Neuropsychologists work with that, too," he said. "There's been brain damage, there's a physical cause. We still don't know enough about it, but they're working on it."

"Like a therapist," I said. "Retraining muscles, or whatever's called for."

"Much more than a therapist," he said. "Figuring out what can be retrained, and what paths are open—what can be done about the paths that are closed off in the brain or the nerves— she sets guidelines for therapists. Among other things. I mean she did set them." He stopped and took another breath. "Sorry. God damn it."

I said: "You've got a right to feel something."

"You're trying to help," he said. "No reason to load my griefs on you." Another pause. "Anyhow, she helped people. She didn't do anything else, not really."

I nodded. "Well—professional rivals? A dissatisfied patient? What was her private life like?"

"Professional rivals—no way," he said. "Maybe, somewhere, there's a neuropsychologist disturbed enough to want to knock off people who have the jobs he wants. But he'd have to be very, very weird. No."

"Patients? A therapist she rode too hard, maybe?"

"Her patients adore her," he said. "Adored her. God damn it, Knave, adored her."

"It's all right," I said. "You've lost her. You'd be expected to feel something."

"Oh, I suppose," France said. "It's—it's hard, Knave. She used to—to—to tell me how to be. What to do. In—difficult situations. I'd go to her for advice, I really would; you wouldn't think she knew enough, but she did. Now—now she's left me to do it for myself."

I nodded. "Her patients adored her," I said. "All of them?"

His eyes shut and opened. "That couldn't be expected. Illness—trouble, trouble like that—makes people irritable. It's only natural. She had some—they'd yell at her, they'd say all kinds of things." He shook his head. "It wasn't serious."

"Tell me about some of them," I said, and he did, and he was right; it wasn't serious, or it didn't look serious. I'd check out any that looked even faintly promising, but there didn't seem to be the Hell of a lot there.

"A therapist, maybe?" I said.

"Now, with therapists," he said, and he smiled. It was a gentle, faraway smile. "With therapists, you really do have it: they adored her. Some neuropsychologists get very tough with therapists. They ask for the Moon, and they expect to get it. Or—what's worse—they draw up a plan of treatment, walk away and never check back at all. The plan's all they contribute, and if it isn't followed, or if there are changes—not their worry."

"And Cornelia?"

"She did it right, Knave," he said. "She really did. She gave orders where she had to—she made them suggestions where suggestions would work better, you know—she followed up, she wasn't too tough, and she didn't just say six words and forget about the patient. She did it right."

"The therapists thought so?" I said.

"The therapists adored her," he said. "God damn it, people liked her. I wished—I used to wish—I had her trick with people. Even the patients who yelled at her. Knave, nobody could have wanted to kill her. Nobody."

But somebody had.

What the Hell, I told myself when I went away—maybe Folla.

SEVENTEEN

There were sixty things to do, of course—check on the patients France had mentioned, do a little more digging on the life of Cornelia Rasczak, talk to Euglane about how France was bearing up, and whether, just possibly, there was anything in his belief about alien examiners that linked up with Folla, or Cornelia, or anything else at all.

I did none of them. Instead, I went home and called the Master—and was told by a strange voice that he was occupied. Deep female voice: friend, secretary, light-and-love? Better, perhaps, not to ask. I said it would wait, I'd phone again, and checked my watch.

Five-forty P. M.—seventeen-forty, if you insist. I reached for the phone, intending to call Gjenda and see whether I could patch up the relationship that had looked so promising before everything had started to happen—and found myself punching in Mirella's code instead.

The thing blipped twice, and an irritated voice said: "What? I am off duty, damn it."

"Mirella, it's me," I said. "Knave."

The voice changed timbre instantly. In the sweetest imaginable tones, the tones of a contralto assuring Rhadames that she, not that pitiful slave Aida, was his only true love, she said: "Oh. *Gerald*. How are you?"

"Confused," I said. "Can we possibly meet somewhere?"

The voice stayed honey-sweet. Honey with added sugar. "Why, Gerald," she said, "you're *rushing* me."

I took a deep breath. "That may happen," I said. "Why rule it out? Why rule anything out? But, for a change, this is professional."

"Now look," she said, and the honey had gone. "I said I didn't change my mind. You are not going to talk me into—"

"I don't want to talk you into anything," I said. "I want you to talk to me. I've been checking the police files—but there are some questions I can't ask just anybody."

Honey. "And I am not just anybody, Gerald?"

"You're somebody I know," I said, "and somebody I think I can trust to be honest."

"Dinner," she said after a second. Not a honeyed tone: Mirella Normal. "And we talk after dinner. Till then we are social."

I grinned at the phone. "Perfect," I said. "Murray's—"

"There's kind of an antique place I like," she said. "Even the name is, like, historical. We could try that, it's maybe a little quieter than Murray's Basement."

"Sure," I said.

"Forty Street and Josephson Road," she said. "I could meet you there, okay?"

"That's fine," I said. "Seven-thirty?"

"Seven-thirty?" she said. "In the morning?"

I sighed. "Make it nineteen-thirty."

She agreed. "You can't miss it," she said. "It's called the European Union."

Mirella ordered, so help me, a crocodile filet. I'd had no idea there were crocodiles on Ravenal, let alone crocodiles being raised for food—Hell, I'd had no idea crocodiles *were* food. She gave me a very toothy smile.

"They want to eat me," she said, "I can eat them. Why not? They're pretty good, you should try one."

Why not, indeed? But I settled for what the place called rissoles and I, out of a Classical background, called burgers. Made from nice, peaceful beef animals, who would never have dreamed of wanting to eat me.

The place was a nice, somewhat claustrophobic little room, crammed with tables and eaters, but surprisingly quiet—good sound management, I supposed. It was dimly lit, which many find romantic and I find bothersome; I have a fondness for being able to see what the Hell I'm eating. But there was decent music going, from somewhere—a selection of Austrian folk songs, of all things, sung by a gentle tenor voice accompanied by a wind trio.

"Every night a different country, the music," Mirella said. "Countries in Europe. That's a continent back on Earth, or something."

"Well, part of a continent," I said. "I'd love to stop in, the night they do Switzerland."

"Must be some Switzerland songs someplace," Mirella said.

"Yodels, I think," I said, and we discussed music for a while, and other things for a while, and when we were finishing up—Mirella with something-or-other flambe, and me with a small selection of fairly decent cheeses—she said:

"All right, so you have something on your mind, so get it off."

I cut a bite of cheese—something I remembered from my last visit to Ravenal, a thing called City Four Smoked. It's not bad, and ought to be better known off-planet. "Harris France," I said. "I've talked with him, and I've dug up the public facts, and some of the private ones. But you know more about him than I do."

"He's a nut," Mirella said flatly. "People who kill people are nuts."

"Mirella—"

"Maybe they do it for money," she said. "Maybe for love, or whatever. Maybe for jealousy, which is a nut thing all by itself. But there are things you do, and there are things you do not do. Killing somebody is a thing you do not do. You do it, who cares what the reason is? You are nuts."

"Well," I said, and watched her stoke her furnace with a spoonful of flambe, which dripped slightly, "there's always self defense."

She swallowed, and sighed. Deeply. "I don't mean self defense," she said, "and I don't mean soldiers. Be serious. Killing people is nuts."

"Basic sanitation?" I said.

"Somebody needs being put away, you put him away. Maybe in the Colony." The Colony is Ravenal's version of an ancient idea—Devil's Island. "Maybe in a nut hatchery. You do not kill him."

It's true that Ravenal has no death penalty, and they get a lot of work out of the Colony population. "Well—"

"It is A, B and C," Mirella said. "You kill people—and I am not talking self defense, or soldiers either, there are special cases for everything—you are taking something nobody can

92

give. Money people can make. Life you get once."

It's not a discussion that has any end to it, and never has been. "About Harris France," I said. "Before he was a nut—or before you knew he was a nut—what was he like?"

"He was away up there," Mirella said. "With the big shots. Me, I walk post in an empty house. Do I know what a big shot is like?"

"There must have been talk," I said. "Gossip. Stories. There always is."

She spooned up the last of the flambe. "Oh," she said. "Stories. You want to go around believing this kind of thing? I mean, people say anything."

"They say what they feel, mostly," I said. "The kind of stories that get told about a commander tell you something about what he's like on the job. They fit what people see."

She nodded. "Could be," she said. "About Harris France—I think back and the stories were, he is a tough kind of a guy. He says six words, he does not say seven. He wants it done, he wants all of it done, not just the piece that shows."

"Demanding?"

She nodded. "You could say. But not a screamer, you know? A fair guy. You screwed up, you had reasons, he might understand the reasons." She thought for a second. "He might not, too. Guy lost a set of prints once."

"Well," I said, "you can always get another copy out of file."

Mirella laughed. "No—look, this *was* file," she said. "People born here, like me, we get printed automatic, when we're maybe six months old. Something like that. But people come here, we just do not print everybody comes in."

"Customs has enough to do as it is," I said, with some feeling.

"So we had a case—a murder case, what else? We would go print a tourist for traffic tickets?" Mirella said. "There were two tourists might be involved, it looked like. Never mind details, but we had to get prints. And the guy got one set, he lost the things." She shook her head in wonder. "I mean, on the way back to the station with the set—the tourist was printed in her hotel, we make it easy for them, right?—on the way back to the station he suddenly did not have the file."

I blinked. "What the Hell happened?"

She shrugged. "Who knows?" she said. "Did the guy just drop it on the street, and a sweeper got it before anybody really noticed? Did he lose it some way in the car? I got a question for you, and it was the question was in France's head, I guarantee you: did he ever take the prints at all?"

"You think maybe she bribed him to forget about taking them, and claim they were lost?" I said. "But somebody would go out and get her prints again, wouldn't they?"

"Maybe," Mirella said. "And maybe she was buying time. And maybe he really did take them, and they got somehow lost. I do not know this guy who lost them, and I wouldn't say word one about it. But anything is possible."

I nodded. "And what did France do?"

She laughed again. "First, he sent out and got another set from the tourist. Who screamed like Hell, but it had to be, right? Second, he busted the guy lost the set so far down he will be ten years making Private First."

"He got mad?"

"Live steam was coming out of his ears, what I heard," she said. "What I heard he said to the guy—name of Gutch, I remember that, Killeen Gutch—he said, by rights he should be shot dead. He had his way, somebody screws up that bad would be shot dead." She paused, and I let her say it. "Hey. So maybe his wife screwed up real bad. So he shot her dead. Makes sense."

"Somehow I doubt it," I said. "But this was one time only? His ears didn't steam every couple of days?"

"One time," Mirella said. "Not often you get that much of a screw-up. But I will say, not often he even got mad, either. Tough, yes. Also fair. Mostly, he would listen, and maybe even understand. That is not such a usual thing, away up there where he was."

EIGHTEEN

I poked around for more, and got a little, but you have the basic picture. Privately, I wondered how Harris France had thought his invisible examiners had reacted to his blowing up at a duty policeman. It wasn't surprising he hadn't done it more than once.

Hell, none of it was surprising: France had been what I'd seen him to be, and what he almost had to be, given what Euglane had told me—a man under tight control, tough enough to keep the control, and as careful to be fair in any situation as he could be.

Which told me absolutely nothing about whether he'd used a beamer on his wife. The Master had been right: motive was the key. My digging hadn't turned one up, and my talk with France hadn't done anything helpful in that direction either.

But somebody had wanted the woman dead. Maybe all murderers were (as Mirella had said) nuts, but even nuts had motives, most of the time. And this wasn't a killing at random, not in a locked, sealed, chained and bolted house.

Most motives are personal. Some aren't; assume Cornelia Rasczak was the well-liked person I'd been reading and hearing about, all right—and concentrate on the impersonal ones: these come in two sizes.

1. She was placed somewhere the killer didn't want her to be placed. In other words, she held a position, or had some sort of standing, that the killer wanted vacated.

2. She knew something the killer didn't want known.

There's a small subset to 2: the victim knew something the killer didn't mind other people knowing, but didn't want the *victim* to know. That particular little oddity doesn't come up often, but you can't ignore it.

I thought about 1 for a while, but not very long. Professional rivalry, at that strength, didn't seem to exist, according to France. I'd do some checking, but, provisionally, 2 seemed more likely.

What could she have known?

If France himself had been shot, I'd have had a thousand instant possibilities: any police officer knows the Hell of a lot of things that other people don't want known. But it was Cornelia who was dead; and what would a clinical neuropsychologist know that might pose a threat to somebody else?

She dealt with therapists, and all of that would normally be a matter of record: programs drawn up, lists made, reports of all kinds. And she dealt with patients.

Patients who might be anybody, and might have any kind of secret.

Why would they have told those secrets to their doctor?

Well, maybe if I knew what the secrets were, I'd have an answer for that. And finding that out meant looking at the patients, in detail.

First thing in the morning, then—well, second thing, after climbing slowly into a state of being awake, cleaned, fed and dressed—I went on back to the police station. Somebody there had to have a list of Cornelia Rasczak's patients.

The somebody turned out to be an ancient, overweight Sergeant-Major named Griselda Fank. I showed her my pass from Michael Morse, and she grunted at it from behind an old and overloaded wooden desk.

"This paper doesn't say you can carry our documents away," she said at last.

"I don't want to carry them away," I said. "I want to copy small bits of them."

"Copy machine's busy," she said, without looking up from the paper.

"I'll use pen and paper," I said, and showed her a small supply.

"In the file room," she said. "No chairs or tables, but the material can't leave the file room."

"I'll write standing up," I said, and that exhausted her invention. When I asked her for access numbers for the files on Cornelia Rasczak she gave them to me at once, in a slow and tired voice.

Fourteen patients. I could list all the names, but what's the sense? I'll list just two: Harnett Groves, and Hester MacEvoy..

Harnett Groves was the first one on the list. He had, he told me, Gilles de la Tourette's Syndrome. "People are pretty understanding," he said. "Go back a few centuries and I'd be burned for witchcraft, or anyhow get into a lot of bar fights. But people here do understand." He grinned. "Mostly."

He was a small, birdlike fellow in his forties, with a thin mat of grey hair and small brown eyes, and with very quick sudden motions, and a habit of blinking his eyes about four times a second, which was disconcerting until you got used to it. He also had a habit of brushing at his cheek with one hand—the first few times I thought he was trying to wipe away some smudge I wasn't seeing, or had an itch, but his hand went up to his cheek every few minutes all through our talk.

"And Dr. Rasczak was helping you?" I said.

"She was doing everything she could," he said. "There isn't much help, even today and even here. There's a new operation—I could go into details, I could draw you diagrams—but it's only for certain types of the syndrome. Certain Touretters. People like me—I've got the wrong balance or something. Thyroid, I mean. For some thyroid balances, they tell me, the operation won't work; very bad side effects. Very bad." Hand to cheek. "They tell me, some day soon they'll have an answer." Another grin; they came and went very rapidly. "I've been waiting for some day for twenty years now."

"They tell me it's a complicated kind of thing," I said.

"It seems to be," he said. "It seems to be. It seems to be." He blinked a few times. "Sorry. But when I heard she'd been—killed, I mean not just died but somebody killed her—it wasn't the kind of thing you could believe. Kill Dr. Rasczak? Why?"

"That's what I'm trying to find out," I said.

Another fast grin. "Why not ask him?" he said. "This husband of hers, I mean. He did it, is the way I've heard it. So why not ask him?"

"The police are doing that," I said. "Maybe they'll get an answer. But I'm trying to find out about Dr. Rasczak. She'd been your doctor for—" I had the numbers from the files—"four years."

"One of my doctors," he said. "Neuropsychologist isn't like a medical doctor. They know a lot of the same things, but it's different. She could advise, she could put things in some kind of perspective. I have doctors—I tell you, I have doctors the way some people have—I don't know. Customers. It's like I'm a store, and somebody comes in every day."

"What did she do for you?"

He grinned. "Everything she could," he said. "She knew tricks. I mean, I have pressure of speech sometimes—that's when you talk too fast, you can't slow down or stop. She knew some things—breathing, even sometimes looking out a window—they break the chain for me. Most of the time."

"Tricks," I said, and he said:

"That isn't all. This thing—Touretting—it isn't one thing, it's a hundred. A thousand. Tics. Speech. Even breathing, though I haven't had that." Hand to cheek. "Yet." A small pause. "She knew it—like she had it herself, almost. Knew what it was like, and she knew ways to get around it. To get back to normal. What everybody accepts as normal."

"Did you discuss your personal life with her? Your working life?"

"My working life, I'm a salesman," he said. "I'm pretty good. I think people buy just so they can shut me up." A grin. "We found ways for me to talk to people a little better, a little easier. Without the pressure or the dangers, most of the time."

"And your personal life?"

"She found ways for everything," he said. "My personal life, I've got a few friends, I enter duplicate bridge tournaments. Hearts, I play Hearts a lot. That's about it, nothing much to discuss, but she found strategies, ways for me to handle the cards more easily."

"Nothing else?"

He grinned once more. "Friend, there *isn't* anything else," he said. "I'm a simple guy, and I lead a simple life. A small apartment for two, that's all there is."

I noddded. "For two?"

"Me and Gilles de la Tourette," he said. "My constant companion."

Hester MacEvoy was number four on the list, and I reached her by early afternoon. She was about Harnett Groves' height as nearly as I could judge, perhaps a little shorter, but she outweighed him three to one, a round and lumpy woman with straggling grey hair, and dim, grey-blue eyes. Her hands looked like strong claws, and her jaw looked soft and weak.

She was in a wheelchair when she came to her door, and I said I was sorry to disturb her.

"Don't be silly," she said. Her voice was a very faint foghorn, and she spoke slowly, the words dragging just a little. "You're company. I enjoy company."

She wheeled back to let me by, and I went in and through a small dark hall to a tiny, even darker living-room. There were books everywhere, on shelves that went high into the dimness, and a tall coat-stand in one corner with a sort of dark-grey woman's cloak hanging from a top peg. She wheeled in behind me, having shut the door, and told me to take a seat.

"I've already got one, you see," she said, and gave me the most miserable smile I'd seen in several years.

"I'm sorry," I said. "As I told you on the phone, I'm here to talk about Dr. Rasczak."

"Cornelia," she said. "Yes. Cornelia was a great help. I don't know where I'm to find anyone else who can help the way she did."

"What did she do for you?" I said, but she was going right on.

"I could tell her anything," she said, almost dreamily. "Such a fine woman. So sympathetic. I had no secrets from Cornelia, because she understood. She didn't laugh at me— they mostly laugh at you, you know, though they hide it and just pretend they're taking notes."

Secrets? I said: "I promise I won't laugh. I won't even take notes." I seldom do, except in my head where I can always get at them. "What kind of thing was it that she understood?"

"It's because I wasn't born here," she said. "I'm from Kingsley originally. But Mr. MacEvoy held the Chair of Military History at the Scholarte—well, at Leibniz, you know. That's a college in the Scholarte."

"He doesn't hold it now?"

She laughed. The laugh sounded just as miserable as her smile had looked. "Lord bless you," she said, "he passed over eight years ago. But how am I to go back to Kingsley after all this time? I'm fifty-six years old, and everyone I know is here. And there's the pension. So I stay. But they don't like outsiders here. There are plots."

"Plots?"

"They laugh at you if you're from somewhere else," she said. "Especially me, because I have a midbrain disease and I'm in a wheelchair. I can drive my old car, and I can handle things. My hands look peculiar, I know, but I can use them well enough for anybody." She looked at me, daring me to object. I didn't object. "Cornelia didn't laugh," she said. "Never, not once, not even inside."

I pressed, just a little. "And you told her about the plots?"

"Oh, they don't really hurt me," she said. "Sometimes I think I'm just imagining such things, you know. But she really was a great help about the aliens."

NINETEEN

I took a deep breath. "Aliens?"

She smiled at me again. It was an expression that could drive a man to suicide—or at least to apology. I started to say I was sorry I'd brought the subject up—which I hadn't, and wasn't—and she said: "You have a nice aura. I can tell you. Your name is Knave, you said?"

"Gerald Knave," I said, and for some damn reason added: "Ma'am."

"Yes," she said, sounding a little vague. "Knave. Knave. I think I can tell you."

"Go right ahead," I said.

"They want to get in," she said. "In where we are."

I nodded. "They're not in now?"

She frowned. That looked more natural on her face than the smile had. "Of course not," she said. "They're *aliens*. They're from outside." She waved a hand—a weak motion, as vague as her voice. "Outside everything."

I thought of Folla—from "other spaces." It was brilliantly obvious that the woman was mad. But even mad people can be accurate, sometimes. They may think two plus two make sixteen and a third, but they may be perfectly sound on four plus three.

So I asked her, carefully, how they were trying to get in, and she said:

"Every way. They come and talk to me. They try to make me open a door for them." Another frown, a big one. "I don't understand that at all," Hester MacEvoy said.

"What kind of door?" I said. "What is it they want you to do?"

"They want me to build something," she said. "I can't build things for them. I have a midbrain disease, and I'm in a wheelchair. Anybody can see that. What do they think I am?"

"Build something?"

"With my own two hands," she said, and raised the claws to me. I nodded again.

"What kind of thing?"

"I *said*," she told me impatiently—slowly, but the impatience was clear—"I *said* I don't understand it at all. I can't build things for them. They ought to know that." Her smile was small and distant. "They seem to know a lot, to hear them talk."

I took a breath. Maybe it meant nothing, but maybe there was something here. I'd talk to Euglane—and to the Master. "Hear them talk," I said. "Do they come and talk to you?"

"They talk," she said. "I hear them. Clear as I can hear you. Clearer. But they can't come in yet. They need me to build something, first." A big smile, the first that seemed genuine. "I won't do that," she said. "Do you think I would do that? I won't."

Another angle, maybe. "You say—they tell you things. Who is this 'they', do you know?"

"Dube," she said. "Mostly I talk to Dube. Or he talks to me. Maybe she. You can't really tell with aliens."

"Right," I said. I repeated the name. "Dube?"

"Tell the truth, Mr. Knave, I don't think they even *have* names," she said. "Not really. But he said I could call him Dube. He said it was sound." She paused and frowned, remembering. "Sound-coded something," she said.

I swallowed. Hard. "Sound-coded individuation," I said.

"Right," she said, unsurprised. "That was it. Sound-coded individuation. Dube."

Oh, Lord.

Hester and I had quite a long talk, and she agreed to talk to other people if I sent them around. "It's company," she said with that horribly depressing smile. "I like company."

I told her I'd do my best to see she got some, and I went away. I'd forgotten to hook in my pocket piece, so I looked around on the street for a phone, but Hester's neighborhood was quiet-suburban, small houses that looked just a little worn, lawns, dogs and cars. No handy phone booths. I'd be better off at home anyhow, I told myself.

There was a shopping street a couple of blocks off, and a cab-stand on it. I got home as fast as possible, and I started punching numbers even faster.

*   *   *

Euglane's number gave me a recording: "I'm sorry, but I'm with a patient just now. If you'll leave a number I'll get back to you just as soon as I can." I didn't bother to leave one—I'd get him later. I took a deep breath, hoping the Master wasn't also occupied with something, and checked my watch. Four-twenty. All right, sixteen-twenty. Anything was possible.

The thing blipped once, and his rasp said, as always: "Who?" It is no way to answer the phone. I've never mentioned it to him.

"Gerald Knave, Master," I said. "There's been a development."

I heard him draw in his breath. I hadn't heard him that excited in several years. "Folla?"

"A friend of his," I said. "I think. It may be nothing. On the other hand—"

"Gerald," he said, "I am at work. Whatever you have encountered, it will require discussion at some length, I imagine."

"I think it might," I said.

He chuckled. "Indeed," he said. "Please come here at once. We can talk while I work."

I got an address from him, and left.

He was set up in a small office in a distribution center for Playtime Wispies, and despite everything it took me a couple of minutes to adjust to the sight. It took me about a minute, sixty long seconds, to notice him at all.

He was surrounded by boxes of spools and a big square reader equipped to speak its screen, and none of that was surprising. The reader was set on a desk, with the spools piled around it carelessly, and Master Higsbee sat behind it in what looked like an overstuffed armchair, his cane leaning on the left arm of the thing. There were a couple of stiff chairs in the room, too.

And then there was a medium-tall blonde person, standing near a small table set against the left wall. She had grabbed my attention right away: she was dressed in Playtime Wispies, flat-heeled soft shoes, and nothing else.

The table was heaped with an untidy collection of what looked like more Playtime Wispies.

They were all colors—pink, coral, black, ivory, pale green and more. The ones being worn were a very pale pink, and there wasn't a great deal of either the bra or the little panties.

I must have stood in the doorway for longer than that minute. The Master had been listening to the reader tell him something, but when I shifted my balance in the doorway he looked up. "Ah," he said. "Gerald. This is Roquelaire Hanna." He waved a hand at the girl in the Wispies.

"Call me Rocky, everybody does," she said, and smiled at me. Her voice was a little thin, but it was the only thing about her that was in less than perfect proportion. "Hello, Gerald."

"Knave," I said through my teeth, and, to the Master: "Your investigation?"

"Of course," he said. "We have been trying various combinations."

All right. "Combinations?" I was trying hard to keep my mind on conversation. This was not easy.

"The thefts have been of display clothing, from models in stores throughout the city," he said, as calmly as if there were nobody in the room but the two of us. "We have been attempting to see how the theft could be managed most easily, with a variety of lingerie, a variety of clasps or ties, and so on." He gestured toward Roquelaire Hanna, casually. I couldn't have made a casual gesture toward that woman if I'd practiced for years. "Ms Hanna serves my purpose better than a plastic display model," he said. "She can cue her location by voice, and inform me which type of lingerie she is wearing."

I grinned—at him or at her, who knows? I couldn't help it. "It sounds like interesting work," I said.

"The problem is a simple one, as I told you," he said. "But there are subtleties." He turned to her. "You said A53?"

"That's right," she said. "Bra and panties."

The Master got up. He took his cane and made his way slowly and easily over to her. When he stopped, she took the cane, without moving more than one arm and hand.

He said: "One moment, Gerald," and reached with his right hand, for the little pop-clasp that was set between her breasts. He popped it, moved to grasp the material just to the left of the clasp, and pulled. The bra—strapless, of course—came away.

"Time?" he said.

Roquelaire Hanna looked over my head—at a clock over the door, obviously. I had to concentrate to notice what her eyes were doing. "Just over nine seconds," she said. "Nine point two."

"Thank you," the Master said, handed her the bra, took his cane, and returned to his chair. "Gerald, what is it that has happened?"

I hated to say it, but it seemed best. "We'd do better without an audience."

She'd been putting another bra on, a green model with straps. She clasped the thing, stopped and waited.

"Perhaps so," the Master said. "Roquelaire, we will have to continue this at a later time. Perhaps in the morning. I am sorry, but a disclosure of some importance is occurring."

"Just give me a call," she said. She gathered up the Wispies and left, dressed in bra and panties. I waited for noises from the hallway, but heard none except for her soft-soled footsteps. There couldn't, I told myself, have been anybody in the hall just then; or the employees of Playtime Wispies were more blasé than I could make myself believe.

"A helpful girl," the Master said after a few seconds. It wasn't quite the word I'd have picked, but I nodded. He shut his eyes for a second—he does that, perhaps ancient habit—and opened them. "Now," he said. "What has developed?"

I told him about Hester MacEvoy, in detail. When I was through he said: "You do not know the precise nature of her illness?"

"She said a midbrain disease. There are a couple of hundred, at last count."

"And some of them," he said, "involve mania, of various sorts and to varying degrees."

I nodded. "Which is not the point," I said. "Three words are the point."

"I agree," he said. "'Sound-coded individuation'. Not a phrase anyone would hit upon easily, by chance."

"Folla used it," I said. "This Dube, whatever he is—or she, or it, or they—used it. It would be the Hell of a coincidence if there were no connection."

He raised a finger at me. "Caution, Gerald," he said. "You are assuming too much."

"That Folla and Dube are both real, and both aliens from the same—little sheaf of spaces? Either from 'other dimensions' or from the spaces between, in our set? It seems a natural—"

"And so it is," he said. "The phrase is striking, and we can take that much as a good assumption, at the least. But you are assuming more, Gerald: you are assuming that Folla is Dube."

Maybe he reads minds. It would be just like him never to mention it. "Well," I said, "it's possible."

"So it is," he said. "It may be factual. And it may not." He raised the finger again. Lesson time. "But it is no more than possible. We know next to nothing; we should not leap to certainties where none exist. As Ms MacEvoy said, perhaps they do not even own names; they are individuals, but may distinguish themselves in other ways."

"In which case," I said, "*they* might both be the same person. Or thing. Or something."

"No: they individuate; we can assume that much," he said. "To what degree we must remain uncertain, but they may be as separate as you and I, Gerald. As separate as you and Ms Roquelaire." He chuckled. "Which separation," he went on casually, "I have no doubt you will do your best to lessen, should opportunity arise."

TWENTY

I didn't bother cobbling up a reply to that, I just let it go. "So either Folla is back," I said, "or a friend of his has popped up."

"Yes," he said. "I think it reasonable to assume some closeness between the two, at the least; both not only speak our language, but use the same unusual phrase."

"Which neither one would exactly have picked out of casual conversation," I said. "The question is, what do we do now?"

He smiled. "We speak to Euglane," he said. "He is a perceptive fellow, but precise wording may have escaped his close attention. We ask him exactly what the 'alien beings' his mad patients report to him have said, in their words as reported—if possible, we ask for recordings from the relevant talks with his patients."

"Confidentiality—"I began.

"It is common practice," he said. "And it is good practice. But identity can be edited out of such records, Gerald. The job will be laborious—but clearly it must be done. I am sure Euglane will agree."

I wasn't, having had some experience of how carefully any doctor guards confidentiality. Back before the Clean Slate War, a doctor who broke it could have been sued—the ancients had laws for everything, including how a doctor ought to behave, for God's sake; but then, the ancients seem to have had something on the order of one lawyer for very one and a third normal persons, a luxury the Comity is somehow managing to do without.

Today there aren't laws like that—either you trust your doctor, or you find another one, which does seem the simple way to handle the matter—but doctors are very determined on the subject. I'd been surprised into asking Euglane to breach confidentiality, back in Murray's Basement, and he'd gone ice-cold on me for a few seconds.

And editing out identity might be an interesting job; wiping or changing names would be easy, but changing the voice rhythms and general speech patterns, even if the vocal ranges were changed, would be a neat trick.

Well, the Master thought there'd be no trouble, and just maybe there wouldn't be—for the Master.

I tried Euglane's number again, and the thing blipped three times before I heard his voice: "Yes? I am Euglane."

"Gerald Knave," I said. "I'm with Master Higsbee, and there's been a development we'd like to talk over with you."

"Regarding Harris?" he said.

I had almost forgotten there *was* such a person as Harris France. "Maybe," I said after a few seconds. "What we know is, it involves alien beings."

There was silence for almost half a minute. "I see," he said. "Or perhaps I don't. At any rate—I have just left my last patient for the day. Where do you suggest we meet?"

I spent a few tough seconds fighting down the temptation to invite him over to the Playtime Wispies office. "Your place, or mine," I said. The Master, from his chair, put in:

"Or mine, of course, Gerald."

"Why not?" Euglane said, having heard the voice. "'It's been some weeks since we've visited, Master. Can you set a time?"

I looked at the Master. He said: "There will be traffic abroad. You do not drive in City Two, Gerald. A taxi—we should allow the better part of an hour, much of it spent in locating one."

I looked up at the clock Roquelaire Hanna had been watching. Seventeen-ten. "Eighteen-fifteen," I said.

"I will provide a small dinner," the Master said. "Tell Euglane that I do recall his preferences and his needs."

"Please thank the Master for me. And—six-fifteen P. S.," Euglane said. "Is that the way you prefer to say it, Knave?"

"Close enough," I said, and fetched up some polite goodbyes, as did he.

In the cab—which we managed to find after only four or five minutes of casting around on the crowded street—City Two hasn't really got pushing-and-shoving crowds, but just after five (seventeen) any working day it tries its best to pretend it has—the Master said: "You have not visited me at home in several years, Gerald. You will note changes."

"You've given up the fish?"

He looked almost shocked. "Of course not," he said. "But there will be four at dinner; I have contracted an obligation."

I remembered the female voice I'd heard when I'd tried to phone him earlier. It was hard to believe, but—"You've gotten married?"

He gave me his chuckle. "I have not," he said. "Her name is Hilda Ramsgate, she is thirty-seven years old, and she has had recent difficulties. She required some small assistance, and I have provided; she is staying with me for a time." Another small chuckle. "There is no thought of marriage," he said. "Nor of any sort of—liaison. You will see."

But the first thing I saw, when I followed the Master through his massive oaken doorway into the entrance hall, was the damned wall of fish. The hall opened into a living room with a couch, three comfortable chairs, and a couple of tables—and, at the far end, the glass wall. It was lit from above, and not brightly, but the savage little fish were perfectly visible. I hoped to God somebody had fed them recently enough that I wouldn't have to watch the process.

"They are not pets," he'd told me once, long ago. "Keeping a pet is an offense against the independence of all living things. They are exemplars."

Well, whatever they were, they were extremely nasty little horrors. I have never known anybody else who would even think of keeping piranhas as a hobby—for one thing, they need special temperature control, special lighting, and a lot of very careful consideration generally. And of course feeding them isn't a matter of buying a dollar's worth of fish food flakes every so often.

They were drifting lazily around behind the glass, and looked torpid, which was a good sign. We went into the living room, and the Master gestured toward one of the chairs. As I ambled over to sit down—the chair didn't quite face the wall of piranhas, which was a relief—he called out: "Hilda!"

I'd heard her footsteps before he'd raised his voice, and in about a second she appeared in the doorway that led to the kitchen. "You have—a guest?" she said in a rough baritone I'd heard once before; it was still female enough that I'd known she was a woman in one sentence over the phone.

"Very good," he said. "You detected the breathing, of course."

"Breathing and motion," she said. "He walked to the—the light-blue chair. I think he sat down."

"The dark-blue chair," the Master said. "A difference of a few feet only. You are doing very well, Hilda."

She gave him a brief smile—like a spasm. "I'll get there," she said, and he went to the couch and eased himself down, leaning the cane next to him.

"You will indeed," he said, and smiled at her. She couldn't see that, of course, but she could hear it in his voice.

Standing in the doorway, she looked perfectly capable of bracing herself against the sides and bringing the whole damned house down, like Samson. She was a little under my height—which is six feet even—and she was built like an all-in wrestler; under the brightly flowered jumper she had muscles on her muscles, and her shoulders and arms were very impressive for size and apparent strength.

Her face was square and strong, and when she spoke she showed the largest and whitest teeth I'd seen in years. Her mouth was big and generous, her nose a small round snub, her hair a simple, neat mat of red-brown curls. Her eyes were closed. She looked younger than thirty-seven, but not by much.

"Hilda Ramsgate," the Master said without rising, "Gerald Knave. Gerald, my house-guest, Hilda."

"Ah," she said. "You're Gerald. I've heard things about you."

"I talked to you on the phone yesterday," I said. "What things?"

She said it again: "Ah." Then: "Yes, when I hear you clearly I remember. It's nice to meet you." She did that little spasm of a smile again. Well, I might find out what she'd heard some other time. Or not, of course. I said:

"My pleasure."

"May I explain, Hilda?" the Master said. "Gerald will be curious."

"Go ahead," she said. "It's no secret, Sir."

"Hilda became blind five months ago," he told me. "She wishes to learn to deal with her situation, as I have."

I nodded. "She can get her eyes replaced," I said. The Master never had, and I'd heard him give seventy different reasons why. One did not badger him on the subject. But I'd thought his attitude was—like almost everything else about him—unique.

"It might be possible for her," he said mildly. "But she feels—Hilda, would you explain? And sit, by all means."

She was still standing in the doorway. "Thank you, Sir," she said, and walked—trying to do it casually and easily, but moving slowly—to the light-blue chair near mine.

She backed to it, feeling not with her hands but with the backs of her knees, and sat down, trying to make it look natural, and almost succeeding. She turned her head toward me.

"It's my own fault, Gerald," she said. "I thought I was—as *he* says— smarter than the universe." The odd smile again.

"How so?" I said.

She shook her head slowly. "I was a chemist," she said. "In my work, precise color differentiation was important. I came across mentions of something called Calorate-six. You may not have heard of it—"

"Oh, God," I said. "Three drops into each eye, and your rods and cones are six times as efficient. See with greater precision. Discriminate fine shades." It had been something of a fashion, first on Apelles, where odd and expensive fashions sometimes do take hold, and then on several worlds. I hadn't heard of it on Ravenal, but why the Hell not? Intelligence is only intelligence; sense is a different thing altogether.

Back before the Clean Slate War, away back there among the ancients, it might not have been possible for Hilda Ramsgate to go out and casually buy Calorate-six. It would probably have been a Prescription Drug—which means that nobody could sell it to you unless you had a Prescription. This was an official order from an official doctor (or dentist, or psychiatrist) telling whoever had such stuff for sale that you were officially allowed to purchase it—a sort of Security Clearance program for various chemicals.

This odd little rule never did make any sense—many things that could kill or injure the buyer could be acquired without Prescriptions—aspirin, for instance, which was a favorite drug among suicides. And some common poisons, like arsenic, could be bought without Prescriptions if they were labeled as weed-killer or some such. (Weeds are unwanted plants. The ancients divided the vegetable world up into wanted plants and unwanted ones, on no system anybody has ever been able to explain.) But the rule, once put into effect, was as impossible to kill as it was to understand.

Today, of course, it doesn't exist; when people put society back together after the War, there were some pieces they felt it better not to include, thank God. When you need a medicine, you may not need the delay and foolery, not to mention the expense, of going to an official person and begging for a Prescription.

The argument an ancient might make in favor of Prescriptions would probably have been: "But how do you know what medicine you need? An official person, who knows all about medicines, has to tell you that."

And sometimes he does, and if you have any sense, and don't know quite what's wrong, or what remedy there is for what's wrong, you'll go and ask. (And if you don't have the sense to do that, it is not up to the rules to lead you around by the hand.)

But if you've had the same thing before, or if you know what it is you need—and quite a lot of people have, or do—why waste time, money and attention?

Well, the ancients were, as the Master had said, a strange collection of people.

Hilda Ramsgate had heard about Calorate-six, and had decided, without enough checking, to try some. A fair number of people on various planets had, and the results had varied from zero to blindness. If you think such a thing couldn't have happened if they'd all had to go and beg Prescriptions, you have more faith in preSpace doctors than is reasonable.

(Of course, if a preSpace doctor *had* handed out such a Prescription, and Hilda had then become blind, she could have sued him. Doctors and lawyers thus became equivalent, and very busy, bothers.)

"I thought it would help," Hilda said. "I should have known better; I should have checked thoroughly. But—well, *he's* right, you know. I thought I was smarter than the universe."

"I'm sorry," I said. "But replacement—"

"It was my own fault," she said firmly. That baritone voice had a lot of firmness in it, when called for. "I'll just have to deal with it."

TWENTY-ONE

I didn't start an argument. Hilda said suddenly: "I should have told you at once, Sir: I fed them at fifteen-thirty."

"Good," the Master said, and turned to smile—fondly, I swear it—to the glass wall of fish for a minute. Then back. "We will have two guests for dinner, Hilda. Would you instruct the kitchen?"

"The usual menu?"

"Ah," the Master said. "I had forgot—I shall have to instruct it myself. Euglane has preferences; and of course the meal will be vegetarian."

"Euglane," Hilda said. "I know his preferences, Sir. I could instruct—"

"I'll do it, Hilda," he said. "There are also Gerald's preferences to consider."

I told him it didn't matter—and it didn't; why put him to the trouble of limping his way to the kitchen and pushing four or five buttons?—but he was firm about it, giving me a smile that said, as clear as large print, that though crippled, blind and aged, he would see to my comfort. For God's sake. He did go off to the kitchen—not limping perceptibly—and Hilda said:

"He's a wonderful man, the Master."

"He's like God," I said. "Wonderful and terrible."

"He's helping me a lot," she said. "And he never complains. Not about anything."

This was not the Master Higsbee I had come to know and sometimes put up with, but I didn't argue the matter. Hilda and I chatted idly for a few minutes, and the Master came stalking back, dropped into his seat on the couch and leaned his cane against an arm-rest.

"Euglane should be here shortly," he said. "Gerald—we may discuss this openly before Hilda; I have few secrets she is not privy to, and none as regards such matters as this; she does not *chatter*—have you any suggestions about a line of inquiry?"

"You said it all," I told him. "His patients. Alien beings. What the patients said they experienced, in as much detail as is available."

"Yes," he said. "But perhaps his own researches—he has, after all, been looking into the question of aliens from other dimensions, whatever that might be taken to mean—might also serve as a ground for discussion."

And Hilda said: "Alien beings? Excuse me, Sir—and Gerald—I didn't mean to interrupt."

"Quite all right, Hilda," the Master said. "Humans seem naturally fascinated by the very notion of alien beings."

"Oh," she said, "it isn't that. But—when I was in the hospital, you know—I had the strangest dream. Only it wasn't a dream, because it predicted a true event."

The Master seemed to tense a little, leaning forward. "A dream?" he said. "Involving alien beings?"

Hilda hesitated. "Well—one being," she said. "And he said a visitor was coming to—to see me. And he was—but it had to be a dream, didn't it, Sir?"

I was a little tense myself, staring at Hilda, who sat quietly in the light-blue chair. "Did this being have a name?" I said. The Master cut in:

"Hilda, you must not be shy of that word. People see. Even you and I can be said to see about something, or see whether something will occur. You must accustom yourself to the word; that is important, Hilda."

"Yes, Sir," she said. "I know, and I do try. But—" She shook her head, and turned her face toward me. "He said his name was Dube," she told me.

And the door chime went off.

All our plans for discussion had, of course, gone straight to Hell. Euglane got a set of somewhat distracted greetings—Hilda was calm and polite, and he'd visited the Master before; there were no introductions to bother about. The Master and I were both a little hurried. "It seems," Master Higsbee told him, when he was seated and Hilda had gone off to find a fruit juice for him, "that we have more news than we thought."

"About Harris France?" Euglane said. He hadn't relaxed, though the Master's place had room for it. His chair had its back to the wall of piranhas.

"About alien beings," the Master said. "There may be a connection. But we can now establish most firmly that Folla is a real and existent being—and that there exists at least one other."

Euglane frowned; it's an odd effect with a beak. "One?"

"There may be many millions," the Master said. "I speak of what we know. You may yourself know more."

That eagle's face looked puzzled. "I myself," he said, "know nothing at all. The beings of Harris' fantasies are—fantasies."

"They may be," the Master said; "that is surely most probable," and I chipped in:

"You said, by the way, that they didn't have names."

"I said," Euglane told me carefully, "that Harris doesn't know their names, nor whether they have any. Has this become important?"

I gestured, vaguely. "It may be," I said. "Your other patients—the ones who have reported some kind of contact with aliens—do *they* have names?"

"The patients?"

"The aliens."

He shook his head again. He sighed, turned very slightly toward the piranhas, turned back and asked the Master: "Do you mind?" and the Master spread his hands, giving permission. Euglane relaxed, fairly quickly.

"It varies," he said after a few seconds. His arms twined over his head. "Some of them have the names of people associated with the patient's past in some way. Or, most commonly, more or less arcane variants of such names. Some have no names at all; some have names whose origin I haven't yet seen."

"Folla?" I said. The Master cut in:

"If that name had come up, we would have known," he said briskly. "Euglane would surely have mentioned it."

I nodded. "True. But how about Dube?"

Euglane thought for a minute. "Dube," he said. "I don't think so. It's not the—the sort of name I'd expect. Names of these fantasy-beings tend to be—polysyllabic, and full of odd echoes. Hotrufan, for instance. Dube is simple, has only one syllable, and doesn't seem to echo much—'dubious', of course, and its cognates, but little more. Has someone reported an alien being named Dube?"

"It's Dube himself—herself, itself, whatever—who's been reporting in," I said. "There's a woman who's had conversations with him. And he isn't a fantasy."

Hilda had come back with the fruit juice. I sketched my talk with Hester MacEvoy. Euglane nodded.

"But this does indeed sound very like the usual sort of fantasy," he said. "Even to the business of—wanting to 'get in.'"

"But it's not fantasy," I said. "That seems to be clear; one phrase establishes it."

Another nod, a slow one. "I agree it's an odd phrase," Euglane said. "Still, it's easier to believe in even a large coincidence than to believe—"

"Ease of belief is not the question.," the Master said. "And there is more. Hilda here has—ah—met the same being Ms MacEvoy speaks of."

There was a little silence. Euglane broke it at last with one word: "Details?" His arms twined, then shook.

"We have none," the Master said. "We were about to inquire after them when you arrived." His head turned. "Hilda?"

She'd sat down in the light-blue chair again (Euglane was on a small sofa of his own, facing the Master and at an angle to Hilda and to me). "Details, Sir?" she said.

"Of your dream," the Master said gently. "Hilda, you said it predicted a true event. What was the event?"

She looked flustered. "It—well, it's nothing important, Sir," she said. "The—the being—Dube—he told me I had to wake up. After we had talked, I mean. For a little while. He said I had to wake up now, because Mr. Garson was entering the building—the hospital building—and had come to visit me, and I would want to be fully awake for him."

"Thoughtful of him," the Master said. Euglane and I were trying to be as inaudible as possible while the Master got the story. "Mr. Garson?"

"He was my superior," Hilda said. "At the lab. He hadn't come to see me before. He only did come that once, I never expected it, really. But I did wake up, and he came into the room a few minutes later."

"You couldn't have heard him approaching?" the Master said, keeping it very gentle, very calm. "While you were sleeping, perhaps—and made his coming a part of your dream, so to speak?"

"I don't see how that could be," Hilda said. "I mean, it wasn't right away. He was just coming into the building, Dube said. It was five or ten minutes before he got to my room at all—he had to ask at the information desk downstairs, and get a pass to visit, and everything."

"And what did you talk about?" he said. "Not you and Mr. Garson—you and this Dube."

"In the dream, Sir?" she said. "He said he would visit me, because he knew I would help him. He said he needed help."

I said: "To get in." The Master turned his head toward me, frowning. Well, I shouldn't have said a word, but I'd been tense.

Hilda didn't seem disturbed, thank God. "To come in," she said. "To meet everybody. He said he needed help to do that. He said he'd help me, too. He told me he would—give me a new sense to replace—to replace my eyes, he said."

The Master took a deep breath. "What sort of new sense?" he said. "And what did he want you to do, exactly?"

"Well, Sir," Hilda said apologetically, "that was as far as we got, you know. Because I had to wake up. It was a dream—but there had to be something real about it, didn't there? Because it predicted a true event."

There was a little silence. Then the Master said: "And has he returned? In another dream?"

Hilda gave him one of those spasm smiles of hers. "Not yet, Sir," she said.

TWENTY-TWO

The Master said gently: "Thank you, Hilda. Would you see about the dinner? It should be in preparation for about half an hour from now."

I am not a big fan of machine cookery. There exist people who claim that, given good machinery and good programs, it is impossible to tell a machine-prepared meal from one made with human hands, and the Master is one of them. I've always been able to tell the difference, but it's not a subject I'd want to bring up with him at any time—if we're going to argue seriously, it's going to be on a subject the size of the heat-death of the universe.

And that evening, I might even have agreed with him. He'd set up an interesting vegetarian meal—tailored to Euglane, which meant not only that there was no animal material involved, but no tubers or roots—and it was absolutely edible, though artichokes vinaigrette will never replace the old standard with drawn butter.

He'd remembered my fondness for chili, and had come up with a vegetarian version, as a main dish, that surprised me by being edible—I think. The truth is, I wasn't paying all that much attention to the food, and neither was anyone else—Hilda just possibly excepted. One day I will have to try that chili with artichokes vinaigrette as an accompaniment; it doesn't sound like a possible combination, but that dinner was no time to test it. I ate without noticing much what I was eating—which is unusual.

Euglane tried to get more details from Hilda over dinner, the four of us seated around the Master's dining-room table. He worked gently, carefully and very, very effectively. He got one, and a beaut, but it took a while

What had Dube sounded like? It wasn't a real voice, it was a voice in her head, even in the dream. What had he looked like? She hadn't seen him, exactly, though in her dreams she did see normally.

"He was just an invisible voice in your head, in the dream?" Euglane said.

"No, I'm sorry, Mr. Euglane," Hilda said. He'd tried telling her just to call him Euglane, with as much success as I would have trying to get her to call me Knave instead of Gerald. The Master called me Gerald, so that was my name. Euglane was an honored guest of the master, so he was Mr. Euglane. He didn't press her, after the one try.

"He was something else, then?" Euglane said gently. "Not simply invisible?"

"I knew it wasn't how he would really be," Hilda said. "I don't know how he would be. He said it wasn't important." She looked worried. "It isn't important, is it, Mr. Euglane?" She turned toward the Master. "Sir?"

Euglane let the Master take it. "It's perfectly all right, Hilda," he told her. "You are doing very well. You should be proud that you remember so efficiently."

She looked almost persuaded. Euglane said, after a second: "How did he appear to you, in your dream? What did he look like?"

She gave us that spasm of a smile. "He was a small dog," she said. "A sort of cute dog. I thought it was silly, but sort of funny, too, just a little talking dog. With a little girl holding him."

The Master and Euglane nodded. I sat there frozen solid.

After a long, long time—maybe all of ninety seconds—I said: "I had a dream myself."

The Master frowned. "You have not mentioned it to me, Gerald," he said.

I felt like finding a wall to beat my head against. "I never thought of it," I said. "It was a dream. It wasn't anything special, for God's sake. Just a dream." I shook my head, feeling remarkably stupid. "I didn't get instructions from Folla—Folla, not Dube. I never even thought it *was* Folla."

Euglane said, mildly: "And now?"

"And now," I said, "I am telling you I had a dream. About a little dog named Folla. A hat-sized little dog named Folla. And a little girl. And my savings account."

I went through it for them—little girl, hairy little dog, big hall, safe, man with pince-nez and all. "There may have been more," I said at last. "That's what I remember. I had no special reason to put it in file, so to speak. Just a dream, God damn it."

"And so it may be," Euglane said. "None of the elements seems—terribly unusual, for a human dream."

The Master was still frowning, but not, I think, at me any longer. "We may be forced to accept coincidence," he said. "That Folla should appear in your dream is not to be wondered at. The rest seems—normal dream-material, as Euglane is saying."

"And the damn dog?" I said. "A little dog, and a little girl. Like Hilda's."

Hilda, for no reason I could see, said: "I'm sorry."

"Dogs are not uncommon features of many dreams," Euglane said. "Doubtless you have dreamed of a dog before, at some time. Many humans have had dreams which include domestic pets. The Gielli have—equivalents, not pets but sharers of our lives. They, too, appear at times in our dreams."

"And all your dreams share the same basic background," I said. "The same single dream world."

"Is this important?" Euglane said, and I said:

"How the Hell should I know? But here we have Folla—and Dube, for God's sake—popping up in people's dreams and saying they want help to get in to us. And here we have a girl and a little dog, twice. Dreams have suddenly become worth looking at."

"So they are," Euglane said. The Master said:

"Dreams as a means of communication. It is not a novel notion—but such supposed communications have usually come from—ah—the Great Beyond, in one way or another. If I am not mistaken, the father of Prince Hamlet appeared to him in a dream; that is the usual course of such stories."

Euglane said: "Ah. Shakespeare?"

"Right," I said. "The frustrated psychiatrist. Dreams are supposed to be prophetic—or carry messages from the dead, or from angels, or some such. But this is something else."

"Indeed it is," the Master said. "The question—and it will have to be answered, somehow—is: What are dreams?"

Hilda stirred. "Sir," she said uncomfortably, "have I made some sort of trouble with my dream?"

"Not at all, Hilda," the Master told her gently. "It is extremely valuable. You are an immense aid to us all, Hilda. Should you dream again—or should you recall anything further about the dream you have outlined for us—it would be helpful if you would tell me at once. No matter when, and no matter what I happen to be doing."

"Yes, Sir," Hilda said, sounding a little better, and there was a small silence. I broke it.

"There's another question," I said. "What do Folla and Dube want to get in to our spaces—to our universe—*for*? They might, after all, want to be friends. They might be explorers. Or, say, whatever passes for scientists, where they are."

"We must decide the color of their hats," the Master said. Euglane looked baffled.

"Black hats are bad people, white hats are good people," I said. "PreSpace slang." He nodded; I could see him filing it away.

"Perhaps," the Master said, "we *can*, in fact, decide. Suggestions?"

TWENTY-THREE

"They haven't done anything threatening," I said after a second. "Folla did me a favor—got me from nowhere to Ravenal in an eye-blink. Everything else has been talk, and talk in dreams at that. If Ms MacEvoy was dreaming, like Hilda, when Dube came along—she didn't say, and I didn't want to press her; she was flaky enough as it was."

"It is interesting," the Master said, "that he was able to move your ship. He is not yet—ah—in, as he says. He exists somewhere outside; he requires help to enter our own little sheaf of spaces fully—and yet he moved your ship."

I thought about it. "He did something real," I said, "in real space-time—in what we recognize as space-time. How did he manage it—and why does he need help to do something else real—to build whatever machine it is he wants built?"

"A conflict," Euglane said. We were sitting in front of empty plates. "Of some interest." The Master said:

"Hilda?"

She reached with her foot for a buzzer and pushed it. After a few seconds a Totum came rolling in, surveyed the situation and began removing plates. Euglane had gone right on:

"If he can move a ship, why can't he move—metal objects, plastics, glassex, whatever it is he needs for his machine?"

"Too small, maybe," I said. "He lacks fine control. Shoving a ship around wouldn't take that."

Euglane chuckled. "You make him sound like one of Cornelia Rasczak's patients," he said. "Somehow I doubt it."

Hilda said, in a soft baritone: "Perhaps—maybe he *can* build the machine. Maybe he's lying."

"It is a poor first assumption," the Master said. "And I see no motive for such a lie. Though, to be sure, discussion of the motives of an alien being is a vain occupation."

"I'm sorry," she said again, and the Master said at once:

"We must explore all theories. Some will prove false, Hilda. It is not matter for apology to have eliminated a false theory, or to have posited one." She nodded. "And Gerald—the idea of a lack of fine control is, I'm afraid, equally false. Locating a parking orbit around a planet is a fairly precise matter, if no more; but it was done with some speed."

"It was done damn well instantly," I said. "Right."

"And yet help is needed," the Master said. "Help has been requested from at least two human beings."

I looked at him. "Right," I said. "And from God alone knows how many others we haven't run into yet."

He smiled. It wasn't a pleasant smile. "Some of whom," he said quietly, "may have provided him with help—or be providing it as we speak."

"Well," Euglane said, "as we've been saying, he may be friendly. He may—"

"It is unlikely," the Master said flatly.

Into the silence, I said: "All right. Why?"

Another smile. "He knows something of human beings—he or Dube, or both. He appears to have known little when he encountered your ship, Gerald, but he may not at first have recognized you as a human being. He went through a brief survey of you, classifying you broadly as human—or humanlike, we cannot be certain—what he called a first cut—which was very general; but he did so in our language. A version of our language, but an understandable one."

"I was all alone," I said, "and a long, long way from any place human beings congregate."

"Human beings may not be recognizable—immediately recognizable—as singlets," Euglane said. "It's been known by humans since before the—the immense War you had, you know—that humans do not exist as singlets, but in terms of other human beings. This is true, in important ways, even for human isolates."

"But he found Ravenal," I said. "From my mention of the name alone. Without waiting for any sort of directions—even if my directions could have made sense to him, even if we shared a coordinate system."

"Not impossible," the Master said. "He had your ship to consult. Your locator would know Ravenal, and its location in terms of other systems."

"He did it awfully damn fast."

"So he did," the Master said. "And thereby did you a favor—a favor neither he nor Dube has done for others."

I shrugged. "They weren't lost."

"But Dube has promised Hilda a 'new sense'—whatever it might be—in exchange for her help. He has given her nothing." He paused and frowned. "This Hester MacEvoy: I do not know the specifics of her difficulty, but might he have promised her some sort of gift as well—and perhaps not yet delivered it?"

"She didn't say anything about it," I said. "I suppose it's possible. As I say, she's flaky."

"He has offered payment for aid," the Master said. "In one case alone, this other, Folla, has given aid without stint; and in that case he may not have recognized you as clearly human."

"That doesn't make him evil," I said. "People expect to be paid for what they do, and why not?"

"Why not indeed?" he said. Hilda was perfectly still, open-mouthed. Euglane was watching—and thinking of something. Hard. I could tell that much from his eyes, and his arms, which were tightening and relaxing, slowly. "But Folla said to you," the Master went on, "that no payment would be required 'at this time'. Dube might have made the same arrangement—or a similar one—with Hilda, or with Ms MacEvoy."

"Why should he?" I said. "He wants something done— whatever sense it makes for him to need help with it. He says he'll pay for it. You can't expect him to amble around scattering gifts."

One more smile. "He is a guest," the Master said. "He is a stranger asking entrance. It becomes him to offer something to his putative hosts."

"That," I said, "is the way people think. Humans, anyhow. For an alien being—"

Euglane said: "It would appear to be a universal. Gielli act so, as well. It becomes a guest to gift his host—a stranger to provide evidence of his worth. The host's time and attention—and his house—our spaces—have value."

"Evidence," the Master said. "Provided value. Not promises."

I shook my head. "Maybe he can't," I said. "Maybe he could move my ship from—wherever he is—but not do anything else."

"Though Dube has promised action to Hilda, it is possible," the Master said. "I do not think my verdict decisive. But it is, at least, a tentative verdict; we have nothing with which to make a better one."

"And, damn it," I said, "he's alien. Really alien. You can't judge his motives the way you judge people's—"

"Gerald," the Master said gently, "I am not judging his motives. I seldom judge motives. I am judging his actions. Whatever they are, the color of his hat depends upon them—not upon his motives."

"True enough," Euglane said. "As with the—the murder of Cornelia Rasczak. Whatever the motive for the act, the act is an act of murder."

"Well—" I said, and thought of Mirella talking about killing people. There are special cases for everything. "I suppose so," I said. "In general."

"We have, then," the Master said, " and tentatively, to be sure—an alien being, with a black hat."

There was, of course, more discussion, but facts, clearly, were missing. Euglane had introduced the murder again, and he kept nudging us back to it.

The thing looked so thoroughly impossible, I said at one point, that Folla (or Dube) looked to be our best suspect.

The Master chuckled. It's not a petty sound. "Yet one further example of his ability to interact with our space-time?" he said. "If we go on so, Folla will prove capable of any act anywhere."

"For all we know, he might be," I began, and he waved a hand.

"That cannot be so," he said. "To begin with, he has limitations. We do not know what they are, but he exists inside *some* universe or universes; any such being has limits."

"For some reason," I said, "that doesn't fill me with any great hope."

The chuckle again. "Perhaps this will improve you," he said. "He has asked for help. He has limits that make this help necessary to him."

Euglane said: "That's moving things along a bit too fast.

He might be asking for this help for any number of hidden reasons; he may not *need* it at all."

"His reasons, however," the Master said, "will involve his needs. Whatever they are—whether those stated or a wholly different set—he has them, and his asking for help is proof that he has needs; and what has needs has limits."

"In other words," I said, "because he's trying to get people to do something—for *some* reason—he needs them to do it."

"At the very least," the Master said, "he needs the process of asking them. Beyond that we cannot, I think, advance just yet."

Euglane said: "Can we advance on another front? Let's say Folla didn't do this thing. To Cornelia, I mean. Let's say some human being did it. Can we begin to see who that is?" He turned to me. "Knave, you say you believe it's not Harris. I agree with you; had he done it, even without his own knowledge, there would be traces in his attitudes and reactions I believe I could see."

"He didn't," I said. "But I have no idea who the Hell did."

Hilda sighed. "People," she said, "can be so horrible."

And that, I'm afraid, was the level of analysis we reached. We spent a lot of time trying to find a point of entry, but we didn't arrive.

It took Mirella to locate one. Somehow, I was not wildly surprised.

PART THREE

JOSEPHSON JUNCTION

TWENTY-FOUR

I spent a couple of days talking to the people who'd been Cornelia Rasczak's patients. I won't bother you with it, because not a minute of it ever turned out to be useful to anything. I wasn't bored—I met some interesting people, and some good ones—but nothing much got done.

And the morning after I'd finished the last of the talks—late enough that the breakfast dishes had been washed, wiped and put away, and I was sitting with a third cup of Sumatra Mandheling coffee, trying to decide on a next move that actually made sense—the phone blipped at me. I put the cup back in its saucer, reached across and said: "Gerald Knave. Hello."

"Gerald," Mirella said. "I didn't wake you up or anything?"

I was going to have to stop her using that name on me, one day. "I've been up for hours," I said. "What's happened?"

"Nothing, which is why I'm calling," she said. "Absolutely nothing—this is my day to be off. I thought maybe you didn't know that."

"Didn't have the faintest idea," I said. "Congratulations."

"Happens every week," she said. "And I have thought of something." Before I could say a word she went on: "Now look: I have not-repeat-not changed my mind. Do not get yourself an idea. But if you're ever going to get it certain that our boy is Mr. X, you are going to have to junk every other possibility. Only sensible, right?"

"Right," I said. "I think."

"And I have got a possibility for you," she said. "Something you maybe didn't think of yet." A small pause. "Not that you wouldn't think of it, you know—by yourself. But maybe not yet."

I grinned into the phone. "Go ahead," I said. "Tell me about it."

"There is a price on it," she said. "Buy me a lunch."

"I thought you were dieting," I said.

"When I think about it," she said. "Right now, I am not thinking about it. On a day off, who would?"

"Who indeed?" I said, and we arranged a time and place.

No new ideas his time, and nothing fancy, but Mirella said she knew a deli that actually stocked edible food. A place called, with typical Ravenal flair, Old-Fashioned Food.

When we were seated in a small booth at the back of the small, dimly-lit room, she said: "Maybe you don't know much about deli stuff. It is not like regular food."

"It *is* regular food," I said. "Or it ought to be. I have been in delis on six different planets—including the old Original. Where, by the way, things have gone downhill; good corned beef is hard to find."

"Well," she said, "pardon me. Here the corned beef is fair. Maybe there is better, but not in City Two."

A Totum rolled up at that point, and we told it to find some corned beef on rye, two largish piles of potato salad, and a couple of soft drinks. "They have a thing here called a Celery Tonic," Mirella said. "You should try it." I told her celery tonic was traditional deli food almost anywhere, though only on Earth was the original (called Charlie Brown's) still sometimes available.

"We make do," Mirella said. "Earth we are not, and maybe a good thing. But we make do." She paused. "And the pickles here, you like deli, you have got to try."

That convinced me, even before the Totum went away to find our food, that the place really was a deli. A customer of any kind of place might boast about its main dish, or its ambiance; only a deli customer boasts about pickles.

We chatted about nothing much for a bit—the weather, small local news—and, after the food had arrived and Mirella had disposed of one enormous bite of her sandwich—having slathered the poor thing with enough mustard to paint a small room—she said: "That idea. Now, I don't want you to think I am changing my mind, because I am not changing it."

I'd been a little lighter on the mustard. I swallowed a bite—and if it wasn't Earth quality, it was a very close cousin—and said: "Understood. You just want me to hurry up and eliminate everything else, so I can agree with you."

She gave me a big grin. "You got it," she said. "On the

nose." Another bite. In a minute or so she said: "So I'll tell you. If Harris France did this, where is the other beamer?"

I blinked. "If France killed her, why would there *be* another beamer?"

"Because he is not stupid," Mirella said. "The door chain, the bolts, the windows—who knows what happened? But another beamer, he would have to have. The woman has a hole burned in—she did not get it leaning too far over a stove."

"There was a beamer right there," I said. "Clean. Fully loaded. Unfired."

She nodded. The sandwich was half gone. She took a bite of pickle, nodded with satisfaction, and said: "So maybe he fiddled his own beamer. Not hard to do. We said that already. But he had to see, somebody shot the woman. Where is the beamer he wants us to think she was shot with?"

"The killer took it away with him," I said.

She gave me a very overplayed scornful laugh. "This is not a civilian," she said. "He has to know better. He can get a beamer very easy, not on the books anywhere. He drops it right there, so it points to somebody else, he is not so completely on the spot. He says the killer took it away, it is just words. He shows another beamer, he has got something."

"Maybe he didn't think of it," I said.

"Your friend Euglane," she said. "By him, a nut would be too stressed to think of anything. But in real life maybe not. Some things he doesn't think of. Some he does. The doors and windows, maybe not. But the damn gun? He is *using* the damn gun. Something has to occur to him."

I nodded. My own sandwich was disappearing rapidly. I tried the pickle. Mirella was right: the place was a real deli. I put Old-Fashioned Food on my list of places to return to.

"Where would he get the spare beamer?" I said.

She shrugged. "Anywhere," she said. "Anybody can buy a beamer. Or a slug gun. But you buy it legally, it is test-fired— for the slug gun, any bullet later on is going to be identified, the test firing is on record. For a beamer not so tight—burn pattern, deductive temp picture, things like that. But the test firing is on record; it will anyhow, at least, give you an idea." The sandwich was gone. She took a forkful of potato salad. "So he didn't buy it legally. It is maybe a little tough for a civilian to find an illegal beamer—an illegal gun any kind. But for this guy, no trouble at all, he would know how, where and who."

I nodded. "So he buys an illegal beamer someplace—"

"Or he gets one like a favor from somebody," she said. "It has to be there are people want to do favors for a Homicide Detective-Colonel."

"He shoots Cornelia Rasczak with it," I said. "And then what?"

"Then," Mirella said, "I have no damn idea. It has to be there. To show he didn't use his own and gimmick it. And it is not there. We looked: believe it."

"Interesting," I said. "And if he didn't do it—" I thought for a second. "If he didn't do it, the problem doesn't exist. Whoever got in and out of the place took the beamer with him."

"Sure," Mirella said.. "Somebody got in and out, there's no problem. Only somebody didn't get in and out, because there is no way."

"An alien being could manage it," I said.

"A what?"

I explained. Briefly. Mirella nodded, her face perfectly sober.

"Also a thing from the spirit world," she said. "Why not? You are grabbing at some very small straws, Gerald."

"Knave," I said.

She grinned. "You want to spoil all my fun?"

I said: "But would an alien being know where to get an illegal beamer?"

"Maybe there is an alien weapons supplier," Mirella said. "A Fence from Beyond."

"What the Hell," I said. "Anything's possible."

"It would be your thing, then," Mirella said, "to eliminate the possibility—to find out where is the other beamer, and where he got it. Right?"

I took in some potato salad. "Not exactly," I said. "There's no way. If he got rid of it, he did a good job, and finding it is a job for six hundred investigators and two years. It might be loose atoms by now, swept up somewhere and thoroughly trashed."

"So where did he get it?"

I shrugged. "Anywhere. If somebody did him a favor, how can I trace it? How can anybody trace it? If he found a fence with a loose beamer for sale—same question. Mirella, who's going to tell me he sold a loose beamer to a police officer? Who's going to tell anybody, ever?"

She shrugged back at me. "Got to be a way," she said. "People do things, they leave traces. Traces can be found."

"To be perfectly frank," I said, "I prefer alien beings."

TWENTY-FIVE

And it was alien beings I was at work on, late that afternoon. This time, it wasn't at the Playtime Wispies offices, but back in his house; the Master phoned me and said he'd had an idea. When I heard it, I knew I should have had the same idea—weeks before.

"Gerald," he said, sitting comfortably in front of his wall of piranhas, "it is possible that Folla did not, in fact, move your ship."

I stared at him. "I'm here," I said. "I was away the Hell somewhere else. How did this happen?"

"There is a laboratory effect," he said. "I have been laggard in remembering its existence, but it presents interesting possibilities."

"A laboratory effect," I said.

"Quite an ancient one," he said. "It was known before the Clean Slate War, in fact, though never quite explained. Mathematical treatments existed, but a mathematical treatment is a description, not an explanation."

I nodded. "All right," I said. "What's the effect?"

"Gerald," he said, "have you ever heard of a Josephson junction?"

I closed my eyes and swore. A long minute of silence went creeping by.

Then I raised my voice in song. It's a long song, but you might as well have all of it, and here it is.

Josephson Junction's the Hell of a spot—
First you're there, and then you're not.
Want to reach an inf'nite speed?
Josephson J. is all you need.

CHORUS:
Josephson Junction—
What a function

Went on a little trip one day,
All by way of the Josephson J—
Sixty microns, quite a dash—
Did it all in one quick flash.

T'other day I gave a holler—
Lost my dawg, he slipped his collar.
Found him in far Ioway—
Dawg fell through the Josephson J

Gal done left me Friday night—
Took mah truck, blinked out o' sight.
Chasin' for her just won't pay—
She winked out by Josephson J.

Oh, I'd go to find my gal,
Bring her back to th' old corral—
But she might be any place
In sixteen-dimensioned space.

Should've used electron glue,
Kept her by me, tied and true.
Now my sky is always grey—
All the fault of the Josephson J.

Josephson Junction's the Hell of a spot—
First you're there, and then you're not.
Junction took my gal away—
Found my dawg, though—Josephson J.

Master Higsbee said, in a voice as hushed as I'd ever heard from him: "What is that? Gerald, what *is* that?"

"That," I said, "is *Josephson Junction*. A song, damn it."

He shook his head, slowly. "It is not," he said. "Once it may have been a song. After your rendition of it, it has become something else, something for which our language, I am very much afraid, has no name."

I do not sing that badly. I don't think I do. "I have no idea who wrote it," I said. "That makes it a folk song, I suppose—I've never seen an author listed. But I have it on a music tape—some late-Twentieth songs. Performed by a woman named Laura Quink, one of the few guitarists I can stand to listen to. The damn tape is filed on my ship—I was even thinking about playing it, for check, when I was being lost. But I didn't feel like Charming just then."

A very slow nod. "I had not known there was a song about a Josephson junction," he said. "I had not, in fact, known that the effect was popularly known among the ancients. It was something of a rarity."

"An electron appears at point A," I said. "On one side of the junction. Traveling in a given direction, at a given speed—defined within what were called quantum limits of accuracy. It then appears at point B, a measurable distance away, traveling in the same direction and at the same speed—without having crossed the intervening space."

"Yes," he said. "It is quite firmly established that this is so. Mathematical treatments do indeed exist. The effect never appeared, so to speak, in the macrocosm; it was thought of as a purely quantum effect, you understand. But it occurred to me that this might not, in fact, be the case."

"That Folla might have found some large, economy-sized Josephson junction—found it or made it—and pushed my ship through it, just like an electron. From point A, eleven thousand light years from human habitation, to Ravenal. Point B."

"Without crossing the intervening space," the Master said. "Hence, without occupying time in its passage; there would have *been* no passage, simply a—discontinuity. The notion clears up several difficulties at once."

"Sure it does," I said. "Folla didn't have a new, instantaneous theory for space-four, because he didn't push the ship *through* space-four. He pushed it through—his space."

"Or some other, but not ours," the Master said. "And, as the transfer of your ship was the only sign that Folla could in fact affect physical objects in our space-time—and was a great bother to orderly thought on that account—we might now theorize, more simply, that he did not so affect physical objects; the effect does not involve our space-time, and might have been managed as a surround, so to speak, for your ship, without touching the ship at all."

"Like digging a hole under it and watching it fall through," I said. "He never had to affect the ship at all, directly—if he could dig the hole."

"Exactly," the Master said. "It is no more than a vagrant theory—it is of course impossible of establishment by any means I can imagine—but it arranges matters very satisfactorily in order."

Two new ideas in one day. A very unusual day.

TWENTY-SIX

Three new ideas, in fact—Euglane, I found out when I got back to my hotel, had left a message.

I should have programmed my pocket piece to accept forwarding—but it's one of the things I keep forgetting. When I got the message to phone him, I cursed a bit, and punched in his number.

He didn't answer phones as quickly as he answered doorbell-announces; the thing blipped three times before his slightly-gruff tenor voice said: "Yes? I am Euglane."

"Gerald Knave," I said. "Returning your—"

"I have spoken with Harris this afternoon," he said. "I called you at once; he is reporting dreams that may mean something."

I took a deep breath. "Don't tell me Folla has been popping up to ask Harris France for help."

"Not at all," he said. "He has had three successive, and very odd, dreams involving a dog. A small dog."

This did not strike me as spectacular. "People do dream about pets," I said. "Even small pets. We mentioned that, after all. Disposed of it, I thought. If the dog wasn't named Folla, or Dube, it's not—"

"The dog has informed him that he did in fact commit the murder of which he stands accused," Euglane said. "It has told him to confess his crime."

"All right," I said. "Maybe he just can't stand the uncertainty, and his mind made itself up, and is taking this way of letting him know about it."

"It has told him," Euglane said—"that is, this dog has told him—that he shot Cornelia with his own beamer, and that he reloaded the beamer and recalibrated the shot counter."

"You said he couldn't have done that," I said.

"So I did, and he could not," Euglane said. "I have told Harris, very clearly, that the thing is impossible, even if he were sleepwalking—for which, in any case, there has never been any evidence."

138

"Well," I said, "he doesn't have to believe a dog in a dream."

"But he feels he does," Euglane said. "The dog has told him that his confession is the only way in which he can retain the favor of his—examiners."

I thought about that for a couple of seconds. I had two questions.

Question one: "How does he paper over the difficulty?"

Euglane sighed. "He doesn't," he said. "He has become sure that the dream is accurate—that somehow he did commit the murder. He is—beyond argument on the subject; he is terrified of the verdict of these examiners, far more terrified than he is of any possible verdict from a court."

"Suppose he confesses," I said. "It isn't the worst thing that can happen. The confession would have to be checked—your testimony about the impossibility—"

"Would be lost in the noise," Euglane said. "It is a certainty—but it's not the sort of certainty a court would be likely to listen to. Not that it would arrive in a court; the confession would be checked, casually, and accepted. Why not, after all?" Another sigh. "I feel sure I can persuade him to rethink the matter—though it will take a little time, and a good deal of discussion."

"Good," I said. "*We're* agreed he didn't commit the murder—Harris France might as well agree, too."

"Exactly," he said. "He certainly shouldn't have to bear such guilt. But I thought the dream would be of some interest, given recent experiences elsewhere."

"It's interesting," I said. "Maybe more than interesting. The man is an experienced police officer—he ought to have come up with a better story about the murder than that one."

"And the dog," he said.

That was question two. "Did this dog have any name at all?" I said. Not that it really mattered, of course, but . . .

No.

Harris France's dream was one of those small irritants for a day or so. The whole thing might have been coincidence—maybe there just *wasn't* any better way of explaining things than the impossibility of the gimmicked beamer, or France's subconscious couldn't find one—and the rest was easy enough to explain, or explain away. I thought of mentioning it to Mirella, and didn't—if anything, it would harden her already steel-solid feeling that Harris France was guilty, and God knows it wasn't evidence of anything: better to shut up about it.

I did mention it to the Master, who said it was "of great interest, but in itself can promise no immediate use"—there wasn't a handle to pick it up by, in other words. A talk with Harris France might be indicated, but there wasn't much I could think of to ask him, if he stuck to his new story, as dictated by a small dog in a dream.

And the next day I nearly accomplished a small accident. I'd gone out shopping for a few basics in a nearby market, and on the way home I damn near got myself run over. I never got a glimpse of the driver of the car.

I was ambling along peacefully, laden with City Four smoked cheese, a carton of something the shop called Authentic Ceylon tea, for which I had mild hopes, disposable serviettes, and tomatoes, alfalfa, and cos and romaine lettuce for salads.. It was about three P. M. (fifteen), and the street was mostly empty. A few cars went whizzing by to my left, and one of them didn't whiz by.

It came straight down the street, coughed and squealed, and shuddered as it took a right turn and headed for me.

I managed to hold on to my package while skipping more or less nimbly out of the way. The car squealed some more, the driver apparently trying to restrain it or get it the Hell back on the road and off the sidewalk, and somewhere I heard a distant pedestrian shout: "Watch out, Foolish!" Who he was talking to, I had no notion, and I had no spare attention to cobble up a reply with, in case it had been me,

By then I was safe, breathing a little hard, in a doorway. The car shuddered some more, and whoever was almost driving the thing—afternoon sunlight reflected off the damn windshield, which was as old-fashioned as the car itself, a big boxy black thing that seemed almost eighty years old—managed to get it turned so it was heading straight up the sidewalk—not at me, but not quite back on the road.

It traveled along the sidewalk for about eight yards,

coughed violently, and found its way left, back onto the street. And it went away.

The Ravenal traffic system, I told myself, had driven either the car or the driver slightly insane. But what the Hell, no harm had been done.

Accidents will happen.

I never even mentioned the incident to anybody, not then. This also turns out to have been a mistake.

Then—two days later, in late evening—the phone blipped at me while I was peppering some thin slices of cod in preparation for a quiet dinner at home. I had a Robbie dicing some carrots, and a potato was baking. I put down the grinder, wiped my hands and went and answered the thing.

That dinner quickly became one on a list—much too long a list—of Meals I Never Got to Eat. I said: "Gerald Knave. Hello."

"Gerald, you will doubtless receive a call from Euglane," the Master's rasp said. "I will therefore make this very brief. Harris France has committed suicide in his cell. Arrange your mind for Euglane's call. Finished."

Click. I stared at the phone for a few seconds, and then hung the thing up. My rented Robbie diced a carrot or two, noisily. I picked up the phone midway through its opening blip.

"Knave, a terrible thing has happened," Euglane said.

"I've heard," I said. "Where are you?"

"At the police station," he said., "Where he's—where he was being held. I cannot understand—I cannot explain—"

"Stay there," I said. "I'll be right over."

TWENTY-SEVEN

His first question was: "How is it you've heard?"

I told him Master Higsbee had phoned me.

"But how did he—well, doubtless he has means," Euglane said.

"He usually does," I said. "All I have right now is the bare fact. I gather he hanged himself?"

"You weren't told that?" he said. We were sitting in what I suppose was an interview room, a floor away from France's cell. "How could you know it?"

"I saw him in his cell," I said. "I saw the bar he hung clothes from. Easy enough to manage hanging himself from it, and there can't be many suicide methods available to a man in a cell. I was surprised there was that one."

"A convenience," Euglane said. He moaned a little. "Just a convenience. I told them Harris was not suicidal. That there was no danger of it. They were anxious to treat him as kindly as they could. For his comfort."

"You were wrong," I said. He moaned again.

"Knave, I was not wrong," he said. "If there had been suicide lurking in Harris, I would have known. We spoke often. We spoke this afternoon. He seemed distant, calm—it worried me. But I knew his mind; he had not previously had such an urge, on any level that was remotely close to action. It could not have developed by itself over a few days—he might have hidden it for that long, while he himself was fighting it, but not longer. If it had grown in him for as long as four days, I would have known of it."

"Somebody else strung him up?" I said. Euglane waved one arm.

"There is good evidence that he did the deed himself," he said. "But he was—pushed into doing it. Persuaded. Cozened. *Pushed*. It was not his own idea. It did not grow in him of itself; it could not; it was planted, and encouraged." His arms shivered, as if he wanted to twine them.

I nodded. "Somebody pushed him," I said. "Pushed him

fairly hard. And he didn't mention that to you, when you talked?"

He stared at me. "I would think he—it's odd," he said. "Very odd. If a visitor, a guard, anyone had so much as suggested it to him—surely he would have mentioned it."

"Not anyone," I said. "Suppose these aliens of his—the examiners who watched him all the time—suggested it to him. They were special. You knew about them, but even so—would he have told you?"

A second or so of silence. "Not right away, perhaps," he said. "He would have—discussed it with them. If they told him not to mention it—Knave, I am not sure. Such a decision for him never came up; he never mentioned that they had any reaction at all to his talks with me, and of course I never pressed the question."

"No," I said. "Why make difficulties you didn't have to make?" I took a deep breath. "I think we're coming to a conclusion about Harris France and his examiners—and about his dreams. His recent dreams."

"A conclusion?"

"You'd see it yourself, if you were under less strain," I said. "The dog—the examiners—Folla and Dube—they're all the same being. Or beings. Not originally—the examiners were his illness. All right. But beings who could enter his dreams and *pretend* to be his examiners—who would know enough from having watched him in dreams before—well, something about France worried them, and they decided to get rid of him. So they talked him into killing himself."

Another moan. Euglane wasn't relaxed, there in a public room—his arms shivered again. "Knave, that's horrible."

"Horrible and reasonable," I said. "It's even possible to see what worried them about France—a little of it, anyhow."

"He was enclosed in a cell," Euglane said. "He did nothing. What could worry them?"

"He didn't commit the murder," I said. "There were people working—you and me and the Master, for instance—to establish that he didn't commit the murder. France himself wasn't sure—but we were pretty persuasive. At least he kept doubting."

143

"Well," Euglane said, "he *didn't* commit that act."

"No," I said. "He didn't. But Folla and company wanted it nicely, neatly established that he had. The longer we worked—and the more Harris worked with us—the better the chance of our establishing that he hadn't. So they tried persuading him that he had—through the dog in his dream—and when you went on attacking the idea, they imitated his examiners, and pushed him to kill himself."

Euglane was shivering all over—and nodding. "They forced him to kill himself," he said.

"They pushed him," I said. "As hard as they could—which was hard enough." I thought for a second. "I think we can come to another conclusion," I said.

"Yes?"

"We know what color hats Folla and company wear," I said.

He muttered it. "Yes."

"Dead black," I said.

I shepherded Euglane through a lot of questioning and paperwork; he really wasn't in any kind of shape for it, but he had been France's doctor, and he had told them the man was not a suicide risk. That took more explaining than he had available, but not even police expect a doctor to be infallible, and he was so troubled, and obviously troubled, that they let up after only a small while.

There were no relatives to notify, and Euglane was also the person the funeral arrangements were going to fall on. I helped with that, too, for a few minutes, but he seemed much more comfortable once he was dealing with formal matters. I kept hoping Mirella would turn up, but it wasn't her case, and though she'd certainly have heard about France's death—police grapevines, anywhere, work about as well as the best grapevines available—she'd have no reason to wander over to the jail and poke around. Even Cornelia Rasczak was her case only in part, of course; she was just hired help. She'd have had nothing to do with Harris France.

It was actually more than ninety minutes before she did show up.

I wasn't too surprised—well, a little—but I was curious.

Euglane was off somewhere by then, beginning to arrange a funeral, and when Mirella opened the door of the interview room and poked her head in, I said: "How did you get in?"

She gave me that big grin. "I am official," she said. "By now I'm off duty, but you are looking at a dedicated officer, right?"

"Dedicated to the Harris France case?"

"Be smart," she said scornfully. "How would I hook into that? But I am involved with a case, and it's important I come talk to a person who is a part of it. Simple?"

"Simple," I said. "Cornelia Rasczak. Harris France's death closes it out, officially, but—"

Another grin. "What else, Jerry? Sure. I figured you would be here. Gielli are not much good with disaster. He'd call *somebody*."

"And you figured me for the somebody," I said. "Right. But Euglane's fine with disaster, generally—what he isn't good with is death. Apparently Gielli really don't like death or violence."

"So who likes death?" Mirella said. "The stone in every shoe. But you and me, Jerry, we're human. We can deal with it."

"We damn well have to," I said. "This is not a simple suicide."

Mirella nodded. "I figured. A guy like France, he does not take himself off. He makes with the strong jaw, he turns to stone and he gets through it. But the word is, he got hanged in his cell." She made a face. "I am not going to believe somebody here got in and hanged him. We are pretty good officers around here. At least good enough, we don't go around killing prisoners, you know? But if not that—what?"

"Oh, he tied the noose," I said, "and he stuck his own head in it. But he was pushed. Somebody—and that's a very loose description—pushed him into doing it, very carefully and deliberately."

"Takes the Hell of a person to push somebody strong as France was supposed to be," she said. "Broken up, sure, after she died—no matter did he do it or not, he has to be broken up. But still strong."

"Strong enough," I said. "France was pushed from inside. This somebody got at his mind—at his dreams. His nightmares."

"Who?" she said. "This Euglane? He would know about the dreams, and the nightmares too."

"Not Euglane," I said. "An alien. A *real* alien—not just a Giell, or some other kind of person."

Mirella thought about it for a second. "What the Hell," she said then. "You're telling me there is something entirely weird going on here? Something off the 3V? When you talked about alien beings before, it wasn't just jokes?"

"Don't shut your mind to it," I said. "Most of this is provable." I gave her a sketch of Folla, Dube and company and their interference with Harris France's delusions about aliens, and his dreams. I tied it in to my own experience with Folla, and, a little, with Hester MacEvoy—she'd had a very brief look at both of those pieces while we'd been eating Old-Fashioned Food.

"This," she said flatly, "is crazy."

"I said not to shut—"

"I didn't say it wasn't so," she said. "I said it was crazy. So or not, is it normal?"

"It's crazy," I said. "But it's so. I'll fill you in—there's a lot of it, and you ought to have it all. But not here and now."

"Give me a time and place," she said. "This, I have got to hear." Then she did surprise me. "You think maybe it's connected?"

"Connected?"

"With Rasczak," she said. "It looks to be."

She explained it, and she'd followed the same path I had: a motive for killing France, safely locked in his cell, almost had to tie in with the fact that he was accused of murder.

"And," I said, "the fact that he didn't do it."

"I see that," she said. "I don't have to like it, but I see it."

TWENTY-EIGHT

I spent a few hours on it—with Mirella and the Master. Euglane, once his arrangements were as far along as they were going to get that day, had gone home to collapse—or to relax himself, I suppose. He was in no shape to think and discuss; he was barely in shape to breathe in and out.

He'd recover; he bent very easily, under some kinds of strain, but he didn't look as if anything much would break him. I called the Master from the jail, invited myself for dinner and the evening—he made no fuss about it, of course, beyond six or seven mentions of his age, weariness and helplessness—and asked him if I could bring Mirella over.

"By all means," he said; "she is a fresh eye."

She was all of that. She greeted the damn piranhas like old friends, and admired them extravagantly. I did not visibly fume.

"Now I have it all," she said after dinner—we'd spent dinner (after just a little more conversation about the piranhas; the Master got expansive, for him, and I said as little as was politely possible) filling her in as thoroughly as possible, and she'd listened well, and asked absolutely no unnecessary questions—"now I have it all, I see where the problem comes from."

"Which problem?" I said. "There are fifty."

"Why France did not do it," she said. "If he did it, why send a dog to tell him he did it in some way that didn't happen? Why bring in his examiners to get him to hang himself?"

"They might," I said, "be afraid he'd tell people they existed."

"Silly," she said. She took a swallow of coffee—the Master likes a Kona blend some days. "This is good stuff," she told him. "You know coffee."

"Thank you," he said. "Gerald does not agree."

I'd once told him that Kona is too sweet for most occasions. He doesn't forget things, damn it.

"So what does he know?" Mirella said, and shrugged. "But how could these examiner types be afraid France would tell people?"

"Not the examiners," I said. "Or not the original examiners; those were fantasies. Illness. But *our* aliens hooked into the illness, and used it."

"Easy enough, if they go into dreams," Mirella said. "He must have dreamed about them, people dream about what they care about, sometimes." She shook her head. "Poor guy. But look: he had chances to tell people. Lots of them—his doctor, Jerry here, who knows who else? He said no word except to Euglane, and that was just the illness stuff, not the real ones who came along. They waited and waited, and *finally* they got nervous? No." She paused. "Besides, suppose he started to talk about it. Who would listen?"

"Euglane," I said.

"Euglane knows they are there, the examiners," she said. "Why would he suddenly think they are really real? Even if suddenly some of them are?" She finished the cup. "Who would listen to this Hester MacEvoy, she started talking about aliens? Or Hilda? Nothing for the aliens to worry about, nothing at all."

"Maybe he did tell somebody," I said.

The Master nodded. "I think it probable," he said, "that you have the sequence reversed. He did not tell someone, Gerald. Someone told him."

Mirella said: "Euglane—no, hold it," and stopped for five seconds. "Right. Took me a minute, it's late. Cornelia Rasczak told him."

"Told him his examiners were now real aliens—because she'd heard enough from Hester MacEvoy to put things together?" I said. "That's going a little far."

"I doubt Lance-Corporal Puffer means to go so far," the Master said.

"Nowhere near," Mirella said. "What she told him—there are real aliens. Period. Maybe she got afraid. Maybe she just thought somebody should take an interest."

"If she had told him his examiners were real," the Master said—"if she in fact knew of the examiners, which we cannot now establish—she would only have been confirming what he already felt. For him they were already quite real—a private matter, but a real one."

"Right," I said. "The idea that there were real aliens wouldn't have been a surprise to him—because he *knew* there were real aliens: his examiners."

"What he didn't know," Mirella said, "was that these examiners were also involved with other people. As far as he knew, they were aimed at nobody but him. Very private, very solo. That they were off talking to this MacEvoy—that was a whole other thing."

I nodded. "All right," I said. "And we know something else: we know why Cornelia Rasczak was killed."

"Because she told him?" Mirella said. "Jerry, that makes no sense in the world."

"In a way," I said. "Because she told him—and that meant she might get to telling somebody else."

"We have what we have looked for," the Master said. "Something Cornelia Rasczak knew, that her killer did not want told—to anyone but Harris France, who didn't matter."

Mirella nodded. "Simple. Reasonable. I like it."

I shook my head. "Damn it, something's wrong," I said. "Folla couldn't have killed Cornelia Rasczak. He couldn't affect—"

"He did not," the Master said. "Except in the manner in which he killed Harris France."

Mirella said: "Hey. This Folla is one ugly customer."

"He persuaded somebody else to do the killing," I said. "Right. And he got the somebody in and out by way of a Josephson junction."

"I think not that last," the Master said. "The scale makes it—in my judgment—impossible."

"Scale?" I said.

"The effect, as we know it, involves very small distances, and very small objects. A quantum effect, to return to the quaint and ancient terminology. It would seem best to think of it not as a bridging of distances—as an effect involving space and time—but as something else, since it involves zero time, and apparently does not call for successive habitation of contiguous spaces—the electron concerned does not traverse the space between the two points. Think of it as information transfer."

"The electron is the information?"

"That, too," he said. "But think of the departure point, and the arrival—the target—point as loci of information. Each is a given, specific set of axes in three-dimensional space—clearly a unique package of information."

I thought for a second. "All right," I said. "So you need two bundles of information—two sets of data: the departure point and the target point."

"Three," he said. "You forget the object which is to be translated."

"Three. So what does scale have to do with it?"

He sighed. "Gerald," he said. "Use your mind. You can think, if you *will* think." I said nothing whatever. "For very small objects, and very small target areas, there are a limited number of possible sets of information; an appreciable precision in arriving at the target area is quite possible. The larger the object, the more possible sets of information exist—since the number of those sets is proportional to the size of the object, and to the size of the target."

I thought some more. "A large object needs more space to fit into—more possible sets of spatial axes. And a space a foot wide—a target space a foot wide—has more possible locations inside it than a space a micron wide."

He nodded. "You can think," he said, "when you choose to." I said nothing at all, again; I nodded back. Why hand him further opportunities? Maybe he could get the nod. "This introduces uncertainty into the targeting," he said. "For an object the size of a human being, and a target area the size of, let us say, a small house like that in which Harris France and Cornelia Rasczak lived, that uncertainty would be very large—a preliminary analysis gives figures on the order of a kilometer in diameter."

I converted in my head: three-fifths of a mile. "A Josephson junction—"

"Would translate a human being from his departure point—or her departure point," the Master added, bowing to Mirella, the piranha-fancier— "to a point inside a circle whose center would be, approximately, the France-Rasczak house, and whose diameter would be about a kilometer. A thousand yards or so, Gerald."

"Not good enough," I said.

"Not nearly good enough."

I held up a hand. "Wait a minute," I said. "My ship ended up in a parking orbit around Ravenal. That's pretty good targeting."

"So it is," he said. "And quite possible: twenty kilometers one way or another might not matter seriously, since you could adjust orbit on arrival—as you undoubtedly did under instructions from Approach Control on-planet. Given a slight preference for an orbit further away than the optimal choice, there would be time and to spare for such adjustment; and you would never consider it. I called that placement 'fairly precise'—and so it was. Fairly, not exactly."

"I adjusted on Approach Control direction," I said. "I always do. Everybody always does. Everywhere."

"Of course," he said. "The transfer could be depended upon to leave you close enough to adjust. 'Close enough' for space, going into orbit, can safely be several orders of magnitude larger than 'close enough' for a room inside a small house."

"So the Josephson junction didn't get anybody inside that house," I said.

"It did not," the Master said.

"Then we're back where we started," I said. "We have an impossible crime—a locked room with no entrance and no exit."

"Not quite back where you started," Mirella said.

"Why not quite?" I said.

The Master chuckled even before she answered. "Now," she said, "you have me. I am convinced. One more head to figure things out." She gave me a grin. "And just maybe not such a bad head, either."

It was the night after that that the dreams started.

TWENTY-NINE

Call them nightmares. They qualify—I have had a few over the years, though I don't make any big point of remembering them. As I said, when I do remember a dream, it's usually too silly to repeat.

The nightmares didn't come every night, and there was never more than one in a given night. If I sat down and described them, you wouldn't be impressed; nightmares are very personal experiences, and what had me sitting bolt upright in bed, staring and sweating in the dark, might not be anything for anybody else but a curiosity. People standing with their backs to me turned around and showed faces that belonged to other people, or to no people I'd ever thought of before. Things nodded and toppled from high, uneven stacks. Alarm sirens went off, turned into voices, and sang old songs at me.

The third time this happened, I managed to keep a grip on myself. I didn't sit up in bed. I didn't wake up at all—I very carefully and determinedly didn't wake up.

In the dream—I was in a hollow, rounded space, a red-brown space that was dimly lit and had few specifics—I said: "All right, Folla. Enough. Quit the gaming and talk."

A voice I remembered said: "Statement: you will aid me."

The terror of the dream—and never mind it—didn't disappear, but it was manageable. I said: "Aid you with what?"

"You will construct an object for me," the voice said. "I request payment. A service—"

"Of Path, Ltd.," I said. "You're presenting a bill?"

"You were transferred to your chosen destination," Folla said.

"I didn't ask you to do that," I said. "I said, let's discuss this. You flipped me here on your own."

"True," Folla said. "Accurate. Shall I return you to your previous location?"

"I'm not asking for that, either," I said. "I'm here. You used something to get me here—"

"Junction," Folla said. "It has been called a tunnel diode.

Of a different sort."

"It exists, on a large scale?"

"It exists, in terms of its own," Folla said. "It can be used. For what you call large distances only, or very small distances also. Distance does not exist, except in your spaces. An object of the right size can be removed to spaces in which distance does not exist, and returned to your spaces."

"Of the right mass?" I said. *Distance does not exist*—that much made a vague sort of sense; I thought of the Master telling me to think of the junction process as information transfer.

"Mass is a quality of your spaces," Folla said. "Of the right size."

This was not making as much sense as I'd hoped it might make, but maybe I could find out a little more. "Can *I* do this?" I said. "Remove an object and return it?"

"Not at present," Folla said. "You do not know how." Almost true, but not quite; in any case, unhelpful, and then I had no more chances. "Statement repeated and enlarged: you will build an object for me."

"What kind of object," I said, "and what will it do?"

"Reply in series. One: I will specify clearly," Folla said. "Two: what it does is not your concern."

I took a deep breath. I wasn't breathing air, but something much thicker, and very dark. "You want to come in to our spaces," I said. "Why?"

"That also is not your concern," Folla said. "I will leave now. Your waking is occurring. Sleep soon again, and I will then specify."

Everything, it began to come to me as I woke, was now part of the same set of puzzles. From Folla to the murder of Cornelia Rasczak to the death of Harris France—and including a variety of dreams and insanities—all the pieces were now connected.

This is usually a help. Trouble arises, most of the time, when you can't find the connections between pieces of the puzzle. But this time, the connections were perfectly clear—or as clear as they could be, given a) that we were dealing with alien beings we could neither describe nor explain, and b) that we were dealing with dreams, which *nobody* has ever been able to describe or explain very well.

This time, I told myself, all the pieces were connected—but all the pieces was shaped like Klein bottles.

I fumbled around for the usual while, and came fully awake after the usual delays, and decided to build a breakfast around a coffee with the hardest-to-spell name I have ever run across: Keyserlingck, which is a variety originally from Queensland, and which has been replanted and lovingly tended on three or four worlds. I only have to spell it when putting in an order, and I order it in large batches. That morning, I only ground enough of it for three cups, got some eggs and a lot of bacon, went and found the pepper-mill, and sat down to eat and mull.

I seldom use pepper in great quantities, except at breakfast—a couple of fried and basted eggs thickly crusted with fresh pepper will act as efficiently as a cold shower, and a lot more pleasantly, if you like having your tongue tingled. By the time I was calming my tongue with the Keyserlingck, I was as awake as I get, and trying to assort the facts we had into something sensible.

Folla wanted to get in to our spaces. His purposes were unknown, but had to be assumed to be bad ones, given his other actions. He could only enter our spaces if somebody built him a machine of some kind—but it was a machine that had to be fairly easy to build, because he'd asked a woman in a wheelchair, without technical training or, I was convinced, a very sharp or well-focused mind, to build one.

Or did that follow? He couldn't affect our spaces directly—but he could affect our dreams, at the least by walking into them and acting in them. (Sometimes, apparently, as a small dog. Why a small dog? Why a young girl carrying the dog?) Could he make Hester MacEvoy brighter? Could he persuade her mind that she could walk around and move with full ease? And if he could, would her mind rule her body enough to get her doing that? Sleep-learning, after all, was perfectly possible—but could ease of movement, after damage, be sleep-learned? He'd promised Hilda a new sense; had this been an honest promise—and what could he have done with, or for, Hester

MacEvoy?

Somewhere, the back of my head told me, somebody had said or done or seen something that answered those questions. Possibly it had been me. The back of my head often tells me things like that—I think it means to be helpful, but for some damn reason it is almost always forced to be cryptic. Union rules, probably.

On the other hand, it may just enjoy puzzling the Hell out of me.

Whatever it was that answered the questions, I couldn't locate it. All right, what were the other pieces?

Cornelia Rasczak had been shot by a beamer, at fairly close range, inside a locked room. Walls solid, windows sealed, two doors bolted and one chained shut. Somebody had got into that room, done the deed, and got out again.

I'd thought of removing the whole front door, but that wouldn't work—the hinges would have to have shown something in the way of damage (or very fresh paint). And the door would still be chained to the wall—though if it had been removed, it could probably have been swung around enough to permit entry, leaving the chain fastened.

It would be the Hell of a job, and it would take some fairly heavy machinery—but, as I'd seen at the France house, that might not have been a problem: witnesses would have been hundreds of yards away, and blocked off by walking-trees.

Suppose you removed the whole front *wall*?

It was a lovely, even a charming idea. It lasted about fifteen seconds, until I started wondering how you'd replaster and repaint the place when you put the wall back, without leaving obvious traces. Of course, the whole house might have been repainted . . .

While Harris France lay asleep on the ground floor? True, there are paints that don't have any kind of strong or lasting odor . . .

But the operation would have taken hours of time, and been a major project for a small construction firm. Almost anything else would have been simpler. Planting a bomb in the house would have been simpler.

Come to think of it, why *hadn't* the killer simply planted a bomb in the house, and gone away?

Well, for one thing, a bomb would have killed both Cornelia and her husband. Harris France was going to die anyway, but at the time Cornelia was killed the murderer had thought a jury would do that job for him—if not kill France, transfer him to the Colony, out of everybody's way for good.

And maybe a bomb was harder to come by than a beamer. Lots of people owned beamers—anybody could, and though City Two was fairly peaceful, as cities go, there were dangerous neighborhoods, and nervous people, here and there, the two sets not necessarily contiguous. But few people owned handy bombs—or could cobble them up out of easily available materials.

And maybe the killer didn't want to do more than he had to—"he" being a term of pure convenience. Call him a minimalist.

Maybe, too, a bomb would have been blamed on somebody who wasn't Harris France. Investigation wouldn't have stopped with an obvious killer, because there wouldn't have *been* an obvious killer. Murder and suicide by bomb is a rare deed, and accident even rarer.

All right: how had he got in and out of the house?

No chimney. No cellar.

No way.

THIRTY

Harris France.

There was no mystery about his death: his examiners—alias, recently, Folla et Cie—had talked him into putting a noose around his neck.

But though that was clear enough, there were things that weren't.

France's alien examiners had been around for years—as I understood it, they'd been with him long, long before Euglane had entered the picture. He'd been having more trouble living with the fact of his examiners recently—the last six months or so—which was why he'd gone to see Euglane. He'd had other troubles, of course—people do—and as time went along, the presence of the examiners—the strain their constant inspection had certainly been for him—had made every other problem a lot worse.

So Euglane had found out about the examiners fairly recently—but France had apparently known about them, and known them, for most of his life.

Euglane, I thought, had missed a bet—he'd looked at the reports of alien beings his patients had for him, and he'd looked hard. But he'd looked once. France's examiners had been an illness—but they hadn't stayed an illness, not entirely. They'd become real.

All of psychology is metaphor—nobody's ever seen an id, or weighed an ego. The examiners had looked like one more metaphor of a metaphor, and so they had been, once. But—just like dreams, now and then—some metaphors can come true, and France's examiners had.

Question: were they—had they become—Folla and company?

That they were now associated with Folla was certain—nothing made sense otherwise. At least, they had been used by the aliens; and though France had certainly had delusions on his own, delusions Folla and company had walked into, it was a little too much to assume that some brand-new being had pushed France into suicide.

I couldn't imagine what difference it made, but France's examiners couldn't be Folla himself. Folla was clumsy; he didn't know enough about humans to have pushed even a victim like France, ready for any sort of pushing that had Examiner pasted on it, with any great success. (There might have been fifty aliens doing the scouting, and then the pushing, and there might only have been one—making himself a crowd in France's dreams—the night-time dreams, the ones he needed his naps to recover from. He didn't dream at all during his escapes, as Euglane had told me long ago; that, I saw, was why they'd been escapes.)

Dube?

It might be, I told myself.

And it might be another entrant entirely—or fifty other entrants. It really didn't seem to make much difference; the basic difficulty was the one we'd been stuck with from the start.

There was no way to get to any one of the alien beings. We had to wait for them to come to us.

This was not fatal, I told myself. Folla (and by extension the aliens in general) wanted something from us, and kept coming back to get it.

That bothered me. Folla or Dube had asked me, Hester MacEvoy and Hilda for help. Maybe others had been asked—no way to tell.

Were the aliens limited to City Two? To Ravenal? To humanity?

They might be popping up in Giell dreams, or Beri dreams—or anywhere, on any world.

Maybe there was something about Josephson junctions that limited the people they could work on.

Maybe there was something about dreams.

Euglane was really in no shape to be bothered, I thought, but I went and bothered him anyhow. I put the back of my head to work on the damn locked room—there had to be an answer somewhere, didn't there?—and phoned him.

He said he was seeing two patients—patients he felt he couldn't put off at all—but the earliest would be coming in around thirteen. "One U. S.," he added helpfully.

It was still morning, so I went right on over.

He relaxed at once, in his living-room, and he had that paper ready for me. The first time I'd met him, he'd wanted to show it to me, and we'd got off on another track. This time he was urgent about it.

"If these beings can affect human dreaming," he said, "then perhaps some of the reports I've been getting have a real basis."

"Your patients dream about—"

"Some of them do," he said. "And I've seen the dreams as referring to their own lives. They do so refer, of course—but there may be more in them than such reference. Your cigarettes—"

"Inoson Smoking Pleasure Tubes," I said. "Perfectly safe—no Earth tobaccos."

"Yes," he said. "They may be phallic symbols. They may be symbols of other things. But they are still cigarettes; they can still be lit and smoked."

I had never thought of a cigarette as a phallic symbol. Lighting one up and burning it to ash seemed the Hell of a strange thing to do with it if it was one. "And the dreams, whatever symbols the patient puts into them, may also have some real elements."

"Exactly," he said.

I sat there and looked at the paper. Bundle of papers this time, in fact—very small print, and crowded. I wondered if all Euglane's patients reported contact with alien beings. I wondered if all psychiatrists' patients did. Probably not, in either case, but he'd built up a sizable case-list.

We went through it together, with some care. Most of the alien beings were fairly standard stuff, right off the 3V. Amorphous blobs, great spiky beings with teeth, villainous Things that looked like humans dyed bright green, and so on. A few of the dreamers had been more imaginative—there was a child's doll that lisped horrors, for instance—but the basics seemed fairly standard, as dreams and nightmares go.

"I looked especially for any alien making a request of the dreamer," he said.

He'd looked, but he hadn't found anything promising. There were some requests in the pile, but they were dream- requests: an alien in a dream had asked the dreamer to do or say something or other, in the dream. There were no requests that carried over into waking life.

"I had hoped you might see something in the cases that I'd missed," Euglane said sadly.

"There doesn't seem to be anything," I said. "I'll give the whole thing another good look, if I can take a copy—"

"I have one for you," he said, and provided it. I tucked it away in an inside pocket, where it made quite a bulge, and went back to my own dream.

"He didn't appear to you," Euglane said.

"He was only a voice," I said. "What he'd been at first, in my ship. If he was also the small dog I dreamed about, he changed his voice for that—but I don't see any reason why he couldn't. If you can turn yourself into a small dog, changing your voice ought to be easy." I thought of something. "He told me I was going to wake up. Maybe he was trying to duck any more questions."

"He may have seen that you *were* going to awaken," Euglane said. "That's physiological—the body controls it. You can wake before your body insists—you can wake yourself up, sometimes—but you can't keep from waking when it does insist: when the body wakes, you have no choice. There might not be much he can do about it—when your body decides to wake up, you're awake."

I asked my two questions: Could something in a dream persuade you that you could do things, physically, when you were awake, that had previously been impossible for you?, and: Was there any way of figuring out whether Folla and company had been popping up in dreams all over the place, or even on other worlds, to other people as well as humans?

On the first question, things seemed to be pretty vague. "The mind controls the body more than is realized, even today," he said. "The mind can create and heal open wounds, without physical agency from outside. It can block, or heighten, all our senses; hyperacuity, for instance, can be produced in a subject by any good hypnotist. Whether it can bypass physical damage, as in the midbrain disease Hester MacEvoy would have—whatever its exact nature, if Dr. Rasczak was dealing with it—I simply do not know. It might be worth finding out just what sort of disease she does have; and, as for physical aid from the mind—well, it is possible."

"Doing something normally impossible for you?"

"There is," he said, "a phenomenon called 'hysterical strength'. Under various sorts of impetus, a human can perform acts which would normally be impossible, of many kinds. A hypnotist—I have seen this done, though in my own practice I have had no occasion to call it forth—may cause a human to use this power. Can it be done by means of sleep-suggestion?"

He paused, and I said: "Is there an answer to that?"

"Not much of an answer," he said. "Little is known about hypnotism, even today; I myself use it sparingly and with great care. The link between sleep and hypnotism exists; but just how close the states are we do not know with certainty."

On the second question . . .

"It might be that he appears in non-human dreams," Euglane said, "though so far all we have is human testimony. If a Giell began to dream of some being making requests of him, requests regarding his waking life, he would know something very odd had happened—our shared dream-world does not abut so closely on our waking one. I will ask a few people who deal with troubled members of other races, and see if anything is visible."

"And how about Folla's appearing somewhere else—anywhere else? Or Dube?" I said.

His arms twined over his head. "How can I say?" he asked. "So far, all the reports we have cluster around two centers: you or Harris France."

"And Cornelia Rasczak," I said. "MacEvoy was her patient—she had nothing to do with France."

"But he might have followed a chain from France to Rasczak to MacEvoy," Euglane said. "It's clear that he isn't just picking people at random: we can define centers."

"We don't have a lot of targets, so far," I said. "You haven't had any odd dreams, for instance."

"I have not," he said.

"Nor the Master," I said, "whatever his dreams are like. I wonder if Cornelia Rasczak had some."

Euglane waved his long arms slightly. Another shrug? "I doubt it," he said. "She became a danger to Folla—and Dube— when Hester MacEvoy told her of the dreams. If she'd had any of her own, she would either have been a helper to them, or a danger, long ago."

"True," I said. "Which means—well, if Hilda is in danger we can trust the Master to look out for her."

"I should think so," he said.

"But Hester MacEvoy—"

"Perhaps it should be looked into," he said.

So I did.

THIRTY-ONE

I stopped off for lunch first—at Old-Fashioned Food, where I found herring in cream sauce, pan-fried potatoes and a dark beer that was, unfortunately, no better than most of the drink on Ravenal, where they don't understand such things. Their coffee, though, wasn't at all bad, and seemed to be a local blend I'd never run into before. I made a mental note to ask about it some day—Mirella would know—and used my pocket piece, which I had remembered (for once) to hook into the system, to phone Hester MacEvoy.

She answered on the first blip, and seemed pleased to hear from me. Pleased, and a little annoyed. "You said you'd find people to come and visit me," she said, the words dragging a little. "I haven't seen them, Mr. Knave."

"Knave," I said, "and I can come over and visit you myself, if you'd like."

Her tone didn't change—it fit the basic expression of her face, as I remembered it—but her voice got louder. "Oh, that would be wonderful, Mr. Knave," she said, and I sighed and told her I'd be right over.

When I got there nothing had changed in the place—it was as if I'd left it twenty seconds before. She met me at the door, sitting in a depressed sort of way in her chair, and wheeled out of the way as before, to let me pass into the same dark little living-room. Books everywhere, coat-rack, woman's dark-grey cloak—everything was exactly the same. The cloak was hung on a different high peg on the rack, that was all.

Something bothered me, dimly, about that fact. But she'd shut the door and come into the room. "Would you like some tea, Mr. Knave?" she said slowly. "It would really be very little trouble."

"Thanks," I said, "I'll pass."

"I like being hospitable," she said. So we had some tea. And some long, flat and slightly stale cookies covered with more sugar than you'd see in an average month.

"It's nice having someone to do for," she said. "Since Mr. MacEvoy passed over, you know, I've been very alone. They don't like you if you come from somewhere else."

"So you said," I put in. "You're from Kingsley, aren't you?"

She gave me that painful, miserable smile. "How nice of you to remember," she said. "Yes. I had the loveliest years of my life there. Until I married, you see. Not that marriage wasn't a delight, Mr. Knave, because it was. A delight." Smile. "But then Mr. MacEvoy had to go and pass over," she said. "Of course, there is the pension, and that's something. Though it's not very much."

"Eight years ago," I said.

"My," she said. "You do have a good memory, don't you? It must be wonderful to have a good memory. I never did, you know. Not that there was any need for it, of course, we always had a nice couple in as help. But since Mr. MacEvoy passed over, I've been quite alone. Quite alone."

What two servants had to do with memory I couldn't really imagine, but there was no sense in trying to find out. The servants weren't around any more, anyhow—not since Mr. MacEvoy had passed over. "The other day," I said, keeping it as casual as I could, "you mentioned a dream you'd had."

She looked at me with very wide eyes. "I did?" she said. "I did? My goodness, I must have been a terrible bore. People who tell their dreams often are, you know."

"Not at all," I said. "I was very interested. You said someone called Dube appeared to you in a dream, and asked you to build something for him."

The eyes widened a little more. She was really a remarkably ugly woman. I wondered briefly about Mr. MacEvoy, but there's no accounting for tastes, and he may have been madly in love. Perhaps even with Hester. "Dube?" she said. "I don't remember anybody named Dube. People here do have funny names sometimes, it's not like Kingsley, you know, but I don't think—"

"Not a real person," I said. "In fact, not a person at all. Some kind of alien. In a dream."

She shook her head, very slowly. Her clawlike like hands gripped the arms of the wheelchair. "Oh my, Mr. Knave," she said. "You must have me confused with some other person. Even a good memory can make little mistakes sometimes. Or so I've heard."

I shut my eyes for a second. When I opened them again nothing had changed. "You didn't have a dream about an alien named Dube, who asked you to help him get in to us?"

The smile again. "I think—" she said— "mind you, one never does know, and of course I have a midbrain disease—but I think—I'd remember having a dream like that. It sounds very strange."

"You didn't have one?"

"I'm afraid I didn't," she said. "Are you very interested in dreams, Mr. Knave?"

"Only in some of them," I said. "By the way, and if it isn't too personal a question, what kind of midbrain disease is it you have?"

"Oh, it's not a disease, really," she said.

All right. Any minute now, she was going to tell me she wasn't really Hester MacEvoy. The real Hester MacEvoy, she would explain, had passed over. Possibly to Kingsley. "It isn't?"

"I had a tumor," she said. "An astrocytoma, that's what they called it. It's a nasty sort of thing, you know, very nasty, Mr. Knave—but they cut it out, the doctors. Only it had done some damage to me, you see, and then there was some more damage, because a little bit of it had to be killed with chemicals. Midbrain damage. They tell me I'm a very lucky woman, Mr. Knave, because an astrocytoma can actually go and kill a person. But mine didn't." Her hands tightened on the wheelchair's arms. "Not quite, it didn't," she said. It wasn't a smile she gave me, but a sudden, startling expression of absolute grimness.

Then the smile.

"But that was a long time ago," she said. "And it's such a depressing subject, not at all fit for tea-time. Are you enjoying your tea, Mr. Knave?"

"It's lovely," I said. "And thank you. Ms MacEvoy, would you do me a very important favor?"

Smile. "Oh, it's no trouble," she said. "I'll get more cookies in just an instant." She put her hands on the wheels, ready to zip out to the kitchen.

"No," I said. "Not the cookies—the cookies are fine, but this is a different favor."

"Yes, Mr. Knave?" She was attentive and watchful. Maybe, I thought, she expected me to ask her to show me her operation.

"If you ever do have a dream about an alien—"

"Named Dube," she said. "That *was* his name, wasn't it, Mr. Knave?"

"Any alien at all," I said. "If you ever have a dream that has an alien in it—no matter what his name is, no matter anything at all—would you call me and tell me about it, as quickly as you can?"

"My goodness," she said. "Why would I do that? It would just be a dream. Not something to be excited about."

"Would you do it for me?" I said. "As a favor?"

She considered it. After a minute or so she said: "I will, Mr. Knave. I don't expect to dream about alien beings, you know—it's not my sort of dreaming at all. But if I do, I'll call you right up about it." Smile. "You will leave me your number, won't you?"

I gave her a card. "I've written my number in City Two right there," I said.

She studied the card for a while. In the dim little room I was surprised she could see it clearly, but there was nothing, apparently, wrong with her eyes. "My," she said. "A Survivor. That must be very exciting work."

"It has its moments," I said.

THIRTY-TWO

I was sitting in a taxi, on my way back to my hotel, when it hit me. I actually said it: "Aha."

I wish I could tell you how I reached the answer, but I can only tell you how I reached part of it—from what (as you'll see) somebody else *couldn't* reach. That told me who had killed Harris France.

How Harris France had been killed—how the somebody had been able to get in and out of a locked (and chained, and bolted, and sealed) house I also knew. My mind displayed for me a picture of the front door, with the small scuffed-or-trampled patch of dirt right in front of it, and the greenflower stretching all around.

When I'd realized who our killer was, I'd said: "Aha." When I'd realized how the job had been managed, I said: "Damn."

I should have seen it before. I should have seen it long before—within about a minute of getting inside the damn house. My only consolation was that nobody else had seen it, either, and that wasn't much consolation. I knew exactly what the Master was going to say when I told him: "Gerald, you see, but you do not observe."

Damn.

I wish I could tell you why my mind picked that moment to toss the picture at me. I wish I could tell you—or myself—why my mind does most of the things it does. But there are Mysterious Entities Unknown to Science, even today, and the inside of my head is where a good many of them seem to live.

Maybe knowing who somehow kicked my mind into telling me how. It's as good an explanation as any.

The taxi stopped in front of my hotel and I got out and paid the mech and found my way through the lobby and on up to my room, and I did not visibly curse or fume until I had reached it, gone inside, and shut the door.

The damned thing was obvious, of course. It has come to me that the answers always are, once you have them. They stand there and say: "Here I am, smiling and waving and dressed in bright stoplight red, easily, even offensively, visible—what took you so long?"

Of course. Getting in wasn't the problem, and never had been; Cornelia Rasczak would have let somebody she knew in, easily. But getting out, and chaining the door shut after you were outside . . .

If the chain on the front door—a small, light chain—had to be dropped down into its little socket to chain the door shut, you grabbed the chain, and brought it to the slot, and dropped it in. The lock might even have been set from inside—automatic locking when a door shuts is common enough, and there's no trouble about arranging it; as I remembered thinking long ago, there are the Hell of a lot of ways to gimmick a lock.

And to work the chain, from outside the door.

The chain, I remembered noticing, was made of iron, like the hinges. So you get a magnet. It has to be a large magnet, clumsy to handle—an electromagnet of some size, perhaps. You need a lot of power to get that chain exactly where you want it, hold it and drop it.

Through a wooden door?

Yes, I told myself bitterly—through a very thin (as I had also noticed) wooden door. In fact, damn it, I knew that a large, powerful magnet had been used. One large enough to need a rig to support it and help move it just the right way.

And how did I know that?

Because the scuff marks of the rig that had held it, flush to the door, were right there, in the dirt, looking like scuff-marks.

Damn.

Of course, the whole operation would have been beautifully visible—which didn't matter, given the walking-trees for a screen, and the distance. And the rig would have been stowed in the killer's car after the door had been nicely chained up, to make Harris France the only possible suspect.

Not at all an accidental locked room—a tricksy one, built to box Harris France in very tightly indeed.. (Box? Frame? Well, it's an odd language, isn't it?)

The killer had even mentioned having, and using, a car. In fact . . .

An old car. A small accident.

What (I asked myself, in some awe) was I doing running around loose? I was clearly dense enough to be a public danger. The damned car had been aiming at me—had missed, and veered away, passing itself off as an accident that hadn't quite happened. Somebody had shouted: "Watch out, Foolish!" and I was suddenly sure the somebody had been talking to me.

Foolish didn't begin to cover it.

The question (I realized, as I brewed myself a calming pot of Indigo Hill coffee) was: What do I do now?

I could sally out and confront the killer—which wouldn't work, I was sure. I had ideas, and I had a little evidence, but a confrontation would only be an argument—and would certainly result in the disposal of the evidence, such as it was. A sensible person would never have had the evidence lying around—but this killer, even with whatever aid and comfort was available from Folla and company, was sensible, clearly, only in spots. And not all that many spots; the killer alternated between being sly and being helpful.

After all, as Mirella had said, you kill somebody, you are a nut.

That reflection, when it came to me, gave me an idea, and I dug out her number and called it. It was late afternoon by that time, and though she was still on duty she'd be coming off it shortly. Maybe she'd have an idea or six.

She answered as irritably as usual: "Hello? It is sixteen-twenty-seven, damn it. What now?"

"Where are you?" I said.

"I am at the house, God damn it—*Jerry*." Less than a second to change gears. "Hello, what's up?"

"I've got something better than questions for you," I said. "I've got answers."

"You what?"

"Answers," I said. "Actual answers. Of course, they lead to more questions, but don't they always?"

She made an impatient sound. "Damn it, I am on duty out here. Wrapping up. Closing out, you know? I am on duty thirty-one and a half minutes more. Will I have to wait, or will you open up on the phone?"

"I'll come out and pick you up," I said. She said at once, and doubtfully:

"By cab?"

"I got there by cab last time," I said. "Drivers here seem pretty good. Not perfect—one of them aimed for me and missed, the other day—but pretty good."

"I suppose," she said. "Look, come ahead. I will be having attacks of anxiety every three minutes. Answers? Really?"

"Answers," I said. "Really."

As I got out of the cab, paid and thanked the mech, the door opened. Mirella said: "Don't bother with handkerchiefs or anything. What we got, we have already got. The place is clean, back in order, we're through."

"Where's Paolo?" I said.

She shrugged. "Left early," she said. "Why not? Got to put the place back, right? And he hates housework. I am not fond of it myself, tell the truth."

"Really?" I said. "I like it, most of it. It seems to be relaxing."

Mirella grimaced. "All right, the truth," she said. "You said you were coming, I told him go home. Why not? Who needs a third wheel around, right?"

"Right," I said, and wondered briefly why I felt uneasy. But only briefly. "Where are we going? It's your town and your car."

"Oh, sure," she said. "But it's your answers, Jerry. And while I am driving, don't start telling me, I will distract. This is too much to listen to halfway. Where do I drive to?"

"Station, and change," I said. "Then—this isn't a celebration, not yet. I promise you a celebration, but this is a working dinner. Or late lunch, or whatever. Pick a spot."

She thought about it for a second or two. Then she said: "You like eggplant parmigiana?"

It was, by God, the Art Cafe, which I'd spent a lot of time in—and working time, at that—on my last visit to Ravenal. I remembered the eggplant parmigiana with affection—it's not a frighteningly difficult dish, but it can be ruined with ease, and somebody at the Art Cafe had the touch for it. We found a booth at the rear, and settled in.

I remembered the wine, too, but not with affection. Mirella said: "In here, the thing is tea. They have sixty kinds, some of them very weird. But they know about it."

So we ordered, and drank pots of what the place called Gunpowder Green Tea, which is not much like any other tea I know. I won't say it can replace coffee, but it is a definite wake-up call to any and all taste-buds. Mirella said: "See? This, they know."

"So they do," I said. "Thanks. At least they know that tea doesn't come by the cup—it barely exists by the cup. It comes by the pot."

"Well, sure," Mirella said. "You mean there are places, serve one teeny lonely little cup tea? Really?"

"There are places," I said. "Not places I am found in a lot."

"I should hope not," she said, took a swallow, and said: "Answers. Tell me."

So I did.

THIRTY-THREE

She listened to my description of how the chain had been lifted, and then refastened, and nodded. "Damn it," she said, "I should have got that. I should."

"Well, you weren't looking," I said. "You were sure France was guilty."

"Nobody," she said, "should be so sure, she doesn't go look." She shook her head. "Another time, I will know better." Then she said: "But one thing you missed. A tiny thing."

I swallowed some eggplant, and then I raised one eyebrow. "Really?"

"No high horsing around," Mirella said. "The eyebrow, I mean. But really, yes. Just very tiny. The magnet rig got used only on the way out. On the way in, who says the door was chained?"

"Well, Cornelia Rasczak might have—"

"In fact, probably not," she said, and took a forkful of eggplant. "Or would France have been surprised to see the chain hooked on? No. And it was a surprise—he knew only when he saw it, not when he called his doctor."

I nodded. "Right," I said. "That pins it down. You've got a good head for detail."

She gave me a grin. "But it is very small, because what difference does it make? In he could get. She could let him in, after all. Right? Out is the big thing."

"It had to be," I said. "But it's not a he."

"You also know who?" Mirella said. "Not a he. Look, if it is this Folla or something, why would he need a magnet at all?" She took in some more eggplant. "Dieting," she said casually, "I will do another day. Maybe."

"I wouldn't worry about it," I said, and took some more eggplant myself. "Whenever you happen to feel like it. If ever." A gulp of tea, and: "Not Folla," I said. "A human being." She looked at me, and I told her.

She made the name sound like an awed prayer. "Hester MacEvoy?"

172

"Hester," I said. "Who told me about Dube—but not all about Dube. Who told me a lot—I think that midbrain disease of hers has loosened her up a little, and when she's not being extra careful, she babbles. She babbled to Cornelia, and had to repair it."

"Slowly, you said she babbles."

"Slowly, but she does babble," I said. "She realized she shouldn't have said a thing about Dube, when I came on back—and she tried to sell me the idea that she hadn't, I'd remembered it wrong. Must have been two other people."

"And?" Mirella said. "So how could you know?"

"Know she did it?" I said. "I haven't got proof. What I have got is the fact that she doesn't stay in that wheelchair of hers, when nobody's around. And she can drive a car—she told me that She's tied in with Cornelia Rasczak and with the aliens. If I'd thought of her as actually walking around, too—normally ambulant—she'd have been in the spotlight from the first minute."

"And you know she is not in the wheelchair all the time," Mirella said. "She gets up and walks around, on the quiet." She swallowed some tea. "So how do you know this?"

"She lives alone," I said. "She used to have some help, but not for eight years, since her husband died."

"Passed over," Mirella said. "Which sounds like he was a football at a goal line. Never mind."

"Or as if he didn't get a promotion," I said. "Right. And there were books on high shelves. Stacked."

"So maybe her husband's books," Mirella said. "He had books, right? A Professor."

"Of Military History," I said. "Right. And maybe he also had an old, dark-grey woman's cloak. Because there's one hanging in her place, on a nice high peg."

"So a visitor left it," Mirella said. "So Cornelia Rasczak left it. By mistake." She stopped with a forkful of eggplant halfway to her mouth, and shook her head. "I would not believe that if an archangel came from on high and swore to it." She ate the eggplant.

"It was there both times," I said. "Same cloak, different peg. It was the different peg that finally lit it up for me. Somebody took it down and hung it up again. And Hester lives all alone. The peg is too damn high to reach from a wheelchair."

"So she gets up and she puts on the cloak and she goes out," Mirella said, "and when she comes back in, she is very neat and she hangs it on a peg all nice."

"And sits back down in the wheelchair," I said, "in case somebody comes along."

Mirella frowned. "Somebody would notice," she said. "Neighbors. Somebody."

"She's not exactly popular in the neighborhood," I said. "She wouldn't be—and she keeps talking about being alone. I doubt people notice her much—and, anyhow, if you're used to seeing a woman in a wheelchair go in and out of the place, and you see a woman in a dark cloak *walk* in and out—you don't think it's the same person. At high noon on a sunny day—maybe. Otherwise—it's a nurse. A relative. Somebody, and who cares?"

"So at high noon in the sunlight, she doesn't go out," Mirella said. "When it gets dim, why not?" She grinned at me. "I think you have got it," she said. "I really think you have got it."

"She went out around three o'clock—fifteen—the other day," I said. "She probably didn't go out looking for me—how would she have known where to look?—but she went out some-place. Far from home, obviously, where people don't know her as Hester-in-the-wheelchair and she can just be Hester. She was driving—a car old enough to be an heirloom—and she tried to hit me with it. She'd babbled to me, too, and she tried to re-pair that, with her car. Then I called and gave her another chance, for God's sake, for something more peaceful in the way of damage control."

"You said on the phone," Mirella told me blankly. "I thought, a joke, you know? She came close?"

"Not close enough," I said. Mirella stared at me grimly.

"You take care, okay?" she said, in a level, stern voice. "You do not get damaged—you hear me?"

"I seem to manage all right," I said. Her expression didn't change.

"I am serious," she said. "You take care."

I grinned at her. "I'll take care," I said. "But—all right, we know how, and we know who. And now what? I haven't got a thing anybody could take to an official—and I don't think I'm going to get anything. No prints, no witnesses—an alibi would be a joke, because Hester doesn't get noticed all that much, and it's a thousand to one nobody would remember if Hester happened to be around on one particular afternoon—"

"The magnet rig," Mirella said. "It might be someplace."

I shook my head. The eggplant was gone, and the tea was gone. A waiter came over—the Art Cafe is human-staffed—and Mirella ordered some kind of flaming Thing. I settled for fruit and cheese.

"The odds are it's gone," I said. "Broken up and trashed. She probably had Folla's help building the thing—maybe thinking it up in the first place—and Folla would be careful enough."

"Maybe not," Mirella said. "Probably it's gone. But we got a shot, anyhow. We can go look."

"And then what?" I said. "Even if we find it—even if we can manage to connect Hester with the murder solidly—the job isn't over."

"No," Mirella said. "There's Folla himself."

"There sure as Hell is," I said.

PART FOUR

DEATH AND HIS BROTHER SLEEP

THIRTY-FOUR

It was on the way back to my hotel that Mirella, stopped at a purple light for some reason I couldn't figure out, said: "We have got to tell people."

"Well," I said, "I wasn't thinking of keeping it a secret. It's early—we could phone Master Higsbee—"

"I mean *people*," Mirella said. "Like everybody. Everywhere, because who knows?"

I gave it a second. It didn't really take that long. "Right," I said. "Folla might be getting help from anybody, anywhere."

"Maybe not," she said. "What his limits are, who knows—but he has some. He keeps hitting people right here, maybe he has to focus right here. But maybe only for right now—so we have to warn people."

I had discussed the possibility of Folla and company talking to other dreamers, with Euglane. I'd wondered then what the Hell could be done if he had been—on Kingsley, or on Earth, or around some handy corner in City Two. "How do we warn people?" I said.

Mirella had the car heading on again. She found a parking spot near a playground—deserted, now that the local sun was down—and said, once she was parked and freed from distraction: "There is not much a government is good for. Not even here, and on Ravenal things are not bad. But for getting out the word—nothing else compares."

I blinked. "Tell the Comity?" I said. "For God's sake. Just to begin with, tell them what?"

"That," she said, "is the first thing we have got to figure out."

We began with the truth. Tell some Comity official that aliens from other spaces were trying to infiltrate our universe? "They'd laugh," I said. "Then they'd make some phone calls."

"To the loony-bin people," Mirella said. "Maybe not so fast they don't: this is not going to be just you and me."

"Well, the Master—"

"He has influence," Mirella said. "A consultant, and I bet he consults for big people. He has the look: believe it."

"He knows some people," I admitted cautiously.

"And Euglane," Mirella said. "He is a Giell, people like Gielli. Also they believe Gielli. He will swing weight."

"Four of us," I said. "Not enough. But maybe—"

"Sure," she said. "There are other people. People maybe you know, the ones who will believe you. Maybe three or four more."

"And people you know," I said.

"Me?" she said. "I am a Lance-Corporal. Who I know, is Paolo. Swings no weight whatever."

"But there must be—"

"Other people? Sure," she said. "Corporals, a Sergeant or two. I know Murray, runs the Basement, is about as important a person as I got." She grinned. "Better to lean on your people, Jerry," she said. "And maybe the Master knows a few, too."

She took out her pocket piece and handed it to me. "Here," she said. "Make the call, we'll go see Master Higsbee."

I grinned back at her. "Now, how would you know I forgot to hook my pocket piece into the system again?"

"*Again* says it all," she told me. "So I watch, and I remember. You got a problem with it?"

The grin stuck, very nicely. "No problem at all," I said, and took the phone.

The Master was sitting down to dinner, but he wanted to discuss spreading the word. Mirella and I, stuffed with eggplant parmigiana and other delights, sat and drank as we all talked; I went with coffee, and was unsurprised to find that the Master also had a stock of Indigo Hill. Mirella took tea. Hilda drank water, all through her own dinner, to the Master's barely hidden discomfort. I filled the Master in quickly on Hester, our murderer; and he did say it, damn it.

"I observe," I said. "I observed the damned cloak. It just took me a while."

Mirella, meanwhile, was looking sternly at my coffee-cup. "You drink enough of that stuff," she said, "you will be very jittery."

"Somehow," I said, "I'll manage."

The Master sighed. "We have four problems," he said. "I ignore for the moment the question of Ms MacEvoy's responsibility for two deaths."

"Two?" Mirella said. "She did not get into Harris France's head. That's Folla. Or whatever. Dube."

"Clearly," the Master said, "the murder of Cornelia Rasczak was the first step in the erasure of both persons; it was more convenient—for Folla and his compeers, and perhaps for Ms MacEvoy—that Harris France either be exiled to the Colony, or be driven to suicide; but it is all—"

"All part of the same picture," Mirella said. "Okay, I get it."

The Master does not like interruptions. Not at all. But Mirella was a guest—and a fellow piranha-fancier. He gave her one glare, and said: "Thank you," in a tone that made her pale just a little.

"Let it go," I told him. "Please." He turned to me with an expression I couldn't read for a second, and chuckled.

"I intend to," he said mildly, and to Mirella: "That out of the way for the moment, then, dear girl, we have four problems." I translated his expression then, and felt uneasy all over again; I don't usually try to deflect his irritation. But I just had.

Hilda was looking a little stunned at the peaceful moment, and I suppose I was, too. She was, all in all, the silentest dinner companion I could remember meeting, over any table. Maybe she just didn't like to interrupt anybody, ever—or maybe she just liked listening.

"We have got to get out the word," Mirella was saying slowly. "We have got to get believed. We have got to figure just exactly *what* word to get out. Three."

"Those are simple," the Master said. "But we must also, somehow, stop Folla—or, at the least, intermit his plans. Watchful waiting—which is the best expectable result from any notification—is a temporary expedient."

Mirella considered for a second. Then she said: "Right. People will get tired and goof off. That Folla will go away by himself, we can't hope for."

"We may hope," he said. "Hope is never forbidden. But—given an event we cannot, after all, reasonably expect—we must find a way to—ah—put a spoke in his wheel."

Mirella took a long swallow of tea—in the Master's house, always Irish Breakfast. "That," she said, "sounds like a job."

"Can it be done at all?" Hilda said.

"We are not without resources," he said. He paused.

"Folla wants to build a machine," I said. "The machine has *some* sort of specifications—materials, probably. We can find out—and put a watch on the materials involved."

"Perhaps," the Master said. "If the materials are, for instance, simple steel, oil, water, alcohol, it will be useless; but some may be more rare than that, or require forming in some way that will leave unusual traces."

Hilda looked up. "We might also look at the purity of the materials required," she said. "Nine-nines iron, for instance—or molybdenum of the same purity, or—well, if he must have materials exactly specified for composition, it might be possible to trace them."

"Just so," the Master said. "That possibility does exist; and thank you, Hilda."

She gave him that odd spasm of a smile, and Mirella said: "Well, that's part of what we want to get out to people, anyhow. Watch for whatever it is he needs."

"So it is, dear girl," the Master said. "But there is a more active path open to us. We can carry our opposition to Folla and his companions, and we must."

"How do we do that?" I said. "We can't get into his spaces, whatever they are, any more than he can get into ours. A Josephson junction isn't a path into his spaces, it's a path that doesn't have space in it at all."

"Quite so," he said. "Although there exist possibilities—you will recall his having said that neither mass nor distance exist as such in his spaces, which provides us with a starting-point for thought."

"Hell of a starting-point," Mirella said. "No mass, no distance, and it is a space? Makes my head itch to think about."

"Treat it as a mathematical abstraction," the Master said. "A space is defined by its qualities; we know—or Folla has told us, which is admittedly not quite the same thing—qualities it does not have. We can theorize from that point, and perhaps arrive at *some* conclusion—though I am not hopeful."

"But you have something else," I said. "I am damned if I can see what. If we can't get to his space—"

"But we can reach Folla himself," the Master said. "Him, or his companions. As he has come to us."

"But those were—" I stopped. "Oh, God," I said. "Dreams. I talked back to Folla—got him to start a conversation with me—last time."

"Exactly," he said. "We will require Euglane's help. But I said some time ago that we would have to discover, in the end, what dreams are, and what dreaming in fact is. We would appear to have done so."

"Wait a minute," Mirella said. "Folla shows up in a few dreams here and there, and from this we know about all dreams anyplace?"

"Dreaming," the Master said, "is a means of communicating with—of visiting, in fact—other spaces. Some of those other spaces are inhabited, it now appears, by thinking beings—Folla and Dube and perhaps more. Communication is vague, and often confused and confusing, and the world—the space—the dreamer enters is used for his or her own purposes whenever possible, and distorted by the dreamer to serve those purposes. All that is admitted, ands it makes analysis no simpler. But if the space we enter in dreams exists as a communicative medium between ourselves and Folla's spaces, then it so exists for humans in general; there is no reason to assume that we are all special cases."

"People dream about everything and anything," Mirella said.

"So they do," the Master said. "They interpret the experiences they have—experiences of other spaces—in terms with which they are familiar, and in terms useful to them, terms they can recognize in dealing with their own lives and questions. Gielli, who share a single dream-world, may see these other spaces a bit more clearly. At any rate, they see them differently."

"Communication," Mirella said. "With other spaces. Visiting whole other spaces. This is what dreams come to? Who'd have imagined?"

"This," I said, "is going to take some thought."

THIRTY-FIVE

"The Gielli share a single dream world," Master Higsbee said.

"So Euglane says," I put in.

"The question is," he said, "is it the same world which we humans enter, in our dreams?"

Mirella shook her head. "Why should it be? They're Gielli—they're different, right?"

"Not that different, dear girl," the Master said. "We exist in the same universe with Euglane; we share the same physical laws; we can communicate, we can act upon each other. Do our dreams also share a universe?"

I thought about it for a second. "I am damned if I know how anybody could tell," I said. "We can't take our dreams out and compare them—we can only compare descriptions, and vague descriptions at that."

"We might," the Master said, "compare specific objects, specific places, as experienced by humans and Gielli—or by humans and any other beings. But I agree; as humans, we use the world we encounter in dreams for our own purposes—interpreting what we experience in the light of our own needs and wishes, defining our experiences individually. It would not be possible to compare anything resembling objective data. The Gielli doubtless also use their shared dream-world, though to what degree their use is distorted by *their* needs and wishes I do not know. Euglane might know—but the question is not worth exploration. There are too many unknowns on our side of the equation."

"And no way to cross over from one side to the other," Hilda said. "There are no measurable objects in dreams—objectively measurable. We can't compare Euglane's dreams with mine, not and get anywhere."

"So where does that leave us?" I said.

"With a question still more interesting," he said. "We may assume that the world we enter in dreams has a real existence—though we distort it greatly. We may assume tentatively that this is also true of the shared Gielli dream-world; the two worlds may be the same, but no matter, for the present." He turned his head to Mirella, to Hilda, then back to me again. I don't know why he does that. "Folla exists in a different world—a different—ah—sheaf of spaces," he said. "The question is: does he exist in either our dream-world, or the Gielli world—if the Gielli world is in fact different from our own."

"Damn it, he has to," I said. "He pops up in dreams. He has to exist to do that at all."

"Ah, but you have missed the point, Gerald," he said. "Is the dream-world his—ah—home space, so to speak, his natural universe? Or is he a visitor there, as we are periodic visitors there?"

"So the next time he shows up," Mirella said, "we should ask him for a passport? Find out where he lives?"

"Somehow," he said, "I doubt that he would provide a reply—or that, if he did, it would be easily comprehendable. But this question is, in fact, decidable."

There was a little pause. His head swivelled again. Damn it, I told myself, he was enjoying this. He knew something we didn't know.

"Let us suppose that Folla's home space—the home space of these aliens—is our dream-world," he said. "What follows from this? Surely, at once, two facts: first, that it might be possible for him to enter many, many thousands of dreams (though he has not)—and second, that he is familiar with our waking space."

"Well," Mirella said, "so maybe he can go into lots of dreams. We only know—how many?—four people he's talked to, or this Dube talked to. MacEvoy, and Harris France, and Jerry here, and Hilda. Who says he didn't talk to fifty thousand other people, anyplace?"

"I say it, dear girl," Master Higsbee told her. "He (or Dube) has asked for aid from Hilda, from Ms MacEvoy, and from Gerald; whether he also asked for aid from Harris France we cannot know."

"So?"

"He needs a mechanism constructed," the Master said. "He has asked for aid from people who do not, as a rule, construct mechanisms. Ms MacEvoy, in particular, seems a very bad choice—but, given Ravenal, given even City Two, there are easily eight thousand choices superior to any we know he has made."

"So he doesn't know anything about people," Mirella said. "So he's just shooting in the dark."

"No," the Master said. "Think: we know that he was in contact with Harris France some time ago, in contact with Hilda during her hospital stay, months in the past. He has had time to approach many people; and he is still requesting aid of Gerald. Apparently he can only reach certain people; why this is, we do not know."

"A Detective-Colonel in Homicide," Mirella said, "A Survivor, a—chemist, right?" Hilda nodded. "And a woman in a wheelchair. So what is the common link?"

"Two are male," Hilda said, "and two female. Might this be significant?"

The Master shook his head. "Anything might be significant," he said. "There is no way for us to know on what basis contact is possible' we do not know how Folla experiences our spaces, or what it is he sees—if seeing is his mode of experience, to be sure. There is one facet of character all four do share—a high level of what might be called determination. Strength. The inability, if you will, to surrender."

"Stubbornness," Mirella said.

"Just so," the Master said. "Hilda owns it, as her decision to accept her blindness and live in terms of it will show. Harris France seems to have been a most decisive, firm, and decided person. This stubbornness, if that is the word, is one of Gerald's most noticeable characteristics."

"And Hester MacEvoy?" Mirella said.

"It would be far easier for her—as she has been described to me—to leave her life here, to return to Kingsley, to live out her life in the shallows of invalidism. She has not done so."

"So he picks stubborn people," Mirella said. "There are a lot of stubborn people."

"There are certainly other qualifications, so to speak," the Master said. And the fact is, given our ignorance, we cannot judge of his needs—of the needs of these aliens—from the people known to have been accessed; they are too varied." He shook his head. "No," he said. "He has chosen those he must choose, and has hoped that one, at least, will be both capable and willing."

"Like MacEvoy," Mirella said. "She is willing to go shoot her own doctor. Maybe she is also willing to build this machine, whatever it is. She says no, but what does it mean she says anything?"

"He still searches," the Master said.

Hilda looked up, uncomfortably. "He does search, Sir," she said. "So he hasn't got his machine yet. But perhaps something should be done about Ms MacEvoy—just in case."

Mirella made a sound that was about half laugh and half snarl. I hadn't known she had it in her, and in its way it was a pleasant surprise. "Like maybe get her arrested, at least," she said. "The woman killed somebody. Maybe we should do something?"

THIRTY-SIX

But we tabled that—for a brief while. Mirella had been thinking about dreams.

"I have heard," she said suddenly, "if you dream you die— then you do not wake up, you just drop dead in your sleep. Does anybody know is this true?"

The Master chuckled again. "I cannot imagine a way to decide the question," he said. "Who could testify to its truth, but the dead? And there can be no testimony of its falsity; there are dreams of dying, and dreams of an afterlife—there exist even dreams in which the dreamer attends his own funeral. But there are no establishable dreams of death itself; we cannot say anything clearly about an experience no living being has yet had."

"People have been clinically dead for a few minutes," I said. "That's been happening for centuries."

"What difference exists between 'clinically dead' and 'dead' we cannot know," he said. "But if it is reversible, it was not death; that much is a beginning."

"Tell the truth," Mirella said, "I do not truly want to be dead, and I am not much on being clinically dead either."

"Nor am I, dear girl, nor is Gerald," the Master said. "But the chance must be taken; we must treat with Folla. The alternative is to allow Folla and his fellows freely into our spaces— with what results we cannot know, but they are unlikely to be pleasant ones."

"Telling people—" I said.

"Will maybe help out for maybe sixty days Standard," Mirella said. "People get tired, people goof off. Then what? We cannot call Wolf every sixty days. The third time, nobody will listen."

I sighed. "So we're going to go and make a stand in our dreams," I said. "Well, it's a new experience."

"Gerald," the Master said, "some weeks ago you told me that you had a novel situation for me. We are all now beginning to see how very accurate your statement was."

"That's my Jerry," Mirella said. "He hit it on the nose, right?"

The Master chuckled again. Damn it, it's not a pleasant sound.

Euglane was in fairly good shape when we reached him by phone. He'd had some time to adjust, and he was adjusting fairly well. The Master filled him in as quickly as possible, and Euglane suggested we all head over to his place. "There is equipment here that may be helpful," he said. "And if more is needed, there are labs at Lavoisier to which I have access."

"Labs?" Mirella said. "I am not much good with lab stuff."

"I'll help you, if needed," Euglane said. "It will be neither difficult nor threatening."

Mirella sounded doubtful, but she said: "I take your word, okay," and we piled into her car, the four of us, and headed on over to Euglane's.

Four of us. Hilda had stayed firmly in the background all through our talk, but the Master asked her to come along. "It may be that your contribution will be a major one," he told her.

She looked, and sounded, more doubtful than Mirella had, but all she said was: "If you think so, Sir."

Mirella drove. I wouldn't put it past the old helpless blind Master to be able to drive a car—through City Two traffic and in Ravenal's complex traffic system—but he sat in back with Hilda, and let me share the front seat with Mirella. There was no conversation en route, just a general, stuffy atmosphere of worry.

And when we got to Euglane's place, the first piece of equipment we used was the phone.

"It is a holding action, perhaps little more," the Master said. "But it has value—and its value depends on our speed."

There were five of us—not really enough, as Mirella and I had agreed. But there would be others; I knew one or two right on Ravenal, and the Master, to nobody's surprise, knew what sounded like the entire top five per cent of the population of City Two, whether you ranked by intelligence or influence. "Some I have worked with," he said, sounding as casual as a human being could sound after the list he'd given us. "Some I have met socially—despite my infirmities, I maintain what social life I may—and a few are old friends and acquaintances, reaching back to our days as students."

I passed over the infirmities in silence—he was still using his cane, and it still handicapped him about as much as a pocket-handkerchief handicaps people—but I did have a little difficulty with the picture of Master Higsbee as a schoolboy. I suppose he must have been, once upon a time in the Pleistocene Era.

Euglane suggested calling a few of them first, but the Master shook his head. "It is not needed," he said. "They know my word is good, and they cannot fear I would exaggerate. I shall explain matters to them at a convenient time; let us simply *begin*."

So we started to run up Euglane's phone bill. What we wanted was a connection to two people: the Governor-General on Ravenal, probably on his estate outside City One, and the Emperor of the Comity. In a pinch, the President of the Dichtung would do as stand-in for the Emperor, though the Emperor—as an elected official—would be closer to the people generally.

One does not pick up the phone, dial a number and connect with these folk. One does not (except by extraordinary effort) connect with them at all, except at an unhelpful distance. In the end—forty minutes later, which may, for God's sake, be a speed record—we mounted a two-pronged attack: a friend of Master Higsbee's ("I was able to help him with a small difficulty, some years ago," the Master said, "and he will remember") who was attached to the Official Household in a fairly close way—and Guin Jenn, who was, as I remembered after a little thought, Surgeon (for her specialty) to the personal household of the Governor-General.

Guin needed a little persuading. "I am not," she said sternly, sounding much less tired than she had when I'd got her to push Michael Morse for me (well, it was mid-evening, and, except for emergencies, her surgical day not only started early but ended early)—"I am not in the habit of chivvying Lord Batesman in any way, or for any object."

"And I am not in the habit of chivvying you, Guin," I said, "and damn well you know it. I've got a situation here—or we have."

"We?"

"Master Higsbee—you've met him, I think—and a Giell named Euglane, whom you may not—"

"Euglane?" she said. "The psychiatrist?"

"The psychiatrist," I said.

"A sensible fellow," Guin said. "I know few psychiatrists, Knave—my work deals with the real world—but I am familiar with his reputation. He appears to do good work, in his way."

That, from Guin, was the equivalent of six medals and a brass band. "Well, we're all facing rather a special situation," I said, "and—"

"Can I reach him somewhere?" she said. "Nothing personal, Knave, but I should like to hear about this from Euglane himself."

"He's right here," I said, stifling a small sigh. "This is reasonably urgent—"

"Knave," she said, "I have never, in some years, known you *not* to be urgent. Put him on, please."

So I did. And, with Guin's help, and more help from the Master's friend—who didn't need nearly as much persuasion—we arranged for the Governor-General to call Euglane's number within the hour.

The Governor-General would serve as our line to the Emperor, by space-four communicator—if we could persuade him. We spent a little time setting up the explanation for him, but not much; Batesman had the reputation of being a fairly sensible type (well, he didn't have to get elected, though he did mix into politics more than his job description showed)—and, Master Higsbee said, he'd had a science background, once upon a time.

"He showed some imagination," the Master said, "according to those who knew him at that time. Much of it will have been eroded by the demands of his career, to be sure; but some will remain. He will not dismiss us out of hand."

"He is supposed to handle big emergencies," Mirella said. "That's his job, right? This qualifies."

"Exactly so," the Master said. "We shall make him see that. Euglane, perhaps you will best serve here."

So it was Euglane who talked to the Governor-General, when he did phone in fifty minutes later—on a shielded phone, the shield imposed on the link straight to Euglane's instrument.

Lord Batesman turned out to be a fairly tough sell, which was no surprise. Euglane was good—very good, using every ounce of his persuasive powers and his inbuilt combination of likeability and trust—but it took some additions from the Master to get the Governor-General to agree to find the Emperor with our message.

The Master was friendly—for the Master—and authoritative, which was no great stretch. The call went on for about half an hour, maybe a little longer, and when it was over we had only the wisp of a promise. Lord Batesman would call the Emperor "in the morning" for the Emperor's planet and time-zone— which (he told us) was about six hours away. "I don't guarantee I'll speak to him directly," he said. "I will try. But he will get your message, whether directly from me or from one of his household."

We hoped for a direct communication; even the best middle-men (and women) are subject, like other forms of communication, to Noise. And we hoped for fast action, once the message got through.

And what had that message been? We knew, after all, very damned little. We wanted this word to get out fast: that anyone who mentioned (to a doctor, to anyone at all to whom the word could be carried) any dream in which an alien being—or a small pet, I added in, since that was the only disguise we'd seen, and it had been used several times—asked for something to be done in the dreamer's waking life was to be advised of what we now knew—and watched, in whatever way the individual planetary setup allowed.

It was a net that had more holes in it than a mining asteroid, and all we really had was a set of hopes; but it was a start.

Now we could go back to Job One.

THIRTY-SEVEN

Euglane had one small rig I admired instantly. "Hypnotism," he explained to us, as he'd once told me, "is not a normal part of my work; but I've found it useful now and then. With great care, of course."

The usual hypnotist has a shining thing—a watch, a light, anything that glitters and is small enough to carry in your hand and move at a regular, reasonably slow speed—the speed varies with the subject, and hypnotists generally experiment till they find the right one each time—a shining thing that you stare at while it moves back and forth, and while the hypnotist talks gently to you.

Euglane had a small light attached to the end of an ancient (and silenced) metronome. He set it, he told us, to the subject's pulse rate. "This is almost always the correct frequency," he said, "and the regularity of the motion is a great help."

A lovely gimmick. And it was going to be useful.

"If we are to be in touch with Folla—with these beings generally—during sleep," Euglane said, "we will have to be able to sleep more or less at will—and, if at all possible, report back on such contacts *during* sleep."

That, I told him, sounded like an interesting order. Going to sleep on command was manageable, certainly—and the little gadget would come in handy, because hypnosis, and a post-hypnotic trigger, is the easy, no-side-effects way to manage that—but reporting back while sleeping sounded like a brand-new trick.

"I do not know that it's ever been tried," Euglane said, "but it should be possible. There exist, after all, many humans who do, occasionally, talk in their sleep."

"Well, yes," I said, "but—"

"They don't say much," Mirella said, "and what they say isn't sense."

"Exactly," I said.

"My cousin Donna was sleeping once," she said, "and she started talking, so I started listening, you know? Some of it was just mumble and hiss, but she did say one thing clear. She said: 'Barrels of mice, in strawberry jars.'"

"And remembered nothing of it when she woke," Euglane said, "and was unable to explain the reference."

"This always happens?" Mirella asked him.

"It is usual," he said. "Where such speech is born, and what it means, we are not certain. But—if speech, then controllable speech, since speech is not a reflex but a learned and complex action; it is not simply producing—mumble and hiss."

"Fine," I said. "But, as it happens, I don't talk in my sleep. Never have—I have it in good authority. And what if none of us do?"

"Good authority?" Mirella said, fixing me with an eye as glittering as a cobra's.

"Another time," I said. Euglane was nodding calmly.

"What has not been tried," he said, "and what I propose we do try, is: a post-hypnotic command to speak during sleep, to describe the dream one encounters, and to describe it audibly and with clarity."

"Will this work?" I said.

"We can hope," Euglane said. "It will take a very dependable hypnotic state, of the sort usually induced by drugs. But I may be able to produce it in you—specifically you, Knave, and Hilda here, since we know Folla can approach you two in the dream state—with a little time, and without the drugs."

"Drugs cannot be used," the Master said. "Such of them as affect sleep tend also to affect the capacity to dream, in one way or another."

"True," Euglane said, "which is why we'll do this the difficult way."

Hilda said, in a very tense voice: "Am I to be hypnotized, Sir?" She was addressing, of course, the Master.

"It will be quite safe, Hilda," he said gently. "You have my word."

She didn't pause more than five seconds. "Very well, Sir."

So we set things up—Hilda first, because she looked to be less of a threat to Folla, if he thought in terms of threats; after all, I'd already told him to quit playing games, which was more resistance than he'd had from anybody else we knew about.

Euglane and Hilda stayed in his inner room, where the hypnotic metronome was, though he'd be using, of course, a pulse sound derived from it, rather than the little light, for Hilda—and where he had a cot set up, and started rigging some electronic gadgetry—and Mirella and the Master and I went out to the living-room where Euglane and I had had some talks, and where he saw most of his patients. The Master did stay behind for a few minutes—reassuring Hilda a little more, I suppose—and shut the door, when he came to join us, very quietly.

As Mirella had passed me in the doorway, she'd muttered: "Good authority? Jerry, we will talk. Soon."

Hilda was a washout, which was as expected—after all, Folla had come into one dream of hers, months before, and though he'd clearly intended to come back, he hadn't managed it to date. Apparently he thought I was a better candidate—likelier to be able to build the gimmick he needed?—and was concentrating, more or less, on that. "I asked her to call for him, in her dream," Euglane said, "and I did suggest as strongly as possible that she dream. There's a limit to the strength of such a suggestion, if it's to be useful."

"Make it too strong," I said, "and the subject will invent a dream, just to please the hypnotist. Self-defeating."

"Exactly," Euglane said, and Mirella said:

"Jerry, how come you know so much about this?"

I shrugged. "I've been hypnotized," I said. "It was the only way to deal with a Fairy Godfrog. Some day I'll tell you about it—too long a story for right now."

"Lots of people get hypnotized," she said. "How come you learned about it? Just curious?"

"I don't like things I can't understand," I said. "So I tried understanding it. To tell the truth, I'm not at all sure I do."

"There exist a hundred theories regarding hypnosis," Euglane said. "A thousand. Many are plausible; none provide certainty of any sort. Despite some interesting mathematics, little is actually known about the state."

I sighed. "Well," I said, "my turn." Folla had never turned up for Hilda, but she was still on the cot—Euglane wanted to give her a chance to rest, held by a post-hypnotic. But she could be moved to an upstairs bed—a very large, wide bed, in fact, since it was Euglane's, and of course he slept relaxed.

He and I got Hilda up the stairs and on the bed—a water-bed ("It's a blessing, in this gravity," Euglane told me)—without waking her. When we came downstairs the Master and Mirella were in the inner room.

He was looking at the wiring. "You measure the depth of sleep?" he said.

"Just so," Euglane said. "For these purposes, essential: I must know, so to speak, how far into that—ah—undiscovered country our traveler penetrates."

"But from this country," I said, "travelers do return."

"I hope," Mirella said. "I still worry: if you dream you die, what then?"

"If I do," I said, "I'll tell you all about it when I wake up."

She scowled at me. "Very funny," she said. "Just take care. Who knows what an alien can do?"

THIRTY-EIGHT

So I lay down, and Euglane started with his wiring. Most of it was hooked to a flexible cap; the cap generated a field that echoed electrical activity inside my head. He eased the cap onto my head and adjusted it a little, not fussily, and I shut my eyes and told my body to relax.

"You've been hypnotized before," Euglane said.

"I know how it works," I said. "You'll want me sitting up, won't you? To see the swinging light?"

"Not necessary," he said. "It's mirrored above you; I'll switch it on."

He did, and when I opened my eyes I was staring at a good, but not too shiny, mirror, with the metronome ticking silently away in the middle of it.

After a little while, I was sleeping, and knew I was sleeping, and looking around for a dream to have. I felt calm and fairly confident, and hoped Folla would pop up.

Trying to generate a dream, even as cloudily as I was doing it in my induced sleep, is an unusual feeling—like trying to invent a tall story to tell somebody in a bar. It's not the kind of thing I've ever been good at—the stories I spin in bars, when I fall into that odd habit, are usually all too depressingly true—and I kept asking myself what dream materials would be likeliest to attract Folla.

That was a useless kind of question, on six or seven different grounds, but I was still asking it when I found myself in a dog factory. Large mechanicals were putting dogs together on a long, old-fashioned assembly-line belt, out of parts they took from bins ranged alongside the belt. The rate was just slow enough for me to follow the steps: a small, hairless torso appeared at the start of the belt, a head was stuck on, then hind legs, forelegs and a tail. The last two mechanicals attached small, pointed and floppy ears, and sprayed the finished product with immense globs of hair, which settled all over the animal, leaving feet and eyes bare. At the end of the belt, each dog stood, shakily for a second, barked twice, and then jumped off, trotting into the shadows beyond my view.

I watched this process, with only very faint surprise, for about a minute and a half, dream-time—say six dogs' worth. Then a dog got fully assembled at the end of the belt, stood, looked at me and said: "Statement: you wish to aid me."

"I wish to talk with you," I said. "Folla?"

"So identified," the dog said. He trotted over to me. "Shall you select a subject for conversation?"

"If I'm going to provide any help," I said, "I'll want to be paid. What can you offer?"

"Question: offer?"

"You offered another human a new sense," I said. The dog cocked his head at me.

"Your sensorium is full," he said. "I can provide that only with changes."

Bargaining time? "What kinds of changes?"

"New material would have to be grown," he said. "Time would elapse, and isolation would be essential."

"What length of time?" I said. "And what would the new sense do?"

"Would you enjoy perception of temporal extension?" he said.

"I would know when I looked at something how long it had lasted?" I said.

"You will see its temporal extent," he said. "Its time of beginning, its existence and its time of ending. The perception will be suited to your experience of temporality."

It sounded like a very handy thing to be able to do, I told myself. Look at something and see when it had started, when it was going to end. "This perception will apply to what kind of object?"

"Any and all," he said. "Partial list: objects constructed, objects grown, other beings of all sorts. Do you wish this sense?"

"Isolation required," I said. "How much isolation, and for how long?"

"Reply in series," he said. "One: total isolation from all other beings and living objects. Two: uncertainty exists. Growth factors are individuated."

"Give me a horseback guess," I said, and immediately translated: "An approximate figure. Minutes, days or years?"

"In your experience of temporality," he said, "between two days and six months Standard."

"How will I know when time is up?"

"When perception begins, you will experience it," he said.

"How?" I said.

"Reply not expressible," he said, which was what I'd expected.

I tried to act as if I were thinking it over. "I'll need time to decide," I said.

"What time is required?" the small dog said.

"Days, and not many days," I said. "How will I find you again?"

"I will watch," he said. "When you have decided, I will know, as soon as you enter these spaces."

"As soon as I dream again?"

"Dreaming is your perception of this entry," he said. "Your dream will advise me."

"Automatically?"

"You will wish to tell me of your decision," he said. "That wish will create a suitable experience in these spaces, and I will watch for such an experience."

"Two questions," I said.

"Questions in series awaited."

I took a breath. The assembly line was still going on; our talk had been punctuated with barks every now and then. "One," I said. "Can I rely on this agreement remaining open, or will you make an agreement of some kind with some other being? Two: why do you appear as a dog, along with a small girl?"

He cocked his head at me again. His ears went up, and down. "Reply in series," he said. "One: No other being has made agreement. Of beings reachable, you alone have discussed to this extent. I will await further discussion. Two: Humans have pets. Small common pets are non-threatening and inspire friendship and confidence. Young female humans inspire confidence and affection."

I nodded. "I'll get back to you as soon as I can," I said. "Now I must wake up."

And I did. Euglane was looking down at me, his face, what I could read of it, dispassionately kind. "An interesting discussion," he said, and I cleared my throat, blinked once or twice and said:

"It worked?"

"Your report was clear, and I've recorded it for analysis," he said. I sat up—slowly; I felt as if I could have used another eight hours of sleep, or at least an hour of good massage.

Discussion time.

THIRTY-NINE

"A dog factory?" Mirella said.

I shrugged. "Why not a dog factory?" I said. "I must have built it, one way or another—we have no evidence that Folla can impose anything more than Folla on a dreamer."

"We have no evidence that he is not at this moment making arrangements with six other humans," the Master said. "Despite his promise, which we cannot wholly trust, it is possible, though I admit unlikely, that he is now treating with another, here on Ravenal, or on Kingsley, or Rimshot, or Earth." He looked around at the rest of us, sitting scattered in Euglane's comfortable living-room. "Or can we derive something?"

Euglane said: "Perhaps we can." There was a little silence.

"Expound," Master Higsbee said.

Euglane looked inquiringly at me, and it took me a second to get it. Then I nodded; Mirella knew a little about Gielli, and she wouldn't be too disturbed by the change.

Then, as he relaxed, it occurred to me a) that Euglane had asked my verdict on possibly disturbing Mirella with the sudden appearance of his long arms and legs, and b) that I had accepted that fact as normal.

Well . . . it was something to think about. Later.

Much later.

"Let us assume," Euglane said, when he had the kinks out a little, "that Folla—that these beings in general—can access, so to speak, any human being at any location. If this is true, he did not appear in Knave's dream just now."

"Probabilities?" the Master said.

"Exactly," Euglane said. "He needs, or wants, to—'get in'—to have this machine built for him. If he can access any human anywhere—we are still unsure of other beings, not human, but the distinction is not relevant to this chain of reasoning—then he will, first, be accessing those who can most easily perform the task, and, second, be accessing as many humans or other beings as possible. He would be occupied with many such encounters; that he would be free to appear in Knave's dream when called, with little delay, is, as you have realized, Master, very highly improbable."

"He could be anyplace all at once," Mirella said.

"Polylocation," Euglane said. "Folla, spreading out over our spaces to attack at thousands of points simultaneously. It's a frightening picture, Lance-Corporal—but no."

"So why not?" Mirella said.

"Folla is Folla," he said. "He is not several beings; Dube is Dube. Individuated, he has said—and 'so identified'. If individuated, he is not collective. He is the same person each time."

"So Folla is assigned to us, here," Mirella said, "and sixty other aliens are assigned to sixty somebody elses, in some other place. This is not possible?"

"It is very unlikely," Euglane said. "Folla was not on Ravenal to begin with; the being who appeared in Ms MacEvoy's dream, and in Hilda's, was Dube, and of the identity of Harris France's being, once it became a real alien rather than his illusion, we have no data. We assume that being to have been Folla, Dube or another of the same sort. But Folla would have come here after having sent Knave here. And—this is, after all, Ravenal. Someone fully capable of building a machine for these aliens—someone who could manage the job with ease—would be easy to find, anywhere in the Scholarte. Any mechanician, perhaps electronics technician, perhaps metallurgist, perhaps—"

"I see," the Master said. "And Dube, as we've been realizing, chose the crippled widow of a Professor at Leibniz. Folla, clearly, is not better-informed."

"A Professor of Military History," Euglane said. "Scarcely the sort of discipline that would be handy—even if Ms MacEvoy were fully acquainted with her late husband's specialty, which we don't know."

"I doubt it like Hell," Mirella said, "just on what I hear about her. But so maybe Dube makes a mistake and tries her out—how much can he know about humans? Does he know there *is* such a thing as a metallurgist, say? Maybe by him this woman in a wheelchair is an expert, and just right."

"No," Euglane said. "In order to gain her cooperation at all, he helped her to walk. He knows enough about humans to know that her wheelchair does not provide an optimum condition for any work he needs done." He paused. "It seems probable that he knows of metallurgists, or whatever his machine requires; he is to provide specifications for its construction, and must have acquired those specifications from some experience of materials and possibilities in our spaces. But, whether or not that is so, the limitation of the wheelchair applies: he chose her because—for reasons we don't know—he had to choose her; his pool of possibles must in fact be very limited."

"Maybe," Mirella said, "maybe he needs a chemical analyst. He came into Hilda's dream, after all."

"So he did," the Master said. "Into hers, and Ms MacEvoy's, as Folla entered Knave's—a widow with physical troubles and no apparent helpful specialty, a chemist, and a Survivor. He also seems to have some tie to the late Harris France, a police official. We cannot judge of the needs of these aliens from the people known to have been accessed; they are too varied." He shook his head. "No," he said. "Euglane is right: as I have said, he has chosen those he must choose, and has hoped that one, at least, will be both capable and willing."

"Like MacEvoy," Mirella said. "Who is maybe willing, can we say for certain?" Which brought us back to *that* little puzzle.

Arresting Hester MacEvoy was going to be a job. Such hard evidence as we had—without bringing in Dube—was not going to be persuasive to an average judge, jury or prosecutor—and mentioning Dube at all didn't look like a cheerful thought.

"I can see it now," Mirella said. "What the idea would be is, we are all a little bit nuts. We have visions. Maybe, just maybe, we are harmless and do not have to be locked up."

"All right: what do we do?" I said. "I agree something has to happen; she said she wouldn't build the damn machine—but she also said she couldn't, because she was in a wheelchair. Which turns out to be true only now and then. So what the Hell do we do?"

Hilda was standing at the top of the stairs. For a large person, she was really remarkably quiet; none of us had noticed her. She cleared her throat, and gave us all that little spasm of a smile. Her deep voice was very quiet, almost apologetic "We frame her," she said.

FORTY

So we did.

Persuading a lot of officials that Hester MacEvoy could get out of her wheelchair—which was the basic point; if we could do that, I thought, police could do the rest, because Hester, stubborn or not, wouldn't stand up under questioning very well; she was a little too flaky—didn't sound possible; the trick was, obviously, to get her to demonstrate her mobility before an audience. And I didn't think asking her to get up and do a few dance steps was going to work.

Rushing into her place and shouting: "Fire! Earthquake! Flood!" was better, but what if she simply put on a burst of speed and wheeled the Hell out? Perfectly possible—people in wheelchairs can move like streaks, when practiced.

But there was another way . . .

Euglane had to use his persuasive skills again, because Guin Jenn wouldn't have responded well to mine. She'd do me the occasional favor, always just a bit amused at whatever the Hell I happened to be involved with, but actual neurosurgery was something she didn't like playing games with. And I couldn't appear in the picture at all, when things got going—Hester was already worried that she'd babbled to me, and if I popped up, no matter how confused she happened to be at the moment, all her alarms were going to go off. So we planned it, carefully, that night, until we had everything nicely set up and agreed on by the two on-stage players.

Guin, when she'd arrived, had had a lot of objections, even when she'd agreed to the basic notion. "Non-invasive procedure?" she'd said scornfully. "Knave, what, exactly, is a non-invasive neurosurgical procedure? Do I cast spells for the woman?"

"If we offer her an operation," I said, "she'll refuse it. She'll come up with a reason—she's used to her life, she doesn't want to run any surgical risks, something. She can walk *right now*—she has no reason to check into a hospital and have her head sawed open."

"And this—idiotic story?"

"She'll have to accept that," I said. "No risk, no trouble for her—and she has to look as if she *wants* to be able to walk. She has to be minimally plausible—offer her a cure and she has to take it, if it's risk-free—whether or not she needs it."

"I don't like it," Guin said.

"I'm not all that fond of it myself," I said, "but it'll work. We're calling her bluff."

"But the whole idea of the procedure is such nonsense—"

"I know," I said. "It has to be—because the whole meaning is that there's no reason in the world for the procedure to make her walk. Unless she already can."

Euglane and Guin were to head over there the next afternoon—calling first, and spinning the story. Euglane was a noted psychiatrist, and a confrere, he was to tell Hester, of Cornelia Rasczak's; Cornelia had told him of Hester's problem, and he'd heard from another old friend (Guin) of a new procedure for such cases.

"Brain tissue has been destroyed," Guin had said to us. "Am I a miracle-worker, that I'm going to regrow it for her?"

"You're going to develop new pathways," Euglane said. "By induction."

Guin laughed. Scornfully. "Do I chant while I do this?" she said. "Burn incense? Stagger through a ritual dance to something-or-other?"

"You wear sterile gloves, perhaps," Euglane said. "You put on a surgical mask. You look distant and professional. There are many sorts of rituals, Dr. Jenn."

"I only hope," she said, "that word of this—escapade never surfaces. I would never, ever, live it down, you know."

"No fear," I said. "We'll never spill it, past a few selected police people—and Hester will be in no position to babble."

It was the next afternoon because Guin had, she insisted, a revision of a neck fusion to do in the morning. "I'm going to be in no shape for anything complex after that," she said, "but I suppose I can handle simple nonsense." And the time in between was interesting, if that's the word.

We all had to go to our various homes, after all, and go to sleep.

The Master and Hilda went on home, Hilda looking determined—her normal expression, I suppose—and the Master assuring her that there was nothing to fear: "Folla has promised he will wait upon Gerald's decision," he told her. "If he break his word and come to you, you will of course temporize. He requires aid, Hilda; he will do nothing harmful in any way."

She said it again, of course: "If you say so, Sir."

Guin went home to rest up for her neck fusion job, disturbed only, as far as I could tell, by the pure idiocy of the story she was going to be delivering in eighteen or nineteen hours. Euglane seemed calm and even assured. And if Mirella fretted at all, she wasn't fretting about Mirella.

"Suppose he gets in a rush and comes to say hello to you?" she asked me, when we were driving me home in her car.

"I'll say hello, see you soon," I said. "He'll have to wait his turn—I don't want to fence with him at all until I have some sort of word from the official Comity."

She didn't sound persuaded. "So suppose this Folla doesn't want to wait?" Mirella said.

"That," I said, "is his problem. As the Master was saying, he won't hurt anything—he wants help."

"Just be careful, okay?" she said.

And, if anybody dreamed anything, helpful or threatening, he or she never mentioned it. Folla was apparently keeping his word to wait for me; it occurred to me to wonder if Folla *could* lie. He'd promised Hilda a new sense, and he'd promised me something novel, too, but the fact that he hadn't delivered didn't quite mean that he wouldn't, or couldn't. Lying is a complicated thing to learn how to do; making a careful statement false to fact requires some grasp of what's meant by "fact", and, given that Folla wasn't really used to a space-time that had mass and distance in it, and might also be a little vague as to what we meant by "time", lying seemed unlikely.

I actually thought all that. The howling clue buried in it passed me right by, at the time; I thought it was a small side-issue. Some days I am not as bright as I am other days.

Well, the next afternoon did arrive, finally, and they took Euglane's helmet, and most of the wiring and monitors that went with it—they crowded the back seat of Guin's car with it. Mirella and I bade them a fond farewell, that next afternoon, from Euglane's apartment; the Master was at the Playtime Wispies building, and Hilda back at home—feeding the piranhas, I supposed. "You will of course inform me of events," Master Higsbee had said when we'd broken up the night before, and I'd said that of course I would.

I'd helped load the car. Mirella had come along for no reason I could see. "Another day off?" said.

"I am on investigative leave," she said. "The France case is supposed to be closed out, but I have got them believing there are loose ends."

"Well," I said, "there's one—the murderer. Film at eleven."

She stared at me. "What when?" she said.

"PreSpace slang," I said. "It means—wait for the tapes. Full sound and color." Because, of course, Guin had been carefully rigged with a nicely invisible spy camera, its lens apparently a small decorative pin on her rather severe grey jumper.

"If this doesn't work," Mirella said, "what do we do?" She was driving back to my place, following the wildly complex Ravenal traffic laws with, as far as I could tell, no trouble whatever. She even had enough spare attention for conversation.

"We think up something else," I said.

"And Folla is just going to wait around?" she said.

"Well," I said, "we'll think fast." Once again a large clue had bit me on the nose, without my having noticed the fact.

And in a few hours, my phone blipped, and it was Guin and Euglane, downstairs, reporting success and on the way up.

They interrupted a small snack I'd cobbled up—blinis and caviar, and pots of Gunpowder Green tea—I'd had a little time that morning for shopping, and laid in a supply, most of which I'd frozen, in preparation for getting it into stasis on my ship. Mirella had never encountered blinis before, and I don't think she'd ever encountered first-rate caviar, and we were having a fine, diet-free time whiling away the wait.

"You should have seen it," Euglane said, when they were nicely settled and I'd started a new array of blinis (for Euglane, with some slivered, salted and toasted wax beans I'd been crisping for a salad). "She bought the story without a blink—it was really a very good story for such a person—and once she had the helmet on, and everything 'connected'—it's surprising what a few blinking lights will do to persuade a human that something important is occurring—we went most solemnly through the 'procedure.'"

"And she walked?" I said. "And you got it on tape?"

"Pure idiocy," Guin said. I dished out some blinis, spooned out some caviar, and folded in the toasted wax beans for Euglane. Guin took a swallow of tea, and began on the food. "You're improving, Knave," she said. "Simplicity—it's the key to good nourishment."

Well, I'd once tried to impress Guin with the Hell of a complex recipe; not that I'd ever succeeded in impressing her at all. But—"Nourishment?" I said.

"Caviar is high-energy food," Guin said. The medical viewpoint, maybe. "And yes, we have the scene on tape. Which I very much hope you will to show only to those people who can keep their mouths shut."

"They won't be interested in you at all," I said. "How did it go?"

"Watch the tape," Euglane said, and fished it out of a pocket, unboxed it and slipped it into my display screen. "Perfectly satisfactory, I feel sure."

FORTY-ONE

Satisfactory was the word. We ate blinis and caviar (or wax beans), drank tea, and watched Hester MacEvoy, with her incredibly depressing smile, usher Euglane in—Guin, camera-rigged, was just behind him, but we couldn't see Guin, of course. I saw the damn cloak hanging on a nice high peg as Guin went by it, and then we were in the dark little living-room. The tape was good enough even in that light; we were getting detail and full color, as well as sound.

Euglane went through the story nicely—I have the feeling that any good psychiatrist probably has the makings of a fair actor—and I applauded Hester silently; she looked almost as hopeful and distant as she should have looked, if she'd actually been pinned to that chair. She wanted to know how long the "induction therapy" would take, and what results it would have, and where she'd have to go to get it. I could see her piling up possible objections, but it took careful looking.

"We can provide it here and now," Euglane said. "Dr. Jenn is quite practiced in its use, and I will assist. The induction field will last for about fourteen minutes—" Never quote a simple figure like ten or fifteen, I'd told him; it won't sound plausible—"and the effect should be immediate."

Hester stared. "Im—immediate?" she said slowly.

"Your muscles may need a little practice," Guin's voice said. "Probably not much, Ms MacEvoy; according to Dr. Rasczak, there's been very little loss over the years. The musculature is still basically healthy." She sounded as if what she was saying made actual sense, and I turned to grin at her as we watched. Her expression was so completely a scowl that I buried the grin in a hurry.

Euglane explained carefully that he and Guin would assist Hester out of her wheelchair for a short walk across the room and back. He made that sound plausible, too. Hester looked doubtful—working at it, just a little.

"Suppose something goes wrong?" she said.

Guin's voice: "It's a simple, non-invasive technique, Ms. MacEvoy. If something goes wrong, the technique won't work; and in that case, to be quite frank, you'll be neither better off nor worse off. The technique will either work or it will not; and—based on Dr. Rasczak's records and measurements—we feel quite sure that it will." Decisive and professional, just as if she'd been talking about something real.

There was more talk, and a little more objection from Hester—but her bluff had been called, and there was nothing for her to do, in the end, but play out the hand. The foolery of putting the helmet on her head, hooking up wiring, getting the blinking lights going, and so on, went by without anyone visibly smiling—or scowling, for that matter.

And, after fourteen minutes' worth of blinking lights, and absolutely nothing else, Hester walked—a little less timidly, past the first three steps, than might have been completely plausible, but she did a fair job of pretending it was her first vertical foray in years. She mimed great weariness—total exhaustion, in fact—after about thirty steps back and forth, and Guin and Euglane put her back in her chair.

"You'll need practice, of course," Guin's voice said. "But the technique clearly does work, Ms MacEvoy. We'll return, probably tomorrow—either Euglane or I will phone you first, of course—but in a very few days you should be walking normally." I thought she might have sounded a little more triumphant about the thing, but the crisp professional tone worked well enough.

"It's wonderful," Hester said mournfully. "How can I thank you enough?"

"Rest and relax," Euglane said. "We'll see you tomorrow, I hope."

There was a little more on the tape, and we watched it, but it didn't matter. When it was over, I looked around and congratulated the actors.

"I very much hope," Guin said, "that no one will ever mention this again."

"The police have got to see it," Mirella said. "With an explanation—you know that, right?"

"Lance-Corporal," Euglane said, "I'm sure you and Knave

can handle the explanation for them; neither Dr. Jenn nor I will be needed for that. We'll be available to confirm, of course; but from this point on, you can transport the ball."

"Carry the ball," I said, and Mirella said:

"I got it, I got it." Then, to Euglane: "Sure. We'll do that."

And we dropped the subject, cheerfully —Mirella and I would get the tape into official custody in a short while, and the persons who would visit Hester he next day would be police persons—and went back, less cheerfully, to Job One: Folla.

Euglane hadn't heard from the Governor-General, and I suggested that he put in a call. He agreed—"From my office, in half an hour or less. By sixteen o'clock—four L. P." And he and Guin took themselves off.Meanwhile, I asked Mirella, what the Hell were we going to do to stop the alien invasion?

"Alien invasion," Mirella said. "It's like old-time science-fiction, all of a sudden coming to life on me."

"Well," I said, "we know about Folla and Dube. They might be the only two aliens—but they might be the first of thousands."

"All by themselves they are enough," Mirella said. "Anything that can pull some of the tricks they pull—getting into people's dreams, arranging Hester's head so she walks, pushing a good cop into suicide—moving a ship, for God's sake, all that way in zero time—does not need a cast of thousands to make trouble."

"So how do we stop them?" I said. The ghost of an idea was nagging at me, but it wasn't more than a ghost.

"We shut the door," Mirella said. "Somehow, we have got to make it so they can't get in."

That much was obvious, damn it. And then, very, very slowly, I began to see how. We were going to need Euglane—and we were going to need the Master.

FORTY-TWO

"The key," I told Master Higsbee over dinner, "is in the whole idea of travel—and travel time. In dreams."

We'd gone back to Murray's Basement for dinner—people wandered by now and then, but the noise level was high enough for privacy. This time, I tried cubes of beef in a mild cheddar sauce, peas in a butter-and-garlic arrangement that was, in several small details, both new to me and worth careful attention, and zucchini, of all things, in a red sauce that seemed to have chili in its ancestry somewhere. Mirella stuck to her french-fries, along with octopus fried in batter, and the Master went for the Classical: cubes of beef and bread in a spiced cheese sauce.

Watching the Master manipulate the skewers and make his way around the vats kept Mirella in a state of blank astonishment. "You're sure he's blind?" she said, while he was away loading a plate. "I mean, he has got the cane, but how much can a cane do?"

"He's really blind," I said. "Truly. The cane's just for his leg. He can load the skewers by touch—and by smell, I think, picking out what to load, and picking out which vat to use. He keys on the vats by heat signal. How he gets around the room—avoiding tables and chairs—I have no damn idea. I would not put it past him to have got a braille map of the place before he ever came here. There is not much I *would* put past him."

"He is something else," Mirella said. "How come you know him? He hired you on for something, once?"

I swallowed some peas, and chased them with the spiced wine I'd remembered from last time. "More the other way around," I said. "I was a brand-new Survivor, and I had the idea I could use some helpful hints. The Master got mentioned, and I came and looked him up. That was a lot of years ago."

Mirella took in some wine, and nodded. "Helpful hints," she said. "I bet he gave you some doozies."

"Mostly," I said, "he told me I could find my own answers.

He told me that often enough so I found out I really could. He finds his own answers, God knows—he just finished a job for Playtime Wispies, he told me."

"Playtime Wispies?" Mirella said. "Hey, could I ask him to get me a few? I never yet tried one."

But that had to wait. Master Higsbee, carrying a plate in one hand and working his cane, almost idly, with the other, got back to us and sat down. I didn't see him feel for the chair with one leg, but of course he did; he was just very, very good at it.

He'd offloaded the skewers at the vats, as everyone did, and he took a couple of bites before he said anything. Then he nodded. "Satisfactory," he said. "A fascinating restaurant, this."

"Nothing like it," Mirella said.

"Now," he said. "Travel. In dreams. Gerald, you will have to expand on that just a bit."

The ghost of an idea I'd had was coming back to me. But I had to start by clearing the ground. "I talked to Euglane about two hours ago," I said. "After he'd called the Governor-General."

"I would assume that Lord Batesman had wished to do a very little research before he talked again to Euglane."

"Right," I said. "He'd done some checking around—a few planets, at any rate."

Master Higsbee gave us a little smile of satisfaction. "I did say that imagination would not be wholly dead in him."

"So you did," I said, "and it isn't. He followed through. The Emperor will get the word out—and according to a very fast check by Batesman, there have been exactly zero instances of somebody being asked to do something, in a dream, that affects his waking life."

The Master nodded. "It would, of course, be an extremely difficult thing to check," he said. "We have nothing like sufficient data—but even a small indication is grist to our mill."

"Batesman said, according to—"

"Lord Batesman, please, Gerald," he said. "Politeness is a necessary counterpoise to the manifold frictions of the world."

All right. "Lord Batesman told Euglane that he'd checked around with some of the oddity groups here and there. Not all of them, not even most of them—it'd be two months' work—but a few of the ones he thought most likely. On Kingsley, Earth, Illawarra, the Haven system."

Mirella said: "Oddity groups?"

"There are people who believe in contact with aliens," I said. "People who believe they've been contacted. There always are—there always have been, whether you call them aliens or devils or God knows what."

"It is a common affliction," the Master said, "to think yourself the object of some strange and unknown being's rapacity. You are quite right, Gerald: before space travel, there were devils to conjure up out of imagination; since, devils and alien beings have shared the stage."

"Anyhow," I said, "he checked. Nothing resembling Folla or Dube—by those names or any others—turned up. Just the usual run of monsters and demigods—the kind of thing Euglane's been collecting all these years."

"Again," the Master said, "a small indication, but a cheering one."

"It begins to look," I said, "as if Folla and Dube really are limited to Ravenal. Possibly limited to City Two."

"Possibly even, just maybe," Mirella said, "limited to not a lot of people in City Two. MacEvoy, Harris France, Hilda—"

"And me," I said. "The same list, four people long. Maybe they really can't go anywhere else—or not yet."

"But they can," Master Higsbee said. "Folla was present eleven thousand light-years away, at your ship."

"True," I said. "And nowhere else. Maybe—just maybe—whatever it is about the four of us—stubbornness or whatever, plus something else—maybe there's something peculiar about our ears, or our toes—it had to be me he could get in touch with. Once I'd got lost, I mean, and turned up where he could perceive me. Me, he could find, once I'd put myself out there somewhere—though location doesn't seem to matter to him, much."

"And the others were here," the Master said. "He was able to come here, clearly, not because he could find you, but because he could find another of his sort—Dube. Dube had been here before, speaking to Hilda, and to Hester, and that probably in her dreams, though she never quite specified."

"One thing," Mirella said. "Again: why isn't Hester building his machine right now?"

"She said she wouldn't do that," I told her. "I doubt she meant it, quite—she went and killed Cornelia Rasczak, after all—but she may have been hesitating. And whatever the machine is, it'd be a job of work for one small, out-of-condition woman alone. And it would cause talk—whatever materials she had to get, somebody might notice." I thought for another second. "I think she was hesitating," I said. "Remember, Folla said no other discussion had reached the point I got to with him—and I don't think he can lie, I really don't."

"Folla would like someone better, to be sure," the Master said. "And that he has not found someone better we can be sure; or he would not be interested in you, Gerald."

"The odd thing," I said, "is that he talked to me twice—on my ship, and in a dream—without asking me for help."

"Not odd," the Master said. "His first encounter with you was a puzzle for him: he did not clearly know you were human. And when he reached you again, he was performing a—a check. A ranging shot. Making certain that this human among humans was in fact the same being he had before encountered."

I nodded. "Right," I said. "And now we get to it—but let's adjourn, once we finish dinner, to a quieter spot."

FORTY-THREE

"Time first," said, when we were settled in my hotel room, with coffee available. "Folla appeared to Hilda months ago. He said he'd come back. He never did. He waited six weeks or so between the first time he met me and the first time he turned up as a small dog in a dream. He gave me some help in that dream—my head distorted it into using a wire or something to pull the front off a safe, but I think he must have had the magnet and chain in mind."

"So far," the Master said, "we repeat old material."

"But," I said, "it's the time that kept getting to me. I kept seeing the clues, and not observing hem. Look: time in dreams is very strange. It doesn't just pass the way time does out here in old, familiar, three-dimensional space. It can cover three years in a minute and a half, or take thirty seconds and stretch it out over what seems like months."

"This may be the effect of our own distortions," the Master said. "Even in waking life, the passage of time, though even, does not always *seem* to be so."

"It may not be distortion, too," I said. "Time may be entirely different in the dream spaces."

The Master shook his head. "Not entirely," he said. "It remains unidirectional, from past to future, so to speak. But I gather that you feel Folla may be behaving so oddly simply because his time rate differs from our own."

"His time rate, or his experience of it," I said.

"So he waits, and then he shows up," Mirella said. "So why does this matter?"

"It gives us a little room to plan," I said. "To prepare. But it's not the important thing— the important thing isn't time, it's travel," I said. "Folla—and Dube, apparently—can get to a few people here. We can't be the only four humans alive who share whatever it is—there are a hundred inhabited planets, more or less, and some of them are even more densely inhabited than Ravenal."

"Soon or late," the Master said, "they will begin to search

otherwhere. They will develop what they lack, be it capability or understanding, and their search will widen."

I nodded. "If they can," I said. "And we have to assume they can—or can learn how. But when they do, we can stop them."

"Nice to know," Mirella said. "How?"

"The warning we got out is the start," I said. "We'll amplify it—we'll send the Emperor the full story, in detail. That will keep the thing alive—it'll get built in, and a lot harder to forget. We're going to have a murder case to tie into it."

"So how does MacEvoy tie in—not for us, we know about it, but for the Comity people?"

The Master was smiling; he'd seen this, of course. I gave him a grin—who knows? He might get it, some way—and told Mirella: "Hester can walk. We have tapes. And we have the firmest possible testimony that she can't. How was this managed?"

She thought for a second. "It might work," she said.

"It'll work," I said. "When—whenever—Folla and company pop out, anywhere in the Comity, we'll be ready. We'll stop them, just the way we're going to stop them now."

"You have some method for doing that," the Master said. "I will confess I have not seen it."

I gave him a bigger grin. "The Josephson junction," I said. "That's the key."

He sighed. Not as theatrically as Mirella, but he made it count. "Gerald," he said, "the effect is, in the ancient terminology, a quantum effect. That Folla can utilize it on a large scale does not mean that we can do so. It is true that the knowledge that a thing can be done is a very great help in accomplishing it—but a period of years would be required for any development of he effect on a large scale—years at a minimum. This is not a minor quibble, Gerald; it seems fatal to your notion."

"Well," I said gently, "maybe not. Suppose we could set up a Josephson junction—so that when Folla popped up, he was in its focus. At point A. Suppose it was keyed to send him to a point B we selected—somewhere very far away. Not to the spot he found me in—he knows where that is, and how to get here from there. To someplace else. Say the Magellanic Clouds. Greater or Lesser, take your pick."

He sighed again, but this time it was a real sigh. I had something, and he knew that—an he had no idea what the Hell it was.

It was a memorable moment.

"Very well, Gerald," he said after that. "Expound."

"We know that a Josephson junction can be built big enough to transport my ship sixteen thousand light years. We don't have to know how—we don't need the specs for it. Dreams don't work that way."

"Gerald," he said after a couple of seconds of silence, "you surprise me. You have seen a path out of our difficulties, and it is a good path. You will yet learn to think."

It was like being presented with a medal. Mirella gave the moment its space, and then said:

"Okay, so I don't get it. So just for me, Jerry, expound a little bit more."

I nodded. "Look," I said. "If Euglane can put me into dreamland—which turns out to be a real land, damn it—and instruct me on what to do when I get there—and he can do that, he's done it—then he can tell me to have a Josephson junction ready when I get there."

"So you can have a dream thing in your dream," she said. "So what good will that do? This Folla, he is not a dream."

"He affects those spaces, and he's affected by them," I said. "The things in dreams are real—they're just not what they seem to be. We distort them all to Hell and gone, we use them to tell ourselves things, remind ourselves, warn ourselves, everything—whatever the laws of those spaces are, they let us do the distorting—but if it's a real place, there can be real things in it."

"You can build this junction thing, without knowing how?" she said.

"I know it's possible," I said, "and I know it can be built. So I can dream it. And because I know it can work—it'll work. We'll need specs on our point B—wherever we send Folla—but the Master and I can provide enough data to do the job—in the dream world."

Very slowly, she nodded. "Tell me," she said. "If you dream, say, six pounds of that good caviar, you can bring it over to my place?"

I grinned at her. "It doesn't cross over," I said. "Folla can use a Josephson junction in our spaces, because he knows the mechanics. I won't know the mechanics—so I can only use it where dreaming about it can build it. And nothing in dreams crosses over into our space."

"Except for Folla and his companions," the Master said. "And they only in part—from their own, different set of spaces. The spaces we enter in dreams seem inviolate."

"Probably a good thing, too," I said. "There's enough trouble in all this, as it is."

FORTY-FOUR

And then the Comity put the lid on.

It was basically a Dichtung decision, I think: don't worry all us people. Just shut up about the whole thing, and there'll be no panic, and nothing will happen.

But it might. Yes, the Josephson junction worked, and Folla blinked right out of sight, on his way to—we finally picked a good spot—M33 in Andromeda, which makes the Magellanic Clouds look like back-fence neighbors. And Dube seems to have got the idea; there have been no reports of him, or of any other alien, since.

But there might be. We found a solution, but it isn't going o last forever. People have got to know, Mirella says, and she's right. So here's the report. Now it's in the open, complete with a way to handle the aliens, while we learn more—if we need to, and sooner or later we'll need to.

Mirella thinks people will want to know how the Playtime Wispies thing came out, too. Well, why not?—though, as the Master says, it wasn't much. It seems if you make the little clasps and such just tough enough to manage so they take more than seventy seconds to pop free, the thefts stop. The Master had popped one in nine point two seconds, while I watched, after all—and, whoever was lifting the things, seventy seconds is apparently too damn much work for the end result.

And what the Hell, if you get impatient while unclasping a set of your own or your rosebud's, they do tear without much difficulty.

The Master was at work on something else—he didn't say, and I very carefully didn't ask—when he saw us off. The cane was gone, and he was walking normally, which didn't seem to improve his general mood any.

"You will be celebrating on Earth itself," he said. "I have not visited there in many years, Gerald—after all, what use has Earth for an old and helpless blind man? But I bear them no grudge; if you should happen on any distant friends of mine, wish them well for me. And do try to keep in touch; mine is a lonely and a solitary life, and I should enjoy hearing of your travels." I said I would. Now and then, in fact, I really do.

Hilda was there too, and Euglane. Euglane shook hands all around, and hurried away before we left—he was back with a full patient load.

Hilda got me off to one side for a minute. "He'll be fine," she said to me, in a tiny whisper. "I'm getting around fairly well now, Gerald—and I'll see to his comfort. He's a wonderful man."

I didn't argue the point.

Later, when we were both belted in and waiting for the word from Launch Control, Mirella said: "You know, she'll be good for him."

"You heard?" I said. I'd been sure even the Master couldn't have heard Hilda's whisper.

"Jerry," she said, "I got lots of talents. I am on indefinite leave now, so you will have a chance to find out about some of them."

"I'll watch for them," I said. "Wherever the Hell we go."

"For this one," she said, "it's simple. I read lips."

AUTHOR'S NOTE

Once again, there are a few things to be said.

There exist, here and now, psychoanalysts, psychiatrists, psychologists, psychiatric social workers, and fifty or sixty other categories; as there exist, here and now, neuro- psychologists and neuropsychiatrists of a variety of sorts. I am told that, ca. 2300 A. D., on Ravenal and elsewhere, this plethora of categories has been more or less rationalized; and "psychiatrist" and "neuropsychologist" are used as descriptive of these professions there and then. A full description of the borderlines among categories here and now, and of the various duties of various sorts of professionals in any such category, would take, and has taken, several volumes, and I didn't (and don't) feel the details important to add in to this particular report of Knave's. Those interested can find the current books easily enough.

Anyone interested in the notion of objects as information, and translation from one point to another in zero time and without occupying intervening points, cannot do better than see *Information Mechanics*, by Dr. Frederick W. Kantor (John Wiley & Sons). It will provide any reader with (that overused phrase) a new paradigm for physics. You won't find Josephson junctions there, but they're quite real, and a library search will turn them up for you.

Jeff Harris should again be thanked; so should the E. U. Deli on Orwell Street, Potts Point, Sydney, where much of this one was recollected, or dreamed up, or cobbled together. Thanks are also most affectionately due to the redoubtable Laura Davis, who inspired me to sit down and write *Josephson Junction* one day, for purposes wholly different from its use here.

www.ingramcontent.com/pod-product-compliance
Lightning Source LLC
Chambersburg PA
CBHW031403250626
47155CB00004B/1391